The QUICK and the DEAD

The QUICK and the DEAD

A Jack Prester Mystery

SANDY DENGLER

Five Star
Unity, Maine

Five Star Christian Fiction.
Published in conjunction with Moody Press.

Cover photograph © by Alan J. La Vallee.

December 1998
Standard Print Hardcover Edition.

Five Star Standard Print Christian Fiction Series.

The text of this edition is unabridged.

Set in 11 pt. Plantin by Al Chase.

Printed in the United States on permanent paper.

Library of Congress Cataloging in Publication Data
Dengler, Sandy.
    The quick and the dead : a Jack Prester mystery /
Sandy Dengler.
      p.   cm.
    ISBN 0-7862-1647-6 (hc : alk. paper)
    I. Title.
    [PS3554.E524Q53 1998]
    813′.54—dc21
                                   98-39768

Contents

1

It Was a Dark and Stormy Night

— Edward Bulwer-Lytton, *Paul Clifford*

It was a dark and stormy night, with rain drumming and a fierce wind ripping branches off trees, but that didn't keep anyone from attending the park potluck. They were all assembled in the community building, all laughing and chatting in a cacophony of friendship, all standing in an interminable line that snaked slow-motion past the two long food tables.

Homer Clarence Symes found himself, as always, about in the middle of that interminable line, with his paper plate nestled in its wicker holder, his napkin and flatware sticking out of his shirt pocket, and his mental reflections, as usual, going a mile a minute. Directly in front of him, his wife, Jane, was getting the latest about Dumphy's baby girl, the one with the harelip, and how they can fix such things now so that you can almost never tell something had been wrong.

The middle. Ever the middle. Never up front with guests of honor, where the superintendent and her acerbic husband were just now filling their plates from the plethora of casseroles. Not in the back, where the GS-12 managers, the chiefs and specialists, stood about with beer in hand, graciously letting everyone else go first. The middle.

Homer Clarence Symes sighed heavily.

And then the potluck took a turn unique from every other park get-together Homer had ever attended.

The superintendent, Colleen Abcoff, seemed preoccupied, not to mention infuriated, by some problem, and very sour. That in itself was not unusual. But now, breathing heavily, she paused near the head table with a shocked, angry look on her face. She dropped her paper plate. Three varieties of Beany-Wienie (all homemade) and potato salad splashed across the floor. She wagged her head and pressed a hand to her breastbone as her husband pulled out a chair and helped her sit.

The chief ranger came hurrying to her side and squatted beside her chair, murmuring questions as he took a carotid pulse.

She threw up. That was certainly not usual. Then commenced the convulsions — tremors that became shudders that became violent jerking.

Christine Weineke and Anne Cruthers rapidly herded their school-aged children out the door into the waning evening. The other mothers did likewise, clearing the hall of youngsters. Colleen Abcoff's acute medical problem was not a pretty thing for tender eyes to look upon.

Half a dozen rangers and a naturalist, all people with emergency medical training, Homer knew, gathered tightly around her. They slid her gently to the floor where she lay curled up on her side a few minutes. Homer heard the aid van with its howling sirens.

Leonard Walker knelt at her head, tilted her chin up in approved technique, and, mouth-to-mouth, assisted her breathing. From the double doors, Chris Arlington shouted requests to move aside. The crowd of onlookers parted minimally and reluctantly to permit Chris and Larkey to roll a gurney across the room to her, threading among the tables.

Leonard and Jasmine Ingraham began cardio-pulmonary

resuscitation. The EMTs connected a white machine like a laptop, which Homer recognized as a defibrillator, to large, round, white pads and slapped them to the superintendent's bared torso.

Homer had never before seen a body jolted by 200 joules of electricity, except on television. He realized that it was nothing less than horrid, morbid fascination preventing him from taking his eyes away from the surreal scene. They zapped her repeatedly with the defibrillator and then performed CPR even as they trundled her on the gurney.

No one said anything, but Homer knew. She was already dead when they whisked her out the door.

Jack Prester hated funerals. There ought to be a law somewhere against scheduling a funeral less than thirty days after the guest of honor has died. That way, you would have sufficient opportunity to gather your thoughts, become adjusted to the loss, get the weeping over with, prepare a few sage comments. And if you didn't know the deceased from Joe Blow, or in this case Josephine Blow, you could at least take your time getting from Hutchinson, Kansas — home — to the funeral in eastern Tennessee, just outside Great Smoky Mountains National Park.

It had taken him two days of hard driving. This was May too, full of blossoms and singing birds, the best time of year to make a casual, leisurely pilgrimage to beauty across this great land. He hated to feel rushed when so many things were in bloom.

He clipped the forest green tie onto his gray uniform shirt, shrugged into his green uniform dress jacket, and set his flat hat on his head, its brim exactly paralleling the ground. Smoky the Bear in Class A's. All duded up in his park ranger costume and no place to go — except to a funeral.

9

He rubbed Maxx behind the ears and informed him that it was time to go. Maxx appeared unimpressed. The big black Labrador retriever yawned as he lurched to his feet, stretched mightily with front legs extended, and shook. His lips and jowls and leathern ears vibrated audibly, a long, gentle *blblblblblb*. He belched and slurped Jack's hand.

Vowing to get a dog with a short tongue next time, Jack stepped outside under a gloomy overcast. Maxx the Wonder Dog followed listlessly, his telephone-pole tail drooping. Maxx, it would appear, was getting a little bored with riding in a moving vehicle. After two full days, so was Jack. With none of the enthusiastic squirreling around that he normally engaged in whenever he got to take a ride, Maxx hopped up into the cab of Jack's gray Dodge pickup. He was curled up on the seat asleep before Jack torched off the motor.

Jack took his time driving from his motel to the little church on Route 321 west of Pigeon Forge. He could have gotten a motel in Pigeon Forge or Gatlinburg and thereby placed himself much closer to the headquarters of Great Smoky Mountains National Park. But he was a country boy, born in Colorado and raised in New Mexico. The endless parade of miniature golf courses and motels and curio shops and "museums" and restaurants from Gatlinburg through Pigeon Forge really rankled him. God created nature pretty much as it ought to be, and adding a zillion gaudy tourist attractions was definitely not an improvement upon the original creation. So instead, he found a nice quiet place in the comparatively undeveloped country near Townsend and the southwestern entrance to the park. He had been awakened this morning by a meadowlark burbling outside his window — infinitely nicer than yelling people and honking horns.

He pulled into the church lot and parked at the far end.

Let the old people have the spaces closer in. Not that there were spaces as such. The parking lot was a lot, and it was for parking, but that didn't make it striped and divided asphalt. It was an unfenced pasture of beaten grass, a parking field. Cars settled in pretty much wherever they cared to, unrestricted by white lines. They dotted the field in strange clusters and at odd angles. Access to the street consisted of the whole frontage. Not even a ditch blocked your way — drive anywhere you wanted. A heady sort of freedom, to enter a parking lot in the middle.

He left the door unlocked and cranked down the window for Maxx — not that Maxx appreciated his thoughtfulness. Then Jack joined the mourners inside the church.

He was one of maybe threescore gray-and-green National Park Service uniforms here. The deceased, Superintendent Colleen Abcoff, had worked for the Park Service more than twenty years. She'd made a few friends and a multitude of enemies. Jack recognized a couple of superintendents who had been friends of his own father. There was the regional director, and at least one senator.

Exactly who among this illustrious assemblage were friends, and who were enemies? It was a puzzle Jack would have to sort out. He was supposed to solve the crime, if indeed it was a crime and not food poisoning or natural causes. Preliminary reports suggested poisoning by some mysterious agent other than the malicious little animalcules found in unrefrigerated food.

Since he had never met the deceased, Jack took a place near the rear in the middle of a pew. From here he could see just about everyone in the sanctuary. From the material his boss, Hal Edmond, faxed to him, he recognized some of the people he'd never met. The tall redheaded guy down front was the bereaved husband, Andy Abcoff. He didn't look very

11

bereaved. He even wore a pale green suit instead of de rigueur black. Mourning coat? Sport coat.

He could pick out the assistant superintendent, Diane Walling, because of her distinctively Indian heritage. She had rich warm skin and strong, smooth facial features. She declared herself to be half Cherokee. Hal claimed that rumor described her ancestry as quarter Navajo, quarter Muckleshoot, and half blond parolee from San Quentin. Whatever, she stood proudly at Abcoff's side, her five-feet-seven elevated to a good five-ten by the high heels she wore.

Jack would have to sort out all the Park Service people later, with the help of the brass nameplates over the righthand shirt pocket that are part of the basic Pine Pig attire.

Two semiprofessional singers began a duet, "Precious Lord, Take My Hand." Jack had always loved the song. Mentally he picked up the bass line against their reedy soprano and harsh alto.

With rustling to his left, a familiar voice whispered, "Excuse me." She worked her way past the strangers at the end of the pew and planted herself close to his left arm.

He grinned and whispered, "You made it."

Evelyn Brant grinned back. "Just got in." A pretty woman even when she was clinging to the face of a Death Valley cliff, Evelyn looked particularly gorgeous today. Her short-cropped, wavy black hair lifted gently whenever her head moved, framing her face and those huge brown eyes. She wore a modest summer dress in muted hues of blue, three-inch blue spikes with a huge purse to match, and a diaphanous blue scarf that curled softly around her neck.

With his own medium brown hair and eyes, medium build, and medium weight, Jack felt rather — well — medium, next to Glamour Puss here. And there sure wasn't anything dazzling about the Park Service gray and green uniform.

Ev looked altogether too happy to be attending a funeral. She radiated a sort of glow totally inappropriate to the proceedings. Come to think of it, none of the people here appeared particularly broken up. A casual good nature seemed to prevail, even a sense of relief.

The pastor's message, Jack could tell, came from a man who had never known the deceased. One would have to assume therefore that Colleen Abcoff was unchurched. Hal claimed the woman didn't mix well into the local community, but then she'd only been here for about two years. Rural people usually don't accept a newcomer in less than three. Or thirty, depending upon the newcomer.

The service ended precipitately, less than twenty minutes after it began. Immediately, a low buzz of conversation rumbled across the sanctuary and expanded into a dull roar.

Ev added her voice to the hubbub. "Those two grayhaired people by the casket must be her parents, you think? Her bio says they're from Boston. Hal gave me a wad of preliminary stuff this thick." Ev measured four inches with her thumb and index finger. "Pounds of it. The tall, red-haired man down there is Andy Abcoff. Diane Walling is standing beside him — she's the park superintendent now, right?"

"Acting superintendent until the regional office finds a new one." Jack remembered that Ev's background was navy, not Park Service, so he elaborated. "That is, she's temporary but with full powers. They might not find a permanent supe until months from now."

"Is she qualified to apply for the permanent job?"

"Yes, she is. And I suspect she will. She'd be a fool not to."

"Superintendent of Smoky Mountains National Park is fairly prestigious, isn't it?"

"Top of the pile."

People seemed in no hurry to pay their respects to the remains in the casket. They stood about in clumps, visiting. So Jack escorted Ev down the aisle past knots of chatting mourners and fell into the line filing past the open casket. The queue moved quickly. The whole service seemed hurried, not that Jack minded. The only thing worse than a drawn-out funeral is a six-year-old's detailed narrative of the plot of a G movie.

They arrived at the altar railing and inched toward the survivors and the casket. Jack had never seen Colleen Abcoff in person before, though his father had mentioned her from time to time as she moved up through the ranks via a series of small area superintendencies. His dad, now superintendent at Hawaii Volcanoes, kept track of who moved where in the national parks, but then most Park Service people did.

Even in death, lean, angular Colleen Abcoff looked severe and vaguely dissatisfied. She was heavily made up to mask the blue color her face had assumed. She seemed familiar somehow. With a start Jack realized she very closely resembled the evil queen in Disney's cartoon version of Snow White. Grotesquely long fingernails made her skinny hands look ready to give you a poisoned apple.

Andy Abcoff's voice was about twenty decibels too loud for the occasion. It didn't slur, but Jack would bet alcohol was part of the picture. The bereaved husband sneered, dripping with sarcasm, "Yeah, sure, Bodine. I bet you do." He pronounced "Bodine" as if it were a form of leprosy.

The man standing in front of him, a moderately sized fellow in tweed jacket and, of all things, blue jeans, mumbled something in subsonic baritone.

And then big redhead surprised his in-laws, and Jack, and maybe even the deceased by hauling off and knocking the tweed-clad Bodine into the front row of pews.

2

It Was the Best of Times, It Was the Worst of Times

— Charles Dickens, *A Tale of Two Cities*

"It's the best of times and the worst of times," said Richard Platt as he sipped sparkling cider. "With all these schemes to reorganize the Park Service that are either rumored or afoot, I'm glad I'm getting out. And yet, we may well be on the way to a true renaissance in the parks. I'll regret not being in on that part of it."

If his beard were long and white instead of trimmed and dark brown, Platt would have looked like Santa Claus. He was wide enough and short enough — and had a round, red nose and a belly like a bowlful of jelly.

"Dad says he's glad he's out in the field. You can close a regional office, but you can't close a volcano." Jack sipped his own sparkling cider, no ice.

The overcast of the morning had dissipated into a pearlescent haze. The sun pushed through it well enough to cast distinct shadows. That was nice, because this event was being held in the manner of a lawn party in the backyard of the church, and the only awnings — garish pink-and-white striped canvas marquees — protected the food. Were it to start raining now, three hundred people would have to huddle beneath the tables — not a pretty thought.

Robins were tuning up for summer. A vague, sweet aroma drifted across the breeze, and Jack couldn't identify it except that it was surely some tree blooming. He reveled in the feeling of lush moistness that was spring here. Back in New Mexico — or even Kansas, for that matter — spring brought mud but not this indescribable rich dampness in the air.

He observed that this social occasion following the funeral — it couldn't be called a reception by any means, but it sure looked like something after a wedding — seemed much better attended than had the funeral itself. A dozen little kids ran around, and he hadn't seen them inside. How many people, he wondered, simply showed up here for the food without bothering to grace the church?

The food wasn't bad, either. A variety of beverages accompanied the catered delicacies, mostly huge round trays of maimed body parts of cauliflower and broccoli with dip in the middle. Other trays displayed finger foods in the shapes of turtles, snakes, sea anemones, voltage regulators, wine corks, too much toothpaste when you squeeze the tube hard, doughnuts that have been run over by trucks, and those rubber kitchen gadgets that help you twist jar lids off. Probably the caterer didn't intend for them to look that way. Jack called 'em as he saw 'em.

Platt nodded toward a gaggle of people in casually elegant attire — sport coats and dresses that cost more than Jack's monthly rent. "Newspeople?"

"I'd guess so, since your simple secret service folk would be guarding somebody instead of hanging out together, tanking up on the complimentary snacks."

"What was it they said about some gangster's funeral when a couple thousand people showed up?"

Jack grinned. "The gangster's political enemy said it, am I right? 'Give the people what they want, and they'll turn out for it.' "

Platt gazed off into space, nodding and smiling.

"Excuse me." A young woman stepped up and smiled first

16

at Platt, then at Jack. She directed her question to Jack. "Do you work here at Smokies?"

"No, I don't. Sorry."

"Thank you." She drifted off immediately, obviously searching for actual employees to quiz.

Jack grunted. "Wonder what high school weekly she works for."

"I'd give her an F. If you don't work here but you came anyway in uniform, you must have a reason. And there could be a story there." Platt wagged his head. "Kids these days have no sense. They don't think."

"I didn't see you jump up and down and volunteer any 'I work here! Ask me! Ask me!' "

"I've nothing to say anymore." And his voice betrayed a soft, elegant sadness.

Here came the acting superintendent, Diane Walling, and she seemed to be deliberately seeking Jack out. She walked toward him straight as an arrow from fifty feet away. Platt abruptly excused himself and ambled off.

Jack extended a hand as she approached. "John Prester out of the Washington office, Ms. Walling."

She took his hand with a puny excuse for a grip. That surprised him. Women in the upper ranks usually shook hands more aggressively. "Yes. Your boss, Hal Edmond, called me this morning to tell me you were coming."

"To soften the blow, so to speak?"

"So to speak." She smirked. "We're ready to cooperate in any way we can. We welcome Hal's help with the investigation. I understand you have an excellent track record for clearing cases."

"They say an actor is only as good as his last movie, and an investigator is only as good as his next case. We'll see. Earlier I noticed your chief ranger quizzing Andy Abcoff at length.

17

What prompted the outburst, do you know?"

"Nerves and booze, apparently. Andy is distraught, of course, and trying to hide it beneath a casual veneer. Machismo. Honestly. And Bodine's just as bad. He claims all he said to Andy was that he was sorry, and that Andy didn't believe him."

"That couldn't be all of it."

"That's all either of them admits to. I wasn't close enough to catch their conversation, so I couldn't say." She paused as if considering whether to spill all. Apparently to spill won out over not to spill. "Bodine has never seen eye to eye politically with either of the Abcoffs. In fact, 'bitter enemies' isn't too strong a term. They've been at each other's throats ever since the Abcoffs arrived."

"Two years ago, about. I assume Bodine is local. Who Bodine?"

"Local, yes. Publisher of the local paper. It's not Who Bodine, it's Bodine Who. Bodine Lee Grubb." She wagged her head and lowered her voice. "If that ain't a Bubba . . ." She seemed for a moment as if she were going to smile. Instead her dark eyes narrowed, and her mouth tightened as she looked beyond Jack's shoulder.

He twisted to follow her line of sight. He saw nothing or no one that ought to elicit such a grumpy reaction. A slim, tanned girl with dirty-blonde hair, probably not more than twenty or twenty-one, was talking to the chief ranger, enumerating something on her fingers as she spoke. The woman beside him apparently asked something, because the girl nodded vigorously. Beyond them, a gaggle of what had to be park wives sat around a patio table in animated conversation.

Nearby, a mousy little man with a receding hairline was staring intently at Jack with a blank expression as the dumpy woman beside him prattled. Jack casually stepped aside, and the man's eyes did not follow.

The whole scene appeared normal, even innocuous. He turned back and looked quizzically at Ms. Walling.

She nodded toward, apparently, the blonde girl. "Ready for some gossip?"

"Dish it up."

"That immoral little snippet over there is Lovey Hempett. One of the Krazy Kempers, a family like you wouldn't believe. She's as close as you'll come to a camp follower in the park. Some say she makes thousands of dollars a month, and others say she probably doesn't make a thousand in a year. She's the Abcoffs' cleaning lady. She's probably out of a job now that the missus is dead."

"The mister doesn't need a housekeeper?" Jack took in the girl's well-worn dress, her dingy flats, a pink purse that matched nothing, her total lack of sophistication. If she was raking in thousands a month, she sure hid it well.

"I can't imagine he'd hang around here. He hates the area."

"And the Kemper girl has access to their home?"

"Hempett," Ms. Walling corrected. "It's very complicated. There were four Kemper sisters, and every one of them silly as geese. Maizie married George Hempett and had three girls — Lovey and two others. Lovey's sisters died in a house fire when they were little."

"That's too bad." Jack held a doctorate in criminal psychology. More than most people, he was aware what something like that could do to a person. All kinds of nasty psychological problems could fester.

The gossip mill rolled on. "Rumor has it she took over her daddy's illicit still when he died, but no one can find it. Believe me, people have looked too. Moonshine was George Hempett's middle name."

"Wouldn't that be true of quite a few people around here, by reputation at least?"

"No, I mean 'Moonshine' *was* his middle name. George Moonshine Hempett. Distilling good corn liquor has been a Hempett family tradition for over two hundred years. They're very proud of it. And Maizie up and married him. Like I told you, the Krazy Kemper sisters."

Jack turned for another look. The girl called Lovey didn't look crazy. Exuberant, yes. Bright and lively, yes. But not nuts. Of course, even people who claim they're Abraham Lincoln can appear perfectly normal except for the stovepipe hat. Lovey dug into that pink purse and handed the chief ranger what looked like a business card.

Ms. Walling continued unabated. "Colleen confided to me that she thought Andy might have . . . shall we say . . . compromised Lovey. Colleen was trying to enlist me to spy on them."

"Really?" Jack looked at her. "As if you were a private detective? That kind of spying?"

"One thing you're sure to learn about Colleen, Mr. Prester, is that she hated like sin to spend a penny. She made Ebenezer Scrooge look like the Rockefeller Foundation. Yeah, she was trying to get free surveillance out of me."

Jack digested this a moment. "So? Did you?"

"Of course not!"

"Is her husband a penny pincher also?" He opened his jacket. It was getting warm out here in the near sun.

Ms. Walling blew a messy raspberry, the kind of *bpbpbpbp* a baby would use to convey that it didn't like oatmeal. "He had no choice while she was alive. She made the money, and she controlled it. It's going to be real interesting when the will is read — see if she lets him have it or if she ties it up in trust."

"Kids?"

Ms. Walling shook her head. "Childless. No one to give it to. No, wait. Andy has two by his first marriage. I'd forgotten about them. That should really make it interesting!"

"Speaking of kids, I believe we have mice." Jack nodded, smiling, toward the food table. Three of the children who had been running around were raiding the hors d'oeuvres. Two girls, nine or ten years old, were surreptitiously filling plastic bags with finger foods and passing them to a boy of about ten who carried them off into the woods behind the yard. They were being quite casual and sophisticated about it. "Slick as an ice rink."

"I'll be dipped! The little thieves. I think I know them too. Lovey Hempett's cousins. More Kempers. I'll go put a stop to it."

"Besides, it's late, and the day is pretty well *verhuddled.* Shall we get together for an hour of solid business tomorrow?"

"Certainly. When?"

"Your convenience. I'll call your secretary in the morning first thing."

Smiling, she nodded. "*Verhuddled.* I like that word. It describes so much of my life." She reached for another handshake. "I do enjoy gossip. Come by around ten. I look forward to giving you a whole barrel of the stuff. You can't imagine how much dirt I know."

"Ten." Jack accepted her hand. The grip was firmer this time. "Not gossip, Ms. Walling." He grinned. "Testimony."

She flashed him a happy grin and headed for the food table. The little Kempers saw her coming and disappeared into the woods.

Ev stood about looking beautiful at the far side of the yard, talking to Andy Abcoff. They nodded and parted company. She headed for the food table, and Andy moved slowly this way, stopping every few feet to accept a hand on the shoulder, a comment of some sort.

Jack realized Abcoff was not wandering at random.

He was more or less headed beeline for the Krazy Kemper girl, Lovey Hempett. Was she in on the food filching? Jack had seen no contact between her and her cousins.

He moved off in a sort of intercept trajectory, not to interrupt Abcoff but to get close enough to listen.

Abcoff said something to the chief ranger before Jack could get there. The man and his wife left Miss Hempett and walked across the yard toward the food. Roughly, Abcoff piloted Miss Hempett by an elbow to the shade of a white oak beside the church's toolshed.

Jack heard Abcoff mutter in an accusing tone of voice something about business cards. Now that Jack wanted to hear what Abcoff was saying, the joker kept his voice very low. Jack moved in close beside the shed and dropped down to retie his shoe.

A melodious coloratura protested, ". . . strictly business. I'm gonna clean for them." Soft Southern accent.

He rumbled a reply.

She responded, "I do too need the work, and you know it. You don't think I came here 'cause I just love funerals, do you? Especially her. I'm here to drum up some cleaning jobs. And I'm doing it too. Got three so far."

Jack switched to retying the other shoe. Abcoff's voice dropped still lower. It dripped menace. Jack couldn't make out words, but he detected the inflections well enough.

Her voice rose a few decibels. "Who do you think you are, Mr. Abcoff? You don't tell me what I can or can't."

Abcoff muttered something in a low growl.

She held her ground. "You got no clout no more, and you know it. When she went, you just melted all down to zero,

22

Mr. Swellhead. You weren't nothing to start with." Pause. "Tell 'em any old thing you want. They'll get the truth from me."

Jack snapped to standing as she yelped a muffled little cry of pain and Abcoff snarled. He heard them move off behind the shed, scraping the clapboards. Quickly, his anger rising rapidly and his shoes all neatly tied, he stepped past the oak and around to the back.

Abcoff must have taken martial arts training, or else he watched a lot of Chuck Norris movies. He was pressing the Hempett girl flat against the shed by ramming his left elbow against her throat. His left hand gripped her left wrist so tightly her fingers were white. His right hand was clamped over her mouth. Her legs had already gone flaccid. She hung there, pinned against the shed by his arm, as her eyes bulged and her face turned purple.

Abcoff, his cheek close to hers, had obviously been whispering sweet nothings in her ear. His head whipped around toward Jack.

Jack wished mightily that Maxx were here. Arrests went so much easier with a hundred fifteen pounds of surly black Lab backing you up. "Funeral or no, you're under arrest for assault, Mr. Abcoff. Let her down easy."

"Her neck might just accidentally break."

"Then you'd be arrested for murder one."

Without moving, big burly Andy Abcoff studied Jack a long, long moment, perhaps comparing weight and length of reach. Jack came out on the short end. Abcoff's eyes flicked briefly toward Jack's waist, probably looking for gun and mace. He moved away from the shed slightly, relaxing his grip.

The girl slid listlessly to sitting.

Abcoff waved a hand toward her. "Not assault. I didn't hit

her. We were discussing private matters. Ask her, if you don't believe me. She won't press charges. Besides, you don't have any jurisdiction outside the park."

"Won't fly, Abcoff. Turn around, please, and lace your fingers together on top of your head."

Miss Hempett launched a barrage of gasping, coughing, and gurgling.

"You can't be serious." The man's scowl could have melted a connecting rod.

"Resisting arrest carries its own penalties."

Jack was indeed armed, his two-inch tucked at the small of his back. But Abcoff obligingly negated the need for it by obeying. With one hand Jack grabbed Abcoff's fingers and squeezed them tightly as with the other he did a quick frisk. He had to stretch — Abcoff at maybe six-one was a couple inches taller.

A tingle skipped down Jack's spine as he pulled the 9-millimeter cannon secreted in Abcoff's shoulder holster. He had been much, much too lax about procedures. Had Abcoff in his extreme emotional state decided to uncork, he could have blown away Jack and Miss Hempett both, and possibly even beaten the rap. Jack tossed the automatic into the duff behind him and kept looking for more surprises.

Abcoff's voice seethed. "I have a permit for that. I'm authorized."

"I have a permit for mine too. Fortunately, neither of us had to pull a trigger here." Jack stepped back and retrieved the 9-mil. He dumped the clip and ejected the chambered round, lest Abcoff make a successful grab for it.

Abcoff turned cautiously to face him, his hands still on his head.

Jack took another step back, just to be safe. "Mr. Abcoff, I lost my wife a little over three years ago. I understand the toll it takes. Technically you may be under arrest, but I'm backing off for your sake. I'll write this up and file it. As far as I'm concerned, it can gather dust in the county prosecutor's in-basket. You let yourself get a little too carried away twice so far today. A third time, and we haul it out and dust it off." He slipped Abcoff's confiscated cannon into his coat pocket. "Unless, of course, Miss Hempett indeed decides to press charges."

"I want my gun."

"Later."

"I need it for protection."

"From whom?"

Abcoff smirked. "Bugs Bunny."

"Later."

His scowl not softened in the least, Abcoff looked beyond Jack at something behind Jack's back.

Jack didn't look. He was much too smart for that ancient trick. He grew up watching old Westerns where someone got the jump on someone else that way. No sirree, you see enough Three Mesquiteers and Red Ryder movies, and you're onto that ploy.

Abcoff lurched into motion and strode off past the white oak toward the open churchyard. As Jack turned, keeping his eyes on the hostile bereaved, he could see behind him. Ev stood quietly beneath the oak, her right hand hidden inside her big blue purse. Abcoff paused to glare at her and then went on his way.

Jack sucked in enough of the sultry air to dry a load of wool socks.

Ev exchanged eye contact with him and hustled over to Miss Hempett.

Jack probably ought to have helped, but he felt better watching Abcoff's back as the fellow threaded among the mourners. The man brushed people aside, leaving a dozen confused well-wishers standing in his wake. He aimed for the far corner of the church, headed for the pasture that posed as a parking lot.

Miss Hempett was struggling to her feet. In a raspy voice not at all like the low soprano Jack had heard earlier, she assured Ev she was just fine. Ev hovered over her, Florence Nightingale in floral print.

"Ev? I'm going to see Mr. Abcoff safely to his car. Be back shortly. Want me to call nine eleven?"

Ev shook her head. "I think it's OK."

Jack took off across the churchyard almost at a jog. The unloaded 9-mil flopped in his pocket. There were noticeably fewer people standing about; the party seemed to be pretty much over. He continued around the corner to the parking lot.

He observed Diane Walling headed for the parking area also, fifty feet away from him. She appeared weary and dejected, which made her just about the first person he saw at this funeral who actually looked sad. On the other hand, maybe chasing kids took a toll. She was angled more or less in his direction, and he angled more or less toward her.

Jack stopped. Where did Abcoff go? He had no idea what Abcoff was driving, or even whether the man drove himself here today at all. With no procession to a graveside service, need for limousines would be minimal. How could a guy that big disappear that fast?

Simple solution. He would ask Ms. Walling. She'd know what kind of vehicle Abcoff drove. She stopped beside a white Ford Taurus near him and looked around as if wondering where she put her car.

Or, even simpler solution, use Maxx. Maxx, the poor mutt, was nose-impaired. Unlike Labradors as a breed, Maxx couldn't track. However, even Maxx could follow a trail this fresh, and Jack had Abcoff's gun in his pocket to give Maxx the scent. His truck window was cranked down. He'd just call Maxx and . . .

A big, old black Lincoln — a road tank right out of the sixties — was swinging around a cluster of cars, headed in this direction. Jack could tell by the way it revved as it started up through the gears that it was a stick shift. It was speeding up, its tugboat-sized engine howling.

It was aimed right at Diane Walling.

Jack stood gaping, trying to explain to himself that what he was looking at was really happening. Then he bolted toward Ms. Walling at a wild, undisciplined run. He reached her in three strides, flung his arms around her, and literally knocked her off her feet. They slid across the hood of the Taurus even as it lurched violently.

Jack let go. Together and independently, he and Diane Walling went sailing right on off the other side. He hit the grassy ground and rolled. Ms. Walling slammed into whatever was parked beyond the Taurus. He heard the black bomb's engine in the distance, still revving. It wasn't leaving — it was returning. He distinctly heard it coming this way again. Someone in the churchyard yelled.

Jack managed to yank his sidearm as he twisted around to his knees. Here it came, a house-sized chrome grill being shoved at him by twelve cylinders and a ton of steel. He braced on one knee and fired two-handed at the windshield on the driver's side. Again. The monster swerved away from them, toward them, away again. Jack fired again, trying his best to take out the driver, pretending he didn't realize that the person behind the wheel was a human being.

The vehicle whipped aside and forced itself between two parked cars through a space slightly narrower than itself.

Steel shrieked on steel. Bumping and bounding, it rolled across the field and out onto the highway without hesitation. More than one set of brakes squealed out there.

It was gone.

3

Jack Be Nimble,
Jack Be Quick

— Traditional English nursery rhyme

"Jack be nimble, Jack be quick. Jack jumped over the Taurus."
Diane Walling stood wagging her head at the spectacularly
caved-in fender of the white Ford. "He really tried to get us."
She looked at Jack with fear-clouded eyes. "Was he after you or
after me?"

Jack shrugged. "Or both of us."

By his left knee, Maxx flopped from sitting to lying in order to rub his face and ear with a paw. He still wasn't totally
awake.

Ev pressed so close to Jack's right side that he could feel
the motion of her breathing. "I saw that thing coming at you,
and there was nothing I could do. Nothing. It was so close!
He was hitting the Taurus with his bumper at the same time
you two were going over the hood. And then he floored it out
to that open space and wheeled it around and came roaring
back — I was sure he'd get you on the second pass." She whispered, "Jack . . ."

Jack grimaced. "No license plates."

Ev shook her head. Her hair followed belatedly. "And the
windows were heavily tinted. The driver looked like —" she
frowned "— like a black crash-test dummy."

Ms. Walling studied her. "You mean black like the race
black? Or black like the color black?"

29

"The color. It was dark inside the car."

The Sevier County sheriff's deputy was making out the incident report. That young man opened his clipboard and turned his paper over. "Anything more to add?"

Jack shook his head.

Ev started to say, "What about —" and he surreptitiously elbowed her.

The deputy nodded slowly. "We have the names of everyone present. Witnesses. That seems to be it." He handed Jack a copy of his written report. It was the bottom one — the fifth or sixth colored carbon — and virtually illegible. "Let me give you this, since you're investigating and this is a quasi-official Park Service function. And you, of course." He gave the next-to-bottom copy to the chief ranger, Bill Weineke, who stood beyond Ms. Walling, gawking at the aftermath the same as everyone else.

Bill Weineke, like Jack, had dolled up in his class A uniform for the occasion, but his clothes still looked pristine, and Jack's looked as if he'd been rolling on the ground. You'd think grass stains wouldn't show up so brightly on the knees of green trousers.

Another class-A-clad ranger stepped in beside Bill and handed him a bulging plastic bag. Bill handed it on to Jack. "You'll need this stuff. I was going to give it to you tomorrow when you came in to headquarters, but when this happened I figured why wait, and told Greg to bring it out. If someone's after you, you might need it today."

Jack peeked inside at two handy-talkies in their leather cases, their chargers, two pagers, and some protocols booklets. The chargers were no doubt what made the bag so heavy.

The deputy pocketed his pen. "We're assuming the superintendent's death and this are probably related. Get anything back yet on cause of death?"

Bill shook his head. "Toxicology report won't be in for ten days, at least."

Jack couldn't quit staring at the crunched Taurus. Not only was the fender caved in against the rubber, the headlight was gone forever, and the bumper would surely have to be replaced. He pictured Ms. Walling or himself crushed between the two colliding vehicles — it had come within milliseconds of happening. He shuddered.

"No graveside service, right?" The trooper watched the wrecker back up to the Taurus. "So everyone concerned could be reasonably expected to remain right here for a while. The perpetrator could just sit and wait."

Jack shoved Maxx with his foot. "Maxx, sit up. She's being cremated and the ashes sent home to Massachusetts, as I understand it."

Diane Walling smiled for the first time. "Come on, Tom! Graveside? Can you imagine Colleen Abcoff being buried here? Stuck down here in the South for the rest of forever?"

The deputy chuckled.

They exchanged pleasantries, and the investigative team, such as it was, rather casually disbanded. The deputy named Tom — Jack glanced at the signature and couldn't even get that much from the scrawl — swapped a bit of banter with the tow-truck driver and wandered off to his patrol car.

Bill, with the young man identified as Greg, drove off in a four-wheel-drive park vehicle mostly resembling a box — probably a Jeep Eagle. Ms. Walling said something about soaking in a warm bath for several hours as she headed out across the abandoned field toward her car.

Even most of the reporters and other newsfolk had left. Jack wondered how many were quick enough to get a picture of the Lincoln? Bill claimed he asked around immediately afterward, and nobody boasted of being on the ball. They all regretted missing the picture. And to think the Lincoln had given them not one photo opportunity but two.

Ev somewhat absently watched the tow truck. "When you showed Abcoff's automatic to Maxx and told him to find, Maxx indicated it was not Abcoff in the black car, right?"

"Right. When Maxx headed directly to that empty parking space, then went straight out to the road and sat down, he was saying Abcoff got in a car and left the lot immediately."

"If it were Abcoff in the black car, Maxx would have followed the black car's route past us, the turnaround, and back out the middle, right?"

"Semi-right. It's not certain — Maxx's nose being the disabled sense organ that it is. This is one time I'm not going to trust his opinion completely."

She nodded. "So why didn't you tell that to the deputy? Let him add that to the report?"

"Then I'd have to tell him how I got Abcoff's 9-mil, and I didn't want to do that. I'll tell Weineke about it later."

"Ah." She watched the front end of the white Taurus rise slowly and majestically, not of its own doing. "May I get a ride back to my motel?"

"Sure." Jack looked around. "Where's your car?" And then it dawned on him why she was acting so morose. It wasn't the shock and relief of seeing him and Ms. Walling escape death at all. The white Taurus was hers. He felt a wee bit guilty about the broad gouge his belt buckle had scraped across her hood. But then, one corner of the hood was damaged by the collision, and it would have to be replaced anyway.

His nerves were going to be weeks getting over this. He repeatedly caught himself trying to watch everywhere, with darting eyes and edgy ears. Only three other vehicles remained, his gray Dodge Ram pickup, a teal LeBaron convertible, and a red minivan. The caterers', no doubt. He watched them strike their marquees. The garish pink-and-white tarps floated listlessly to the ground.

Ev completed arrangements with the tow truck driver and exchanged business cards with him, and Jack escorted her to his truck. He swatted the steel-wire cage that substituted for his tailgate. Maxx hopped up into it, and Jack hooked the cage door open.

"Almost dinnertime. My treat, if it's not too early to eat." He held the passenger-side door for Ev. "Actually, it's my treat even if it *is* too early to eat."

She paused, halfway in and one foot still on the ground, watching the lot beyond him. Three Mesquiteers movies notwithstanding, he wheeled to see what had captured her attention.

A cheery-looking woman with short brown hair and an infectious smile was crossing the field to them. Squarebuilt but by no means fat, probably on the youthful side of fifty, she wore a long, sweeping, collarless jacket that made her look sort of like Katharine Hepburn. Far, far away beyond the approaching woman, Ev's forlorn little car rolled out onto the road in the clutches of the tow truck.

The woman bobbed up to them. "Are you Dr. John Prester?"

"Yes, ma'am." He waved a hand toward his passenger-side door. "Evelyn Brant."

"Miss Brant. Delighted!" And she actually looked delighted too, as she pumped Jack's hand enthusiastically. "My name is Laurel Clum. I'm a freelance writer in Oregon. I'm in this area doing background research for my next book."

"A real writer!" Ev brightened like the national Christmas tree when the president throws the switch. "What do you write?"

"Mysteries. I specialize in YA."

Already Jack felt a bit the outsider. "Why A?"

"Yes."

He wasn't sure where he wanted this conversation to go, if at all. But then he probably wasn't going to get to take it anywhere. The two women had already developed one of those instant rapports women are so good at. They were shaking hands in a friendly way rather than a business way, and Jack could not explain the difference, except that he knew it when he saw it.

Said Ms. Clum, "I write under the pseudonym Laurel Morgan. You may have seen my name in bookstores."

Said Jack, "Can't say that I have . . ."

Said Ev, "It would be so much fun to be able to write a book. So your next mystery novel is going to be set here in the Smokies. How can we help you?"

Jack would not have said that. True, he'd always toyed with the idea of writing a book sometime, something nonfiction about the national parks maybe, but he certainly didn't want this woman thinking they would ally themselves in her research pursuits.

And then she said, "I can't believe it. I'm here for two weeks, and the day I arrive an actual mystery occurs. A murder. And now an attempted murder!"

Now Jack *knew* he didn't want her nosing around and possibly compromising the investigation. "Not a murder officially yet. An unexplained death."

"We're going to dinner, Laurel," said Ev. "Would you like to join us?"

"I'd love to. Where do you recommend?"

Ev shrugged. "I don't know. I just got here."

Jack shrugged. "I don't know. I'm staying over on the other side near Townsend."

Ms. Clum shrugged. "I know. How about the Peddler? It has a nice ambience and good steaks. I tried them yesterday. Or the Open Hearth? They're fairly near each other, down by the park."

Jack had the same reaction to the word *steak* that Maxx did to canned dog food. He nodded. "Peddler sounds good. Ev?"

"Let's go." She dug into her purse and came out with a Gatlinburg travel brochure. She hauled her foot in, and he closed her door.

Ms. Clum jogged over to her car, the teal convertible. A rental, no doubt, if she was from Oregon.

Jack stuffed the bag with the radio equipment in it behind his seat, slid in, and hauled his seatbelt down. "I detect stars in your eyes. May I recommend in the strongest terms that you not get too cozy with the lady. Charming as she is, she's going to get in the way if we let her."

Ev was studying her tourist map. "There it is. Right on the river, see? Turn at traffic light number nine downtown. Or the next street after it." She came up for air. "What are you doing clear over in Townsend?"

"Avoiding the lack of commercial restraint so blatant in Gatlinburg. When you had your hand inside your purse this afternoon as I confronted Abcoff, was that a bluff or are you armed?" He drove slowly across the bumpy pasture that so recently had held a hundred cars.

In response she dipped into that cavernous bag and hauled out an automatic pistol.

Jack felt his eyebrows rise. He stopped the truck just short of the road and extended a hand. Expertly she popped the clip and pulled the slide, catching the ejecting round on the fly. She handed it to him butt first. He recognized it as a Sig Sauer, now the standard Park Service issue. It hefted nicely, but it seemed awfully lightweight to fire comfortably. She

35

brushed a wisp of hair off her face. "It took me a while, but I decided on the 228. I like the 9-millimeter better than either the .40 or the .45. And I like its magazine arrangement. You know, Jack," she continued in a tone of voice his mother used on him for her basic reprimands, "you're going to have to switch pretty soon. That revolver you carry is out. No good anymore. You'll like the Sig so much better once you get used to it."

He handed her weapon back to her. "How do you know all this stuff? You have to be commissioned to carry that little puppy legally."

Smugly, triumphantly, she brought out a paper, unfolded it, and handed it to him.

He felt like a father must feel as his firstborn graduates cum laude. "You're commissioned!" He grinned irrepressibly. "How'd you pull this off? It takes months!"

She was grinning too. "I asked Hal to get the wheels rolling the moment I got back from Death Valley. All the misgivings when I took that assignment disappeared. I have you to thank for that, Jack. You accepted me as I was and showed me —" her free hand waved randomly "— showed me new horizons is the only way to say it, trite as it sounds. I owe you so much."

"You're the one who did the work." He gestured toward the paper.

"I've been working at it every spare moment too. I had to back up and start over with some of it because of that job at Mount Rainier. Hal sent me out right in the middle of a course, and I had to repeat it." Deftly she reloaded her sidearm.

"You mentioned how you liked the brave new world out West. Or something like that. New horizons, if you will."

"The excitement, Jack! And the feeling that you're doing

36

something very good. These people we go after think they're God — that they can get away with anything outside the law — hurt or kill others — and we're the only ones standing between them and . . . and . . ." The grin turned to an earnest frown. "I felt empty working in the budget office. A sort of what's-the-use feeling. I feel just the opposite now. I'm doing something of worth, and I can do it well. That's very important to me, Jack."

"But you're still in the budget office, technically."

"That's something else." The grin burst forth again. She whipped out another paper. Obviously she had been waiting, all prepared, for just this moment. "I'm officially on the team. Hal got me transferred over, with a grade promotion. I work for him full-time now. The same pay you started with." She showed him her duty assignment.

Actually, it was the same pay he was still working for. His in-grade step raise wouldn't come for another three months.

"Beautiful!" And now his grin split his face so wide his cheeks got tired. "Welcome aboard!" He leaned over, embraced her in a gladsome, avuncular hug, and kissed her cheek.

And then he kissed her lips. He didn't mean to do that, and he didn't know why it happened. He broke away and sat up straight behind the wheel. "That's a first. I usually don't kiss women with loaded guns in their hands. Tends to make a country boy nervous." He saw a hole in the traffic and pulled out onto the road, headed for downtown Gatlinburg.

She giggled nervously. "I usually put my gun away first. I don't want to scare off country boys." She tucked it into her purse. "I spent quite some time talking to Andy Abcoff this afternoon. He didn't realize I was talking to him in an official capacity. In fact, he pretty much dismissed me as fluff. I'd guess from his attitude that he doesn't respect women. I've seen his type a million times. Anyway, he got quite candid."

"Does he know what happened? Or why?" Jack should be concentrating now — they were talking business. Instead, his mind kept skipping to his memories of Ev when first he met her. Back then she was stiff, cautious, reserved. He never would have dreamed her capable of light banter. She was so different now, so much richer and deeper a woman.

"No. No idea. I realize you think he's all torn up, but I'd say no. He comes across to me as too shallow to care. And egocentric. Self-absorbed. You know when Diane was kidding the deputy about Mrs. Abcoff not wanting to be buried here? That was an inside joke, you might say. Both of the Abcoffs detested anyone with a Southern accent. If you spoke with a Southern accent, they assumed you were stupid and rednecked and not worth thinking about."

"Interesting. Not even presidents who were Rhodes scholars, eh?"

"Oh, you should have heard him get on about Clinton. And Carter too. And about George Bush claiming Texas residency." She frowned. "So, Jack, why would she accept the superintendency of Great Smokies, if she hated being around Southerners?"

"Power, Ev. I saw a list once of the ten most popular national parks. Smokies is number one. That makes it a political biggie."

"Really! What were two and three?"

"Grand Canyon and Yosemite. I think Yellowstone was four. I forget the exact order of the rest. Acadia was one of them."

"There!" She bobbed her head for emphasis. "You see? Until Hal sent me out to Death Valley, I'd never been in a national park. Not one. And here we are in the greatest of them, not to mention Acadia last fall. It's a whole new life for me, Jack."

Jack was third generation Park Service. His father and his father before him knew the parks not just as places to go but places to live in, to visit friends in, to protect. To Grandmother's house we go, over the river and through the woods to Yellowstone or Everglades. Your best friend moved to El Morro, and you knew where it was. "Convenient" meant less than twenty miles to the nearest paved road, which classified Chaco Canyon as inconvenient, and nobody cared that it was. Having grown up in the milieu, he had a terrible time conceiving of anyone's not knowing the parks, let alone not knowing them intimately.

He put aside those thoughts and pressed his point home while he was still thinking about it. "This was the peak of Abcoff's career."

Ev consulted her map. "That makes sense. I think you want to turn right at this next light. No, you don't. Never mind. The way Andy Abcoff was talking, she was preparing to make a name for herself. She didn't think she'd get another promotion or a better duty assignment, so she wanted to go out a legend, you might say. She had elaborate plans for — let's see if I can remember his exact words — 'altering the course of Great Smokies and, in doing that, altering the course of the Park Service.' She wanted to make history."

Jack snorted. "She did that. As far as I can tell, she's the only person in the history of the National Park Service who ever dropped dead at a potluck."

4

"I Have Some Papers Here . . ."

said my friend Sherlock Holmes as we sat
one winter's night on either side of the fire,
"which I really think, Watson, that it would be
worth your while to glance over."
— Sir Arthur Conan Doyle, The "Gloria Scott"

"I have some papers here," said Ev before Jack even got all the way through her door, "that I really think are worth our while." She jammed a wad of Xeroxes into his hand.

"What's this?" Jack closed the door behind him and paused to look around her room.

It was lavishly appointed in the unmistakable style that archaeologists far in the future, digging around the ruins of this enigmatic civilization, would call Understated Ultramodern Motel Culture. Heavy draperies in soft graygreen blocked the golden dawnlight. They matched to a fault the grays of the wall-to-wall carpet and the two casual chairs with brass ball feet.

In contrast, Jack's motel room, twenty miles away near Townsend, was an example of Classic Motel Culture. Warm, dark woodworking outlined windows and doors. The shag carpet was brown to match the woodwork and the chenille spread. Pale sill-length curtains begged to be opened to let in the view of a sunlit meadow behind the motel. And his clothes shared the closet with a water heater.

Ev bubbled onward. "I had early breakfast with Laurel Clum. We had a great talk! Anyway, she brought along some of the reference books she uses — you know, she's working while she's here. Writing on her laptop. This is from her book on poisons."

She gave him two pages dry-copied from a book titled *Deadly Doses*, by Serita Stevens. Ev beamed, carried high on the wings of delicious discovery. "Laurel suggests this is the agent, and I agree with her. It sounds perfect. And the plant is local. Any herbalist — and that's just about any rural person in the area — would know about it. She's come across a lot of people who seem to know every medicinal herb in the mountains."

"Monkshood. Aconitum." Jack perused the pages. "Death in ten minutes to a few hours. Nausea . . . paralysis of the respiratory system . . . convulsions . . . it fits, but so do other agents, Ev."

"Laurel is thinking of using aconitum herself. I mean in her story, not on an actual victim."

"Ev, this is not fiction. It's real life." He scanned the entry again. If indeed Ev and Laurel had somehow hit upon the agent, Colleen Abcoff died in misery. You feel chilled, as if ice water were coursing through your veins. You are probably conscious to the very end, although you cease being able to breathe on your own. You realize your life is draining away and there is nothing you can do about it. And then, last, your heart slows to a gentle halt.

"Good fiction reflects real life, and you know it." She was wearing a blue jumper today that nicely complemented her blue shoes and matching baggy purse. He, being back in chambray shirt and jeans, didn't match her elegance any better today than he had yesterday, not that he tried.

She pulled her radio from its charger, slipped it into its

case, and plopped it into her bottomless purse. "My car should be ready, they claim. Temporarily. They have it running, but they haven't done any bodywork on it yet. The insurance adjuster has seen it, but he hasn't completed his paperwork. Apparently he had a couple to handle, including one of the two cars the Lincoln sideswiped getting away."

"Then let's go bail it out of whatever impound prison it's languishing in. Garages usually open at seven."

They retrieved her sorry little Taurus. Its fender had been pounded out approximately into its original shape. At least it no longer mashed against the tire. And a new headlight was duct-taped to the open wound. Emergency medical technician that he was, Jack asked about internal injuries.

The lad at the cash register claimed there were none significant. He averred it might be out of alignment. Jack interpreted that to mean the frame was sprung. He did not mention his suspicions to Ev.

They stashed Jack's truck at Ev's motel and invited Maxx into the backseat of the Taurus.

"After that Lincoln, what can *he* do to my car?" asked Ev rhetorically.

Jack did not comment on the uncommon attraction plush upholstery like hers held for black dog hair, nor did he point out that his own upholstery was vinyl for a reason. The body shop would vacuum the car out anyway as part of their detailing and repair.

Maxx displayed his gratitude for being included in the happy group by stuffing his big fat head between the seats and shoving his nose up under Jack's elbow — his "Pat me!" gesture. Jack rubbed behind his ears absently. Maxx belched in appreciation.

Ev slowed, first in line for a red light. "When do we talk to Diane?"

"Ten or thereabout. Lots of time. It's only eight." He grinned. "Traffic lights always blush when I approach too."

"I have the worst luck with them."

Their pagers went off simultaneously. Jack's nerves did a little hop. He wasn't used to being paged by anything more sophisticated than someone yelling, "Hey!" across the room. "What's our number — do you remember?" He pulled his own handy-talkie off his belt.

"You're six-nine-eight, and I'm six-nine-nine, I think."

He knew it didn't really do any good, but he rolled his window down anyway. "Comm center, six-nine-eight."

Maxx grabbed the opportunity to crowd in behind Jack's ear and stick his head out the window.

The dispatcher's voice came through just a little crackly. "Switch to channel four to talk to six-oh-three, Leonard Walker, please."

Jack had to squint slightly to read the channel numbers. He poked it up to four. As he called 603, he heard a siren in the distance. The cross traffic in the intersection came to a stop as all the lights turned red. Maxx barked loudly, his immediate response to sirens, beside Jack's ear.

"That's from the south — from the park?" Ev leaned forward over the wheel to see better.

"Six-nine-eight, six-oh-three." He could see the flashing lights approaching. "Shut up, Maxx!"

"Jack," Leonard Walker's voice came through loud and clear. "Get up to the hospital in Sevierville immediately. We're on our way there with a critical patient."

A white aid van came howling through the intersection four bells, headed north.

And then Ev pulled a gutsy move Jack would never have expected of her. As the aid van roared through, she floored the Taurus, squealed a sharp left from the wrong lane, and

43

fell in behind it. She popped on her emergency flashers.

In the back, Maxx clambered off the floor and up onto the seat again.

Jack grinned, astounded. "We're right behind you, Leonard — the white Ford." He looked at Ev. "You and A. J. Foyt. Beautiful!"

"The light wasn't going to change yet for a few seconds, and no one else was starting to move. It wasn't all that dangerous." But the look on her face was one of triumph.

He groped under her seat and found a Kleenex box. "Where's your red flasher?"

"What?" She hunched a bit, gripping her wheel tightly, awash in a happy glow.

"A red flashing light. You plug it into the cigarette lighter and stick it out the window onto the roof with a suction cup. It tells the world we're not just humble ordinary folk."

"I should get one, shouldn't I — oh, no! Not now!" She was looking at her side-view mirror.

Jack twisted around to see the patriotic red, white, and blue of a patrol car's light bar splashing brilliance in the back window. "No, it's OK. I think that's Tom Whoever with the illegible signature." He extended his right arm as high as he could out the window, showing his opened badge case to the car behind. Just to make sure, he called dispatch and asked her to tell the pursuing sheriff's vehicle who they were.

Tom Whoever presently turned off his lights briefly, an acknowledgment, turned them back on, and swung out around both Ev and the aid van, a welcome police escort.

What was it from Gatlinburg to Sevierville? Eighteen miles? Twenty? Not far. They whipped along a congested road down a pleasant valley. It would have been a lovely drive were they not in a hurry and were there not so many other cars around. Ev pulled into the emergency entrance to the hospital ten feet later than the aid van. And, bless her, she parked not behind the van but beside it.

Jack leaped out and swung open the back doors of the van three seconds before the emergency room orderly could get there. Leonard Walker, the Sugarland District Ranger, jumped out and stepped aside. Inside, a cheery young fellow in a navy jumpsuit leaned over, disconnected the oxygen mask tubing and tossed it onto the still, blanket-wrapped form of Diane Walling.

Jack stood aside and let the ER personnel do their thing. In one swift, fluid motion they pulled the gurney out, scissored it up to waist high, and trundled it inside. Ms. Walling was plugged back into oxygen by the time Jack and Ev got through the doors.

The ER room was like ER rooms everywhere, only smaller. A couple of treatment areas, including this one, were partitioned by sliding curtains, and molded white plastic chairs sat around in random, inexplicable places. They had a good emergency team, though. One nurse got a blood pressure reading almost before others finished moving Diane from the ambulance gurney to the table. Another started an intravenous line quicker than Jack would have been able to find a good vein.

Diane was already stripped to the waist. Bloody dressings bound her left arm and left side. A nurse completed the disrobing with a hefty pair of bandage scissors. Less than two minutes had elapsed.

Leonard motioned. "Evelyn? She wants you."

Ev glanced at Jack and moved to Diane's head. Jack stayed close enough to listen in. Show me a good investigator, his father always said, and I'll show you a nosy son of a gun. Ev carefully lifted the oxygen mask enough that Diane could speak.

Diane's voice, muted and weary, murmured, "Evelyn? Take my keys. My cat. Mulligrubs. Sealpoint Siamese. Take care of her."

"Love to. Is she inside or outside?"

"Inside. Never out. Thanks. I trust you."

As the X-ray machine was being shoved out over her, the ER doctor said something about clearing the room, but Leonard was herding them out into the hall anyway.

Sheriff's deputy Tom Whoever pressed in among them. "I have some papers here. Run report from Chris and Larkey." He handed sheets of legal-size paper to Jack and to Leonard.

Jack grimaced. "What do we have?" He glanced at "bullet wounds" on the ambulance report and handed it to Ev.

"Drive-by shooting as she was passing the entrance in her car."

Tom scowled. "My side of the line or yours?"

"Just inside the park, but you're welcome to help out on this one. Mutual aid request and all that."

Jack could just about picture it. "On the way to work, in a place where she'd predictably be at a time she'd predictably be there."

Leonard nodded. "She has a cellular in her car, but there was a couple minutes' delay. She went into shock pretty quick and pretty deep. Couldn't get her act together, she said. A tourist came along and used Diane's car phone to dial out. Did a good job on first aid too — just about stopped the bleeding. I got there the same time the aid van did."

"What could she tell you. Anything?"

"Black Lincoln — the same one, she thinks. The driver wore a black hood or ski mask and gloves. His window was down, of course, so she got a good look."

"At nothing."

"At nothing."

Ev's head bobbed. "I told you he looked like a black crash test dummy. He or she. There's no telling which, is there?"

Leonard shook his head. "After that attempt yesterday, which she's convinced was aimed at her, not you, she dusted off her old service .38. She pulled it when she saw the ski mask and got one back at the guy. Doesn't know if she hit anything."

Tom looked morose. "I have everyone I can think of out looking. It can't be that easy to hide a Lincoln, for pete's sake. So far, nothing."

Diane Walling. They should have put a bodyguard on her right away. They should have been more diligent in seeking the Yank tank. Or maybe the search was as thorough as possible. Jack could think of all sorts of shouldas. Now. "Closed the road?"

"Making hundreds of tourists terribly unhappy. There's an alternate way in, but they got trapped." Leonard sighed. "Bill has a forensics team working it over. They should be done before too long, I'd think."

Jack nodded. "Keep it closed until I get there, would you? I want to turn Maxx loose on it — see what he comes up with."

Leonard nodded and headed for a phone. Ev walked back into the treatment area to find Diane Walling's house keys. Jack got a nasty little thought and suggested to Leonard, while he was on the phone to Bill Weineke anyway, that they put a bodyguard on Andy Abcoff. The man, after all, seemed to think he needed his 9-mil for protection. He could be right.

As they climbed into the mangled Taurus and hit the road again, headed back toward Gatlinburg, Jack was startled to see that less than five minutes had elapsed since their arrival here.

A long, long line of disgruntled tourists was backed up all the way into Gatlinburg, waiting to get into the park. Driver after driver scowled at Ev as she worked her way past them. She and Jack probably should have gone to the motel and gotten Jack's truck. At least he had a red flasher. But he didn't want to take the time.

A helpful young woman in full park law enforcement paraphernalia motioned Ev through the blockade.

Ev smiled. "This is another reason I love this job. The sense of power. Importance. I don't know how to say it exactly . . ."

"I agree." Jack pointed, suggesting a parking spot. "Crossing a police line does give one a feeling of superiority." The car coasted to a halt. "Ev, are your brakes getting mushy?"

"Not that I noticed. Why? It stops when I want it to."

"True." He leashed Maxx up and walked down the road to the site. Bill Weineke stood off to the side. Jack joined him. "Maxx, sit." Maxx, bless him, plopped down by Jack's left knee.

A man of few words, Bill waved an arm about. "Shell casings right along there. I have them here for you to show the dog. They'd no doubt carry the perp's scent. Tire tracks there in the road shoulder — heavy vehicle. Diane was doing maybe twenty, twenty-five. She hit the brake even before the shots and put it in the ditch right up there. Got one off at him. No sign she scored."

Jack framed a mental picture, decided about where the perp would be sure to have his window rolled down, and took Maxx to the far side of the road.

Bill opened an unsealed evidence bag and held it low by Maxx's nose. The shell casings were .45s.

"Maxx, find that person. Maxx, find."

Like Labs as a breed, the dog did love to work. Almost instantly he picked up a scent along the roadside weeds. He tugged excitedly at his leash, eager to head north.

Jack called, "Ev? Follow us?"

Her dark head bobbed an affirmative.

Bill watched the dog with some skepticism. "You sure it's the right scent?"

"Not sure in the least. Good bet, though. Dogs do best with moist air and fresh scent. We have optimum conditions here."

"Yeah, but the guy's in a car . . ."

"That shouldn't matter too much. We'll see." Jack wished he had his longline instead of this short leash.

He let Maxx lead. With a few more investigatory sniffs, the dog set off at a rolling jog up the road, his nose low and his tail high.

Behind him, Bill called, "Open up the road now?"

Jack tossed, "Fine with me," over his shoulder.

Back home he tried to get out and run maybe three or four times a week, his only efforts at fitness. He infinitely preferred running along a country road to sitting in one spot struggling mano-a-mano with a Nautilus. It paid off now. Within a quarter mile he had loosened up. He'd be good for another ten miles or so, and old Maxx, once he got in gear, could go forever.

Well, OK, so the line of disgruntled tourists had some justification for gawking. Here came a guy galloping past in civvies with a dog on a leash, and right behind him a beat-up Taurus with its flashers on and a beautiful woman at the wheel. Not an everyday part of your national park experience.

Maxx turned off the main road at nearly the first opportunity, a sleepy little side road with definitely upscale homes.

Ev pulled up beside Jack. "I think he's got it, don't you? The right one?"

Jack nodded. He was starting to work up a sweat. They turned off into other dreamy lanes, staying away from major streets. The perp, whoever it was, knew the area.

And now Maxx jogged unerringly off onto an unpaved gravel lane. The road climbed halfway up a steep hill, leveled out, and wound around so circuitously that Jack couldn't tell which direction he was going.

He pointed to the ground and called to Ev, "The guy's driving on a rim!" Even at this rapid clip, he could see that. He was going to start getting pretty tired soon. Then what?

Ev yelped, "Get in! Get in!" and pulled alongside.

Jack yanked the door open, yelled, "Saddle up!" and leaped into the passenger side at almost the same moment Maxx did. Maxx clambered into the back as she gunned it and took off, wheels howling in the dirt. The car fishtailed a bit as Jack slammed his door.

Red taillights flashed briefly as they disappeared beyond a bend ahead — taillights on a black car.

Ev's voice was jacked an octave above her usual range. "I saw him just a moment before he saw us. Jack, it's been hours! Was he waiting for us here? He couldn't be!"

"I'm guessing he had to stop near here, pull that wheel, and maybe even take it clear into town. Possibly take his spare in to get inflated. Something like that. The timing would be right. After we nail him, we'll bring Maxx back here. Between Maxx sniffing and me tracking, we'll be able to work out the details — where he went." He managed to get his seatbelt hooked despite the wild lurching as she did ninety-degree curves at fifty. Maxx slammed into him.

"Maxx. Jump!" Jack motioned with his whole arm. Maxx vaulted the seat back and landed *fwump!* in the backseat.

She nodded. "You're good at tracking."

"Dad says I can track a soaring eagle back to the egg it

hatched from. He exaggerates, of course." Jack pulled the handy-talkie and tried to reach the comm center. All he could get was a scratched and broken "You're broken" and "Can't hear . . ."

"You want to get Tom or somebody setting up a road-block somewhere out there, right?"

"Right!" Jack watched her right foot alternately working brake and accelerator. She wasn't using the pursuit technique where you handle the brake with your left while your right operates the accelerator. Either she never mastered it, or she had forgotten about it now. And another thing . . .

"Your brake isn't responding right, Ev. You shouldn't have to shove it down that far."

"Jack, what will we do when we catch up to him? He's dangerous. More than dangerous. He'll stop at nothing!"

"That sounds like your brakes." Jack fumbled in her baggy purse for her Sig. He tucked it in the front of his belt and drew his own familiar, comfortable, effective .38. And even as he felt the rough, heavy grip cool in his hands, he wished he had his .45 instead. It would be much more effective at this range.

They were closing. The Lincoln up ahead took a tight turn on two wheels. Its back end slid sideways and bounced off a tree. Ev's little car was much more responsive and maneuverable, and she was handling it as aggressively as a stock-car driver. Another half mile or so . . .

She shoved on the brake. So little happened that she almost lost it on that same turn.

Jack rolled down his window. If the road cooperated by bending wide to the right, he might get off a good shot. "You know, it's going to be really embarrassing if you can't stop and you end up passing the guy you're chasing."

She took his heckling seriously. "I'll run into him first. In fact, I might run into him anyway."

"Bumper cars? He outweighs you two to one. You'd lose."
He wished the woods weren't so dense or that the brush
didn't come up against the road so closely. He couldn't see
ahead well. And branches would deflect bullets. And . . .

She made a funny little sound as she squashed her brake
pedal down and nothing happened. The car veered, spraying
gravel like buckshot into roadside bushes. She brought it
back. Maxx whumped against a back door.

Jack was going to yell, "Slow down, or you'll lose it!" but it
was too late.

She lost it.

5

"I Am Inclined to Think —" I Said

"I should do so," Sherlock Holmes remarked impatiently.
— Sir Arthur Conan Doyle, *The Valley of Fear*

"I'm inclined to think," the mechanic drawled, "that you all might's well junk it." He wore his ball cap backward. Lots of perfectly normal people do that, Jack knew, but still he suspected that anyone with his hat on backward didn't know if he was coming or going.

Jack sniffed. "Yeah, and you're the one who told her it would drive all right and failed to notice her brake line had a slow leak."

Ev looked over at the insurance adjuster.

The adjuster, a placid, gray-haired man Jack would guess to be midway through his fifties, nodded sagely. "A good point, but I'd tend to agree with him. Now, Miss Brant, there may be a little problem. You were in hot pursuit of a suspect, is that approximately right?"

"Yes."

"And according to the terms of your policy, you don't use your car for work. For your employment."

"That's true. I mean, I never did before. You see, I take the bus to work, so I don't use my car to commute when I'm in DC, and I never drove it to a place before — a park. I always flew." Her voice took on a plaintive tone. "Jack always drives his vehicle to the site, but this was the first time I could do that also. I was so happy. Thrilled. For once I'd have my own car with me. And now look."

Look indeed. They all stood about behind the garage body shop, gazing in morbid fascination at her white ex-Taurus. The damaged fender, headlight, and bumper were the least of it anymore. The roof was partly caved in now, where it hit a tree as the vehicle rolled. The right-hand doors were both crumpled, jammed shut. Wads of grass and mud were wedged into the tire wells and in ends of the drip rails and under the bumpers, stuffed in here and there as the car plowed the ditch. Glass shards lay all over the seat where once Maxx liberally spread dog hair. Her front wheels faced each other.

Jack rubbed his cheek. "Ev, do you remember when I put Maxx to the trail, I asked you to follow us?"

"Yes."

"I believe Bill Weineke is witness to that."

At Jack's right, Bill nodded. "I remember."

"So, Ev, you didn't have any choice. I told you to. Pursuing the Lincoln wasn't your decision. You wouldn't have been out there if I hadn't sent you. You were acting as my agent."

The insurance adjuster studied Jack a long moment. "I see what you're doing. I don't think it'll wash" (he pronounced it wareesh, jamming both syllables together into one). "She's here on business, and she was using it in her line of work, but I'll talk to my supervisor." With a few curt good-byes, the man wandered off and climbed into his Toyota.

Jack could have told you by looking at the car that the man was either an insurance agent or a realtor — his backseat was full of accordion files and stacks of paper.

Bill smiled at Ev, a sort of it's-gonna-be-all-right-little-girl smile. "Talk to Homer tomorrow over at headquarters.

Homer Symes. Homer's in personnel, and he's a whiz at things like insurance. If your company won't spring, he might get something out of some special fund. He knows places to look."

She smiled back, barely, and nodded.

"Need anything?" Bill directed that to Jack.

Jack shook his head. "Just the Lincoln. And the perp. Other than that, we're set."

"Yeah. Aren't we. I'm driving to Sevierville to see Diane later. If you want to go along, I can pick you up somewhere."

Ev wagged her head and forced another of those half-hearted smiles.

Bill nodded and farewelled them then and walked off to his patrol car.

The young man with his cap on backward grunted something friendly and returned to the dark cavern of his shop.

Ev drew in air clear down to her knees and started out the asphalt toward the street. She tucked her camera, hanging idly from its wrist strap, back into her cavernous purse. She had photographed the car from every angle. Jack thought it a great idea. He never remembered to do things like that.

The garage was also a used-car lot and had about as strange a mix of makes and models as you'd find anywhere. Jack and Ev walked past huge old road hogs, little Japanese sub-compacts, a stellar variety of beat-up pickup trucks, and even a red MG Midget, the solitary representative of that whole class of eternally-in-need-of-something vehicles called sports cars.

Jack slapped his leg to bring Maxx to heel and wrapped an arm across Ev's shoulders. "You ate breakfast at six, and it's now almost two. Eight hours. Way past lunchtime. The world will probably not look brighter after we've eaten, but we'll be able to see in the dark better."

She sniggered mirthlessly. "I was flying so high. That commission, and my car here — on an equal footing with you. I suppose that was it most of all — and now . . ." Another sigh, this one down to her ankles, spoke more than words could.

This was a tourist town. Free enterprise and the American way being what they are, Jack reasoned that there probably wouldn't be any bad restaurants here. Competition would have weeded out the losers by now. Therefore, since one was probably as good as another, he dragged Ev to the closest, a log cabin sort of café called Uncle Gene's, right here on the corner. He tied Maxx to a parking meter in front of a big picture window, so he could keep an eye on the mutt, and ushered Ev inside.

The interior decor tried to fool you into thinking this was some kind of old homestead. A shelf more than head high held all sorts of 1930s non-antiques — crocks, jugs, washboards, a rusty reel push-mower. You seated yourself. Jack flopped into a booth by the window. Ev slid in opposite.

Jack nodded toward the window. "Maxx is gonna be stiff as a crutch tomorrow. He was banging around in the backseat like popcorn in a microwave." The dog bellied out on the sidewalk and began licking between his toes.

"So are we, I suppose."

"Probably."

She stared into space, no doubt watching reruns of the past. "We were lucky."

"Let's not get into that argument again."

She snapped back to the present. "You mean whether it was blessing or luck? Jack, haven't you ever noticed that when something neat happens you say we were blessed, but when something lousy happens it's our fault?"

"I didn't say that." But he could see how she might think that. Persons outside the faith tended to. And he was certain he had breathed to her no hint of his absolute conviction: had he been driving instead of her, brakes or not, the Taurus would never have rolled.

And they *were* blessed! What less than God's blessing could you call a spectacular wreck with no injuries?

She stiffened slightly and pointed with her eyes. "Isn't that the man Andy Abcoff punched at the funeral?"

Jack twisted to look. "Want to make it a business lunch and do a little interviewing?"

"Why not?"

Jack scooted out and crossed the room to the corner booth with the lean and supple man in a tweed sport coat and blue jeans. Gentle sun crinkles around his deep-set eyes suggested he was in his late thirties. His strong features and clear skin said, "Younger than that," and the incipient bald spot at the back of his head said, "No, older." He watched Jack approach and stood up.

"Jack Prester, National Park Service out of Washington. Bodine Grubb — am I right?" He extended a hand.

The man accepted it with a nod. "What was your first clue?"

Jack smiled. "The mouse under your left eye. I understand you're not pressing charges."

"If ever I have to bury my wife, I'll expect the world to cut me some slack too."

"Amen and amen. Would you care to join my colleague and me over there? Late lunch and casual conversation."

His deep-set eyes looked tired. "To be honest, I don't remember seeing you there." He nodded toward Ev. "Remember her."

"She's memorable." Jack led the way to the window booth and introduced the two of them. He let Bodine slide in opposite Ev and sat down not beside her but beside him. With Jack facing away from him, Bodine would feel less as if he were being grilled. Jack could get to substantive questions quicker.

A middle-aged waitress with henna hair arrived and dropped two menus on the table. "You lit to stay yet, Bodine? This here's the third table you set at since you got here."

"Likely so, 'less I get a better offer somewheres else. The usual."

"Figured as much." She nodded to Ev and Jack. "Be back in a minute."

Bodine looked from face to face and settled, not unexpectedly, on Ev's. "You two are down here investigating Colleen's death. I publish the local paper. You intend to pump me for as much information as you can get, and I'm going to pry as much inside stuff out of you as I can. That sound about right for the ground rules?"

Ev smiled fetchingly. "That certainly cuts through the time-consuming preliminaries." She picked up her menu, so Jack glanced down through his. "Mr. Grubb, I love liver and onions, and I usually order it whenever it's available. Do you recommend it here?"

"One of my favorites. Gene doesn't overcook it. The owner. Been cooking breakfast and lunch himself till he finds a good day-cook he likes — and hates it. Puts in a sixteen-hour day some days." Bodine's voice rumbled almost subsonic even when he was speaking normally. "And the world calls me Bodine. Hope you will too. Both of you."

Jack laid his menu aside. His eyes had reached patty melt and needed go no further. "Since we've bypassed the preliminaries, Bodine, tell me: what question would you like me to ask you?"

Bodine twisted to look at him. "The question I would most like to be asked is, 'What irritates you most?' and then I'd expound. But the question that would bear fruit, probably, would be, 'Who killed Colleen Abcoff?' "

"Who did?"

"I don't know, but I can speculate. Her husband wants her money, her assistant superintendent wants her job, and Richard Platt, forgive the pun, wants her head on a platter."

Ev frowned. "Richard Platt is the man they were giving the party for, isn't it? The retiring chief naturalist?"

"Not retiring. Forced out, fourteen months short of retirement age. What's the minimum? Thirty years' service and age fifty-five? He's out thousands of dollars in lost pay and reduced benefits. Thousands."

They paused because conversation is difficult when the other dozen people in the place decide to fete a friend. The waitress yelled at the whole room that Hank here just turned sixty. She plunked a cupcake with a lighted candle down in front of an old fellow on the other side and led a lusty chorus of "Happy Birthday to You."

"Now that," Jack confided afterward, "is exactly why no one's going to know when my birthday is."

"I agree." Ev nodded.

He looked at her. "Your birthday is September nine. I looked it up."

She sat open-mouthed.

Bodine chuckled.

With forty years in the service and age over fifty-five, Jack's dad could retire any time he wanted to. He loved the job too much to quit yet. But almost as much, he was calculating pay and pension and sick leave and a score of other variables to get the best deal. "I don't understand why she'd force Platt out. A vendetta? Personality conflict?"

"Worse. Whim. Vagary." Bodine paused as the brick-top waitress took Ev and Jack's orders. He watched her leave and continued. "Two years ago, the chief naturalist was a man named Galen McFarland. Grew up here. Accent thick as a bowl of hamhocks and rice. Richard Platt is a son of old money in Carolina — all his ties are there. Platt managed to wangle his way to the superintendency at Carl Sandburg. Along came sweet Colleen. She decided Galen's life would be richer as a superintendent and forced a swap, Platt for McFarland. She pushed it through by arguing that both men were stagnating where they were and it would be good for them and the Service both to make the switch."

"That happens now and then, doesn't it?" Ev asked.

Bodine snorted. "I'd like to think it happens when a swap will actually benefit at least one of the parties. Galen received certain promises in return for his cooperation. They were withdrawn once he got there. Platt figured he'd finish out his career here and retire with a nice pension. Am I correct in this: your pension is based on your top three salary years?"

Ev nodded. "With the sharp reduction you mentioned if you retire before you meet the minimum. So he lost in both regards. He didn't have three years at the higher salary, and he quit early."

Bodine was wound up now. His thick accent thinned somewhat, and he even used complete sentences. "Colleen forced him out under the pretense that his performance was inadequate. She apparently documented her case extensively. Excuse me. A guy serves eight years as a superintendent — capably, good performance rating — but he can't handle a chief naturalist's job?"

The waitress plopped a salad in front of Ev. "You still beating that old dead horse, Bodine?"

"Ain't dead to them. They ain't heard it before."

The redhead exited, wagging.

Jack prodded, "And McFarland over at Sandburg is just as upset?"

"Nearly so. Had to take a loss on his house here, lost other money on the move, and now he's caught in the downsizing budget crunch. Trapped. And two kids in college."

Ev finished a mouthful. "Now that Platt is leaving, McFarland can come back to this job. Even if Colleen Abcoff opposed it, she's gone."

"Walling is a cut out of the same bolt. She wouldn't let McFarland back in if her life depended on it."

Obviously, Bodine caught the glances they shot each other. "Now it's your turn to spill. What am I missing here?"

"One more thing first." Maybe if Jack got Bodine's mind onto other topics, he'd forget his question. "Abcoff had to have some reason for her treatment of Platt, let alone McFarland. You're talking about a carefully considered series of moves to deliberately ruin the man. I don't see it."

"What's to see? She'd get some malicious notion, and — *wham* — someone's ruined. Or dead."

"You're accusing the deceased of murder?"

"Dead figuratively, like Platt. He's not the first."

Jack's patty melt arrived. The fries were that curly kind. Ev openly admired the generous platter of liver and onions set before her. Bodine's usual, apparently, was the chicken sandwich.

Jack didn't hide the fact that he bowed his head and said grace, but he tried not to do it too blatantly. He knew it embarrassed Ev. The patty melt was as good as it looked. "So, Bodine, what irritates you?"

Bodine laughed aloud. "Since you asked . . ." and he plunged into his favorite topic.

It turned out to be the way locals and outsiders alike dwelt upon the hillbilly image to their detriment. Jack had at times wondered if the locals might not be getting a little tired of the opprobrium, or whether they didn't mind it so long as it attracted flatlanders and city slickers with fat wallets. Now he knew that Bodine at least, and through him the local paper, detested the grotesque stereotype.

And they heard about it from one end of lunch to the other.

6

Being a Spider in Chicago

is a very satisfactory vocation.
— Charles D. Stewart, *Fellow Creatures*

Jack watched a spider spin a web between a fireplug and a lamp-post. Being a spider was a satisfactory line of work. You acted instinctively and didn't have to try to think. Jack tried, but his thoughts were all a-jumble. For example, he tried to picture Bodine Grubb as a child. Man and boy, the fellow simply did not seem to fit in this community. It was a curious anomaly, nothing Jack could identify clearly.

He stood on a street corner in bustling downtown Gatlinburg and pondered what to do next. The lab reports for neither the death nor the shooting were available yet. He had called the hospital. Diane Walling was not strong enough yet for visitors. The sheriff's department had put a twenty-four-hour guard on her, now that the horse was stolen. Jack had all the information Bill Weineke had gathered so far in the official investigation. Bill and his law enforcement specialist were handling the bulk of the routine stuff.

Andy Abcoff was attending to business of some sort in Boston and would return Sunday. Richard Platt was at the regional office in Atlanta signing papers, although why the personnel office here at Smokies couldn't handle it Jack didn't understand.

Ev was off with that writer Laurel Clum, getting a rental car. Those two were as thick as cold chicken gravy. Was the writer kissing up to Ev in order to milk information, or was Ev dazzled to be in the company of a published writer, or . . . Jack's long years of study in psychology failed to teach him any more than the fact that he did not fathom women.

And he knew that anyway.

He had just dropped his class A's off at a dry cleaner who did no dry cleaning. They sent the work elsewhere. Brazilian rubber barons once sent their laundry to Portugal, and California land barons sent theirs to China. Where would Jack's go? Idaho maybe.

He gave Maxx's leash a gentle tug. The mutt stood up stiffly. Jack was about to return to his truck when he stopped.

Fifty feet away, a boy sat on the curb hard beside a phone booth, balancing a telephone book in his lap with clumsy determination. Jack recognized the kid. He was the ten year old identified at the lawn party following the funeral as another Krazy Kemper. One of the food thieves. His shaggy, dirty-blond hair sort of clung to his head against its better judgment, its ends poised and ready to fly if ever he washed it. His T-shirt and jeans needed washing too. In fact, if cleanup were Jack's job to do, he'd toss those sneakers in the washer as well.

The boy was thumbing through the Yellow Pages. It was his eyes, though, that told a story. There were tears in them, tears of anger and frustration.

Jack squatted beside him, far enough away that he wasn't crowding the boy, and motioned Maxx to sitting. "Need some help?"

The kid's voice nearly broke with fury. "There ain't no doctors in this stupid book! They think they're so uppity they don't have to tell you where they are!" and he called them a word that questioned their legitimacy.

"Medical doctor?"

"What other kind is they?"

Jack made mental note not to mention his Ph.D. — the kid would never understand. He pulled the phone book off the boy's lap. It had been wrenched out of the holder that was supposed to keep phone books from being removed, and it was considerably worse for the experience.

The boy was a master at transferring anger. He shifted it instantly to Jack. "I went clear through the D's, case they got it in the wrong place accidental."

"Let's try under P. Physicians. What kind of doctor do you want?"

"I told you! The medicine kind."

"Mm." The "Physicians" list was less than half a page. "I think I'm asking the wrong question. What's the problem, and we'll pick out a good doctor that handles that kind of thing. Who needs the doctor and why?"

The boy didn't trust him. That was obvious. The kid looked at Maxx a moment. Apparently he trusted Maxx more. "Broken leg. My uncle busted his leg."

"Did you call emergency services?"

"He told me come into town and call up a doctor, not no services. Have the doctor come out and tend him."

"I don't think doctors do that anymore — make house calls. You have to come in to them."

"Well, he can't 'cause he can't walk. Besides, we're only six or seven miles out. Gimme the book." He yanked it off Jack's knee and dragged it back onto his lap.

Jack stood up. "Pick out a doctor, and we'll call him." He fished a quarter out of his pocket.

The boy could read but not well. He followed from line to line with his finger, ignoring the display ads. "Here. I remember this one's name."

"Read me off the number." Jack punched them in as the

boy recited them, then handed the receiver down to him. "There you go."

He listened to the kid argue with the receptionist for maybe two minutes, and felt the strongest urge to interfere, but he kept both hands stuffed in his pockets. When the boy figured out no doctor would come, then Jack could help. Not until then. The angry little fellow kept protesting the need to call random numbers such as nines and ones.

Exploding with an obscenity that startled Jack, the boy suddenly, wildly, threw the receiver aside.

Jack yanked on the cord to keep the receiver from coming back and nailing the kid squarely in the ear. He fished the receiver in and cradled it. He squatted down again, closer this time. "Let me help you, OK? You and your uncle."

No response. The kid stared morosely at the unswept gutter.

Jack stood up and punched in 911. "What's your uncle's name?"

"Harold Gaines, Junior."

"Do you know the address? Does he have a mailbox?"

"Gets his mail at the post office."

"No phone, I assume, since you came into town."

No response.

Jack identified himself to the dispatcher. No, they had no address record for a Harold Gaines, Jr., or a Harold Gaines, Sr., for that matter. A lot of houses on the back roads, she informed him, had no functional address. There was no way she could dispatch an aid van until she had a location.

"Hang on." Jack looked at the boy. "The lady says we can't get an ambulance out to him until they know where he is."

"He lived there nigh onto his whole life!" The boy hauled himself to his feet. "They sure ought to know by now."

"Most paramedics are younger than thirty." Jack must be losing his powers of persuasion. It took him another couple of minutes to convince the woman that someone without a Southern accent could be an EMT. That taken care of finally, he managed to talk her into dispatching an aid van to the street corner here. He thanked her and hung up.

Jack leaned casually against the phone booth. "They're coming. Know what an EMT is?"

The kid didn't answer. He was desperately fighting an unmanly crying jag — and losing.

"Medical people who arrive first at the scene of an accident. Ambulance people. I am one. The doctors won't come out, but EMTs and paramedics do. I'll drive along and help."

"Ain't nobody gonna help Uncle Harold." This was clearly not the boy's idea of the thing to do. He had received his orders, and he had failed the assignment. No doctor would come. His skinny, scrawny little shoulders sagged.

But the ragged head didn't. The fire still burned, the anger still smoldered. The boy's spirit was not the least bit broken. He stood resolutely beside Jack not because he wanted to, Jack knew, but because he had no other options.

Jack pointed down the street. "That's my truck, the gray Dodge four-by." He reached for a shake. "Jack Prester out of Hutchinson, Kansas."

The boy hesitated only the slightest moment before accepting the handshake. He gripped well too. "Wade Manchester."

"And this is Maxx. He's trained as a police dog, but he only obeys when he's in the mood. He never bites anybody who's not a criminal suspect."

Without fear or hesitation, Wade reached out and rubbed Maxx's broad head. "Silky, ain't he? Shines. You brush him a lot?"

"I don't have to. He's just that way. Labrador retrievers have especially oily coats so they can swim in cold water comfortably."

With wildly splashing red and blue, the aid van came rolling down the street. It stopped beside the phone booth, and the cheery fellow with shaggy blond hair, Someone Larkey, rolled down the passenger-side window. "What'd your uncle get into this time, Boy?" He smiled at Jack. "Howdy."

"Shaking the barn roof, and he fell off. Ever'body does that ever' now and then." The boy sounded defensive.

The ambulance attendant nodded at Jack. "Good to see you again, though the circumstances ain't the best."

"They never are in this trade. I've been meaning to stop by and talk to you. You responded to the call at the potluck a couple days ago, didn't you?"

"You two know each other?" Wade looked from face to face.

"He's with the park, Boy, but he's OK." Larkey looked at Jack. "How 'bout you and Boy leading, and we'll follow you. We never been to his uncle's place, but I think hit's kinda back."

"Sounds good." Jack jabbed the boy's arm. "Come on, sport." He jogged to his truck with Maxx at one side and the boy at the other. Wade heeled a lot better than Maxx ever did. Jack motioned Maxx up into his cage, hooked the cage door open, and unlocked the passenger door. By the time he had trotted around to streetside, Wade had hopped in, leaned across, and unlocked the driver's door.

"Buckle up." Jack flopped into his seat, torched it off, glanced in his side-view mirror, and waited until a battered stakeside truck passed. It carried six crates of chickens. "Which way we going, Wade?"

"Out that way." He had trouble latching the seatbelt, but

with a few fumbled stabs he made it. "That Larkey feller is Aunt Kate and Uncle Dick's boy. I'm Estelle's."

"Kate and Estelle are sisters, right?"

"Yeah. You know what he was saying, don'tcha?"

"Sure. He was saying, 'If somebody's rig is going to get hung up in some ditch out beyond Woop Woop, let it be yours.' "

"And you gonna let him get away with that?"

"I won't get hung up in any ditch."

Wade was frowning. "Where's Woop Woop? Turn there."

Jack had to cut in front of a pickup to make the turn in time. "It's Australian slang for way out beyond town. My wife was Australian."

"Ever been there?"

"Couple times." Once to wed her, once to bury her, once in between. And his heart still ached.

He changed the subject. "I take it your uncle doesn't need a doctor very often." Behind them, almost leisurely, the aid van with its flashing lights followed.

"Ain't never needed one that I remember. Always took care of things hisself, or else he had Lovey. I don't think hit's a plain old broken leg. I think hit's something more. A plain old broken leg he could take care of hisself. Like when I broke my arm. See?" He held high his left arm. "Lovey and Uncle Harold set it, and hit's like new. My teacher she said that was terrible and hit'd be crooked forever, but she was wrong."

"Your uncle sounds like a real good man."

"He is, yessiree."

"Lovey. Lovey Hempett?"

"She's Aunt Maizie's girl. My cousin. She knows medicine. She gave me stuff called boneset, and it healed up fine."

"Medicines — like plants that grow around here." Jack felt a bit conspicuous being followed by the aid van with its full complement of lights flashing.

"Lovey says you don't need to spend no money on doctors' 'spensive pills when hit's all growing out there in the woods."

Several miles out of town they turned again beside a barn painted on one side only — the Mail Pouch side. Two miles later they turned off onto a dirt lane Jack would not even have noticed. They made two more such turns and ended up in a parallel row of ruts so obscure that hooty owls were in danger of getting lost. If this was six or seven miles out, Jack ate goldfish.

Rounded, lowering hills crowded in on both sides. To the right a small creek burbled, just beyond a split-rail caterpillar fence. How old was the fence? It was green with moss and festooned with lichen, and a top rail was broken here and there. It zigzagged along beside them for almost a mile.

Jack didn't need directions, because there was nowhere else to go. "Forgive me asking, but what about school?"

"I go to school." The lad glanced at him slyly. "When Uncle Harold ain't falling off the barn roof I do."

"Fair enough. Where do you catch the bus?"

"That barn with the Mail Pouch on it back there."

"Long walk."

"Jess and Lug got farther."

The defile opened out into a dank, placid little valley framed by cottonwoods and tupelos and the darkly wooded hillsides. A cabin-sized, unpainted wooden house hunkered among tar-paper barns and sheds and one of the world's great collections of rusting junk. Abandoned and partially disassembled vehicles sat about everywhere. Even without really looking, this rutted non-road sure wouldn't let you watch the scenery. Jack noticed an ancient Allis Chalmers tractor with a steel seat, a rusty old tedding machine with maybe half its original allocation of tines, and auto hulks dating back to the forties and fifties.

They pulled into the farmyard beside the house.

"He ain't in the house. He's back here." Wade hopped out and ran for the barn. Jack listened to his anxious voice fade with distance as he called Uncle Harold.

Take Maxx or leave him? "Maxx, stay." He rubbed the anvil head and left the cage door hooked open. Maxx's tail flailed, and he woofed, questioning the wisdom of being left behind.

The aid van waddled to a halt beside Jack's truck. Larkey slid out. He grinned wickedly at Jack. "Sure ain't your usual freeway."

"Look on it as good practice for when you get a job herding llamas in the Andes." As they headed for the barn, Jack extended a hand. "Jack Prester. Larkey Who?"

"Huey. Hugh Larkey. But hit's just Larkey." Larkey's grip was the vise lock you'd expect of a good old farm boy. "This here's Chris Arlington. He was on that potluck run too."

Jack twisted to shake with the van driver. Chris carried the backboard and jump box. Both men wore navy jumpsuits with volunteer patches on the sleeves.

"This is an all-volunteer outfit, huh?" Jack slipped some in the eternal mud of the farmyard.

Larkey beamed. "Best in the county too. We can work rings around them city types."

"Sure. All they do is hold the patient's hand a couple minutes until the paramedics come riding up with their shiny armor and white horses. You guys have to be able to handle anything, and you've got the whole job for how long? Half an hour?"

Larkey nodded. "At least. They dispatch an ambulance out of Sevierville as soon as we get the call, but hit's still a half hour at least. This one's gonna be more likely an hour or an hour and a half."

"Same thing in New Mexico. We were a minimum of an hour and ten minutes away from a hospital."

"Thought you were from Kansas."

"Only since last year. I grew up in Colorado and New Mexico."

They came around the corner of the barn.

Chris muttered, "Here," and handed Larkey the backboard and jump box. He turned and sloshed through the mud back toward the van.

Uncle Harold was black. That rather surprised Jack for a moment, since Wade was so blond. In mud that would bog a cow, the withered, spare old man lay on his back with a pillow beneath his head and his knees propped six inches off the ground with a rolled blanket. Fell off the barn roof. If so, the old man had not moved an inch since. He lay on the drip line beneath the eaves. A pile of shakes off the corner of the barn looked hand split.

Wade was prodding him and getting no response. Tears were crowding their way up over his lower lids again.

Jack knelt beside the old man and pressed the sides of his hips. Uncle Harold made a vague moaning sound deep in his throat. His speaking voice was probably baritone or bass.

Instantly Wade wheeled and shoved at Jack. "Get away from him!"

Jack stood up.

Larkey dipped his head toward the van. "Chris's fetching the oxygen." He pulled his handy-talkie and keyed it. Somewhere a repeater squawked. Larkey stepped out twenty feet from the victim to discuss the case with his base doctor.

Snuffling, Wade sat close beside his uncle's shoulder and watched as Larkey talked. How much of the jargon could he pick up? Did the boy know that "possible pelvic fracture" also meant extensive, perhaps even fatal, internal bleeding? Probably not. Good.

As he popped the jump box open, Jack caught Larkey's eye. "What about MAST?"

Larkey chewed his lower lip a moment. "Harold here ain't insured."

"That makes a difference?" The blood pressure cuff lay right on top, easy to grab. Jack stuffed a stethoscope in his ears.

Chris arrived with the oxygen tank and a mask. In low tones he described to the suspicious ten year old what he was doing as he adjusted the mask on Uncle Harold, and why oxygen would help.

Larkey started gabbing with dispatch, cajoling her, describing the remoteness and the choppy back road, stalling for time because Jack had to pump up the cuff twice to get a reading. He finally managed to give Larkey a BP and pulse, and it wasn't good.

The dispatcher hemmed and hawed only briefly before she told Larkey to have a smoky fire or a blue tarp out in ten minutes. Apparently, air support wasn't uncommon back in these hills.

Larkey holstered the radio. "We'll package your uncle, Boy. You go build a fire out in the cow pasture, quick. OK?"

"Why?!"

"Just do it."

Jack explained, "So the helicopter can find us back in this hollow. This isn't the easiest place to pick out from the air, you know."

"Helicopter . . ." The kid's eyes went so wide that Little Orphan Annie squinted by comparison.

Jack expected his first words to be, "Can I ride along?" Instead, they were "You can't do that! No!"

"Why not?"

"We ain't got no money for no helicopter. No!" Wade shook his head violently, and the tears returned.

"There are state agencies who will pick up the tab if you're not insured. Go find the kindling and something to start it with. We'll build it out in the open meadow there, so they can see it. Lots of smoke. It's your uncle, and it's OK. Go!"

Wade ran.

Larkey's crowing was no idle boast. These country boys were as good as any volunteers in New Mexico. And Jack had always thought New Mexico's were the world's best. Between the three of them they slid the backboard under without jiggling Uncle Harold. They strapped him down to the board firmly, immobilizing him so well that you could have tipped the board upside down and he wouldn't have shifted a millimeter. They bundled the old man in blankets because he was soaked through and chilled. They took a second blood pressure reading and commented idly on how slow your average MAST ship can be around coffee-break time. It was unfair to the helicopter crew, but they had to displace their fear and worry somewhere.

Jack and Larkey carried the old man on the backboard out to the pasture as Chris followed with the jump box. They set him down five feet from the fire. Larkey and Chris hovered over the fellow, taking another blood pressure reading.

On his own, young Wade had built a fire and a half. Already it crackled and snapped, bright and lively. The clever little pyromaniac was holding a green pine bough just above the burning wood, close enough to smolder, not close enough to smother the fledgling flames. Thick, acrid smoke boiled up through the damp air — enough green smoke to fill the Astro-Dome.

74

Jack grinned. "You're a genius with fire, sport!"

"You said smoky." Wade glanced for the hundredth time toward his uncle. "I sure wish I could've found Lovey. She's in town somewheres, but I couldn't find her. She'd know just the stuff to give him. She'd have him right in no time."

The green pine needles had charred, so he dropped that branch on the fire and reached for another. At his side lay maybe half a dozen freshly cut green boughs.

"Can I stay with him in the hospital?" His eyes were red and puffy, his nose running.

"No, usually not."

"What would they do with me?"

"Hand you over to social services and find you a foster home to stay in until your uncle's back on his feet."

"That's gonna be a while." He drooped, literally and figuratively.

"Months. On the other hand, you can't stay here."

"Why not? Lived here most of my life."

"Not alone."

"Yes, I can."

"Sure, as long as everything's going along all right. But how about when something goes down crooked, like happened to your uncle? What if Uncle Harold fell there, and nobody was around to give him a pillow and prop up his knees and make him comfortable and go for help? What if you hadn't been here?"

Wade stared at the ground a moment. "I can stay with Lovey or Lug and Amy, like Jess does. Jess is my sister, and Lug and Amy's my half brother and sister. They're with Herman."

Jack was going to need a computerized genealogy program to keep track of the Krazy Kemper crew. Or maybe the Kempers would blow up an ordinary computer.

"OK. Get your stuff together, and I'll take you over there."

"Who's gonna milk if I go? And feed the chickens?" But the question went unanswered, because his head snapped up, instantly alert.

Moments later Jack heard it too. The muffled *b-b-b-b-b-b-b-b* became a firm *bl-bl-bl-bl-bl-BL-BL-BL-BL*. The chopper appeared beyond the trees at the far end of the pasture.

Wade stood up, awestruck, and gaped. He dropped the green bough. It smothered the fire almost instantly, to no one's loss. The rapid *blam-blam-blam-blam* grew to an impressive, thunderous clatter that reverberated off the hills, bouncing together and feeding on itself.

The shining blue-and-white bird settled to the ground fifty feet away. Paramedics in white jackets hopped out, all crisply efficient. One of them, a strawberry blonde with shoulder-length curls, carried an IV bag and a steel bracket hanger to be clamped right to the backboard.

"What are they gonna do?" Wade's voice sounded uncharacteristically soft and fear-filled.

"Start a line down here on solid ground before they take him up. It's probably pretty bumpy up there." Jack translated his own jargon as he led the boy in closer by the hand. "Watch. They slip a needle into a vein in your uncle's arm so that they can start a flow of fluids. His blood pressure is really low, and it'll help. And they can shoot medicine directly into him. It's the first thing paramedics do."

Jack recalled the powerful thrust when Wade pushed him away from Uncle Harold, and he imagined the battle going on inside the lad now. But Wade didn't try to yank his hand out of Jack's grip. He watched frozen as the paramedics stuck a huge needle into his uncle and taped it down to stay, but he stood still.

"How about" — Jack looked at Larkey — "Wade rides along in with his uncle, and when I come get him I'll bring your backboard and C collar home."

"Good. Save us a trip in. Don't forget the pillows and blankets. Three blankets. They like to stock the hospital at our expense."

The paramedic with the pink hair stood erect. "Sorry. The boy's too young."

"The old man's never been to a doctor, let alone a hospital. He's going to need the boy for emotional support." Jack reached for the badge case in his hip pocket.

"We're not supposed to —"

On impulse Jack flashed his badge. The National Park Service badge meant absolutely nothing outside a national park, but did she know that? Apparently she didn't, because when he said, "For both their sakes, I insist," she made noises about getting special authorization as next of kin and so on and so on.

The bottom line — for perhaps the only time in his life, Wade Manchester would get to ride in a chopper.

7

There Is No Quick and Easy Way to Rear a Child

— Judith Martin, *Miss Manners' Guide to Rearing Perfect Children*

"There ain't no quick, easy way to raise up a young'n, but some's easier'n others." Wade's stepfather, Herman Tapps, leaned casually against Jack's truck fender.

Jack tried to not to think about the screwdriver in Herman's back pocket.

They had gotten Uncle Harold hospitalized and stabilized and reasonably comfortable. Flashing his EMT certification card, Jack had taken Wade behind the scenes at the hospital, explaining the different units and what nurses' stations were for, then fed him lunch in the cafeteria downstairs where the doctors and nurses and orderlies ate. The kid asked good questions and plenty of them. If he didn't end up in jail for stealing food, he would make a great medical pro of some sort. And then they had driven here to Herman's, dropping off the backboard and blankets and so on at the fire station on the way.

The man continued. "Now Boy there, he ain't easy. So when he wanted to go off with Harold, I said fine and good riddance. Happy to keep Jess. She's good around the house since Estelle left. Keeps the place pretty good and takes care of Lug and Amy. Them's my kids by Estelle, and I got a duty to 'em. But Boy? Always mouthing off and acting tough. Ain't worth the powder to blow his nose."

The boy who wasn't easy to raise sat a hundred feet away at the house, sprawled on the porch and loving up a pair of hounds who were obviously old and long-lost friends.

Now Jack was sure the Kemper genealogy would choke a computer. "So his mother no longer lives with you."

"Shouldn'ta married a Kemper, I know. She run off with Robert Bruce a couple years ago. Left me with all the kids — her two and my two."

"Robert Bruce. Sounds Scots."

"Claims to be a direct descendant." Herman spat derisively.

"And Lovey's mother?"

"Maizie. She's the one that's really crazy. Certified inhabitant of Tennessee State. Lost two babies in a trailer fire."

"And Lovey escaped, as I understand."

"Yep. Maizie weren't never right after that. Lovey kept the place together. She was doing all the cooking from when she was five or six. Then Maizie lost George a couple years ago and went clear off the deep end. Tried to kill Lovey with a shotgun. Was gonna turn loose Lovey and herself both so's they could go to heaven and be with the rest of the family. They say Lovey's still got some of the pellets inside her, in places they couldn't dig 'em out safely."

"Lovey's had a hard life."

"We all do."

"Amen to that." Jack's dead wife Marcia's Australian family were Irish by ancestry and clung to the culture of the Auld Sod. His mother-in-law's favorite saying came straight from the Irish: Life is meant to break your heart.

"Say, I gotta go over to Hatchertown this afternoon, pick up a fuel pump, and get some pullets, they're ready. Since you're here with Boy, s'pose you'd mind picking up the kids at the bus stop and maybe getting me some hamburger or something for their supper? I'll pay you whatever it comes to. I should be back by dark."

Jack felt the distinct impression he was about to get stuck for a couple pounds of hamburger. "Happy to. Wade knows where to get the other kids?"

"Wade? Oh. Him. Yeah. They're on the late bus. The school has Lug and Amy in some kind of program with 'alternative' in it. Keeps 'em late."

Jack whistled and motioned "Come" when Wade looked at him.

The boy really was more responsive than Maxx at times. He gave the hounds a final rub and came trotting out across the muddy yard. The dogs followed him as far as they could, jerking the clothesline ropes that tied them to the porch supports. Jack could hear the porch creak from all the way over here.

Jack smiled. "We're going to go pick up the kids and hunt up some stuff for supper."

"Sure. See you later, Herman."

Herman nodded to the boy, thanked Jack, and said good-bye. He was wandering back toward the house by the time Jack slid behind the wheel.

They drove in silence out to the end of Herman's lane and another half mile down a dirt road.

"Here." The boy waved at a wide spot. "Bus turns around here 'cause it can't turn around at Herman's."

"His yard looks big enough."

"He don't want no bus tearing up his yard."

"Mm." Jack was feeling depressed, and he wasn't sure just why. "Thanks for tying up his dogs when we arrived. I thought for a while there we'd have a royal dogfight with them barking at Maxx. For certain, it'd be too noisy to talk.

How come I'm the only one calls you Wade?"

"Ever'one else calls me Boy 'cause my pappy's Wade too. My pappy, he's Man, and I'm Boy."

"Where's he?"

"Nashville. Ma didn't want to go to Nashville, and he said they was going, so she divorced him. He's gonna be a star like George Jones."

"Music star, you mean."

The boy bobbed his head. "Not no movie star for sure. He says he ain't got the looks. But he sings real good. And when he's a star, Wade Manchester, I'll be Wade Manchester too. But nobody calls me Wade yet." He stared at a rank, abandoned pasture across the road. He twisted and looked behind them. He turned and gazed off again.

"What do you see, Wade?"

He pointed. "Hogs have been into the cattails over at the bottom there, see? All tore up? Real recent. And I was thinking, if a lion or wolf got after 'em, your dog back there would be acting antsy. But he's asleep, so there likely ain't no wolves or lions around."

"Wolves and lions around here?"

"Yeah! See, there's all these wild boars. They're not like pigs. They're European."

"European wild boars? Big, ugly, long-legged things with long snouts. Dark gray hair."

"Right! A herd of 'em gets to rooting, they can tear up a couple acres. They're pretty good eating if you get 'em young. Not much fat. Anyway, the park's turned loose wolves, and they're hoping the wolves will eat the boars."

"Because the boars are tearing up the park."

"Yeah. And the boars eat salamanders the park's trying to save. And the park claims there ain't any lions, but there are. Herman seen one. I'd love to. And I'd love to see a wolf. I seen tracks. They're around."

The big yellow bus came lumbering back the road. It turned into the wide spot, so Jack pulled out and around and drove in behind it in a clumsy, circling pas de deux. The driver, a total stranger, waved. Jack waved back. He had temporarily forgotten the unassuming camaraderie among people who live away from crowds.

Herman had described the children. Jack recognized them as they clambered off the bus. The tall, lanky girl with freckles would be Jess, aged twelve. At age nine, the boy named Lug weighed more than Jess, and he was a good six inches shorter. Jack never did find out what Lug's Christian name was. Little Amy, very small for her age, had just turned five last week. She looked fragile, a doll of a child.

Here were kids in the raw. Jack wasn't used to kids in the raw.

As he prepared his doctoral dissertation on communication with murderers aged ten and under, he'd worked with kids in juvenile halls. He'd worked with parents in clinics. In that self-important manner that psychologists have honed to a fine edge, he studied kids and offered solutions in sterile, carefully controlled, contrived settings.

The bus pulled away, lurching.

Jack got out and leaned across his hood and let the septic, uncontrolled, certainly noncontrived circumstance swirl around him.

Boy introduced him to the kids — didn't do badly, either. He told them about Uncle Harold. He explained the situation. Jack found himself letting the boy do the talking as he sat back and weighed the kids' interactions and psychological structures. More analysis. Marcia used to accuse him of being too clinical, even with their own little Matthew. Maybe she was right.

Jess sighed. "Maybe you guys ought to go get some hamburger, and I'll fetch Amy home and take down the wash. I didn't get it took down yesterday 'cause we were so late. Pa complained about it."

"Maybe," Lug suggested, "we could get something besides hamburger. Something fancy, like hot dogs or something."

Jack looked from face to face. "Let's just go to McDonald's. I'm hungry too. We can get take-out for Herman."

Jess's soft blue eyes opened wide. "We don't never eat at places like that. Hit's too expensive."

Jack stared. "You guys never ate at McDonald's? No fast food?"

Boy shrugged carelessly. "Stuff ain't good for you anyway."

"Come on." Jack motioned to his truck. These kids could get by without MTV and Nikes and CD players and all the other accoutrements of so-called civilization, but fast food? That was taking the term *sheltered existence* too far. "Maxx, come." He slapped his leg to bring the pooch out of his cage in back. "Jess, you and Lug hop up into Maxx's cage there. I don't have seatbelts for all of you, and that's the safest place to ride. Boy, you and Amy ride up front."

"This yere's a doghouse," Lug wailed, but they got in. Jack latched the cage door. He didn't want them opening it at forty-five miles an hour. He motioned Maxx up into the truck bed in front of the cage and slid behind the wheel.

Boy already had Amy belted in and was latching his own seatbelt. "Herman's gonna have a fit." He grinned. "But hang if I care!"

Jack took them to the first fast-food emporium they came to, which happened to be not a McDonald's but a Burger King.

The kids tumbled chaotically out of the truck, sprayed out across the parking lot like a herd of stampeding cattle, and tumbled chaotically in the King's door.

Jack kept telling himself that the people behind the counter probably served rowdy hordes like this all the time, but he didn't believe it.

He pointed to the menu overhead. "OK. You can order anything you want. You can go back for seconds as often as you want. The only rule is, you have to eat anything you order. In other words, you don't ask for more than you can handle. Got it?"

The crowd fell silent. They puzzled. They gaped. Then Boy, the born leader, took over. He read the menu items one by one and had the girl at the cash register explain what some of them were. When she told him they weren't serving the breakfast menu now, he instantly skipped that panel and read on. Amy got him to repeat some of the choices.

He looked over at Jack. "Anything at all we want?"

"Anything up there."

"Don't it matter what the price is?"

"Nope."

"Herman, he's gonna —"

"He's not going to pay for this. I am. This is my treat."

Jess still wasn't convinced. "If I order a double cheese thing there — the big one — is that all right?"

Jack grinned. "You'll love it. They're really good."

It took ten minutes for everyone to sort through this huge overkill of choice. In the end, Boy ordered for Amy because she couldn't decide. Lug started his meal with a chocolate shake.

They settled into a pair of tables in the center of the store. Enthralled by the play area beyond a glass window, Amy had to be coaxed to eat. When Lug offered to take over half her burger, Jack let her abandon dinner and go play.

Jess finished her double cheese whopper. "I'm going to go play too, all right?" She peeled out of the seat without waiting for an answer.

Jack grabbed her arm. "No, for two reasons. One, it's just for little kids. See the sign saying you have to be shorter than that bar there? Besides, little Amy is smothered by all you big kids all the time. This is one thing that's just for her. Let's let her enjoy it."

Before long, a girl Amy's size entered the play area. The two children eyed each other warily for maybe three seconds before they became fast friends. Jess watched longingly. Jack felt bad for her. She didn't enjoy much play in her life.

Lug asked, "Can I get one of their cherry rollovers?"

"Sure." Jack handed him the change. "The lady at the cash register calls them turnovers."

Jess giggled. Lug punched her arm as he left. It wasn't friendly.

Jess popped a french fry and talked while chewing. "Lovey sold that runt pup yet, Boy?"

"I dunno. Hain't seen her since you did."

Jack said, "At the funeral. Is that when you last saw her?"

Jess nodded. "Didn't get much time to talk then. She was off doing other stuff, and then that park lady come after us, and we left. Don't know why she had fire in her eye. They was plenty of food just sitting there. Besides, the caterer's a cousin of Lovey's, so she's a relative of our'n."

Boy had good instincts. He shifted away from the topic. "Lovey's dog, Bugle, is prob'ly the best dog in the county. Bears, coons, boars, whatever you want, she finds 'em. And she whelps good pups. I mean really good pups. Most everyone around knows about 'em, and sometimes even a tourist buys one."

Jess bobbed her head. "Lovey's made lots of money off that dog, just selling pups. And she gets paid for loaning Bugle out. When one of the hunting guides around here wants to really impress a rich client, he'll borry Bugle."

"What's her breed?"

Boy talked with his mouth full too. "Blue tick. Got maybe a tad of redbone in her, but hit don't show. Her pups tend to favor the pappy for looks, whoever the pappy is."

"So she doesn't breed her Bugle to any one particular dog, for instance in order to get the best price for puppies?"

Jess shrugged carelessly. "Whatever's in the neighborhood."

The wide and husky Lug flopped into the seat. The whole table unit shook.

A trace of pride tinged Boy's voice. "Lovey says she's gonna get rich. Make it or marry it, she don't care. Bet she does too!"

Lug sneered. "Gonna hafta make it, 'cause who'd marry that skinny witch?"

"Ain't no witch!"

"Is too. She casts a spell on you, you're dead. She can raise you up from dead too, with some of her potions. Like Eph Meyer's Belgian mare, remember? Hit fell over dying, and she mixed up some plants and stuff, and — *boom!* — the old mare stood right up again. Life or death. If'n that ain't a witch . . ." Lug's voice trailed off as he got serious with the turnover.

With a world-weary sigh, Jess corrected her half brother's excesses. "Honestly, Lug. You and your witch business. Wouldn't blame her if she casts a spell on you sometime. Sure she's life and death, but just 'cause she knows the herbs."

"Death?" Jack asked.

Jess thundered on. "That's where she's gonna get rich,

mark my words. Getting paid for making medicine for people."

"Death?" Jack asked.

"She was thinking once about marrying Mr. Abcoff, the park man, but he was already married just then. But she said she was thinking about it all the same. He has lots of money."

"Death?" Jack asked.

"Like the time Mr. Abcoff wanted to get the rats out of his basement. He said he'd pay her if it worked, and then he tried to get out of it. So she said if'n he didn't, she could mix up something that would bring the rats back. She could too. You mix honey and catnip and smear it around, and a day later you got rats. Guaranteed. So then he paid her. She still laughs about that."

"You're saying she got rid of his rats for him."

Jess's pale eyes sparkled. "She mixed him up some rat poison, and a week later they're gone. Ain't been back since."

8

More Things Are Wrought by Prayer

than this world dreams of.
— Alfred Lord Tennyson, *Prayer*

Nobody can grasp how powerful prayer is, Jack mused. He paused in the middle of reading Luke 6. Here was Jesus spending a full night in prayer before the momentous decision of picking out His special twelve. His choice would shape His church for thousands of years. Indeed, His choice would shape His own betrayal, and apparently He knew that.

Maxx walked over, stuffed his head brusquely up under Jack's elbow, and snorted, vibrating his cavernous sinuses. Jack paused to rub the shiny black head. Maxx moved forward as Jack's fingers worked, until his hand was rubbing the base of the dog's tail. Maxx extended his muzzle and closed his eyes, enthralled.

"There. Now go lie down."

Apparently reassured that he was still a member of the pack, Maxx wandered off and flopped down.

Now if anyone was in solid with God, it was Jesus, Jack thought. He knew His Father intimately and eternally. He thought like God because He was God. And yet He prayed. Prayer to God equated intimacy with God — not just asking favors and advice and giving praise and thanks, but utter intimacy. If that be true — that the more you had of one, the more you had of the other — Jack was in deep sneakers.

His prayer life, never wonderful to start with, took a nosedive after he lost Marcia. It was getting a little better lately, but it sure wasn't anything to write songs about.

Back to Luke.

Someone rapped on his motel room door. Maxx erupted in a spate of barking that probably rattled the windows and made the curtains whip about, but Jack's back was to them.

"Come in." Jack looked up from Luke as Ev followed her knock into the room.

She frowned. "You said you studied the Bible in the morning. Hello, Maxx." She bent over to fend off the exuberant greeting.

He lifted his Bible off his lap, a "See?" gesture, and flung both feet in approximately the same direction, a preliminary to standing up. They hit the floor with a thump.

"Well, you don't look like you're studying, splayed out all over the chair like that. One foot up on the table and the other draped over the side, you look like a teenager on the telephone. How can you concentrate? That's enough, Maxx."

"Maxx! Lie down. Go! This is pleasure, not work." He crossed the room to put his Bible away. "It's a good forty-five minutes from your place to mine, and it's only a little after six. Therefore you haven't eaten yet. So may I take you to breakfast?"

"I was going to take you." She was still staring at the Bible. She wasn't upset exactly, but she looked unsettled with her face puckered like that. "How many times have you read it?"

"I don't know. Fifteen or twenty." He pulled the radio out of its charger, holstered it, and snapped the holster on his belt.

"Aren't you getting a little bored?"

"Never. You throw a full bale of a hay to a horse, if it ate it all at once it'd explode. So it eats its hay over a period of days and gets all the nutrition it needs. Same with Scripture." He got his denim jacket out of the closet — he hardly noticed the water heater in there anymore. "God figures if you got everything His Book has to offer all at once, you'd pop. So He gives it to you in increments, as much as you can handle at a reading. But there's so much there, you find new insights every time through."

She didn't seem convinced, but she didn't comment as he escorted her out.

So eager was he to get out and get going that Maxx heeled without being told. His heavy tail flailed with hope and affection and pure, soul-singing glee as he licked Jack's hand.

Jack could think of one prayer that would make God's kingdom on earth a far better place: *Dear Lord, make me the kind of person my dog thinks I am.*

He locked the door behind him. Nearly all the newest motels had doorknobs that were permanently locked on the outside. Forget your key, and you were in trouble. He liked this one a lot better.

She eyed this curious historical anomaly of a brass knob with the old-style lock plate as a high school senior would look upon a bustle dress. "Why were you sure I haven't had breakfast yet?"

"You are not a morning person, and breakfasts are optional for night persons. I'm flattered you got up so early for me." He stepped off the porch into a glowering morning overcast.

"I wanted to catch you before you left. And I wanted to show you my car. And I just wanted to get out and drive." She walked down to a vehicle Jack recognized — from the garage-and-used-car lot in town — the little red MG Midget convertible.

"I didn't know they lease cars. Or is this a loaner until you get yours back?"

"I'm not going to get mine back. They're writing it off. Too many expensive things to repair." She paused by the driver's door. "I left the top in my room to make more space and just hoped I wouldn't need it this morning. I thought maybe Maxx could fit in the top well. He might have to stay here, though, do you think?"

"Let's see. Maxx, saddle up." Jack opened the passenger-side door and slapped the top well.

Maxx never hesitated. He galumphed up onto the bucket seat and from there scrambled between the two seatbacks into the narrow space behind them. He filled it wall to wall.

Jack climbed in. "He's sure not going to be turning around back there, but he fits." Jack was wedged in just as tightly. And Ev took up her whole seat. No roll bar, nowhere to duck. "If you roll this thing, we're dead."

"I'll try not to." Her voice dripped acid. "Because you're a man, I'm certain that you think you could have done better in that pursuit. That we would either have caught him, or we'd still be chasing him."

"I never said th—"

"I'm certain you think that because I know that every man in America thinks he's a better than average driver. Well, I happen to consider myself a better than average driver also. No tickets, no accidents ever."

"Oh yeah?" He smirked, feeling a bit bad about catching her in an error. "What about Mount Rainier last winter, with your rental car hanging off a cliff?"

"That doesn't count! The other car slid into mine, and there was nothing I could do to avoid it. And I did the best I could this time too. So you will please quite referring to it."

"I will quit referring to it even in jest, which is what this latest reference was."

She stared at him a moment as if she didn't want to believe

him, but she didn't have much choice. "Where's a good place for breakfast?"

"Actually, the little coffee shop right here." Jack pointed across the parking lot. "But if the object is to get out and drive, there's a good place up the road a mile or so."

She bobbed her hair — the slightest nod would do it — and torched off the motor. It sounded like a sports car with a bad muffler and a short in the wiring somewhere. She had never used a gearshift before. That was obvious. It was also obvious that she was determined to master it. She took each step carefully and separately, stepping on the clutch, looking at the shift knob for the desired number, cautiously shifting, releasing the clutch, depressing the clutch, checking out the little gear map on the knob for the next position, shifting . . .

Away they went, fifty miles an hour and eighteen inches off the asphalt. Jack could look up at other people's hubcaps.

He glanced at her face and did a double take.

Here was a woman with her heart in the clouds. She beamed. He smiled to himself at her pleasure. "You know, Ev, you're getting such a kick out of this rental, you ought to consider buying yourself a sports car sometime."

"This *is* my car." She looked at him. "Laurel and I were admiring it, and the young man made a good offer, and Laurel said, 'Oh, take it!' and I thought about it a while, and he took a hundred dollars off the price, and I said yes."

Laurel. It figured. "What year is it?"

"Sixty-seven or sixty-nine."

"Make up your mind."

"It's a sixty-seven body and a sixty-nine motor. And I noticed the windshield wiper motor has sixty-four painted on it. It's a Sprite grill and hood, but that's all right. They're interchangeable." She said it with careful nonchalance.

"Did you happen to ask why it would need a new hood and

grill? That sounds a lot like a collision to me."

"He said something about hitting a deer. It's really commonplace around here, he says, to hit a deer. They eat along the roadside. This café up ahead on the right?"

"Yes." *You believe a used-car salesman with a beater on his hands, but you won't listen to the gospel.*

She slowed, appeared perplexed that the car jerked, and remembered to shove in the clutch. She shifted thoughtfully and deliberately into second and tooled it into a parking slot.

Jack ran his fingers through his hair. If he rode in this little tooter much, he'd need an industrial-strength currycomb. The top of his head protruded above the windshield. Before he walked inside, he used the comb he kept in his wallet. It jerked and hesitated as he dragged it through the tangle.

He told Maxx to stay in the car. At the restaurant door he glanced back. Maxx was plopping down to sitting in the passenger seat, casually looking around.

Ev brought in her briefcase. It and the trunk in which she carried it were about the same size.

They settled into a curved corner booth, ordered, and basked in the warmth of a batch of really good coffee. Why did he feel so strongly that Ev got rooked on the car deal, and why should that upset him so? Like liberated women everywhere, she lost no opportunity to point out her independence. Hits and errors were equal parts of independence. Freedom of choice is the freedom to make a mistake. He had no part in her choices, so why should he want one?

And why did he so enjoy her presence beside him?

Unanswerable questions. Jesus had faced unanswerable questions too, such as, "Which of these people hanging around Me are good material for apostleship?" Were Jack the one picking Jesus' apostles for Him, would he have chosen a couple of foul-mouthed fishermen, a tax collector, a political zealot, a sneak thief? He wondered idly what the rest of the candidate pool must have been like. He was pretty sure at least two of them were ordinary guys, Matthias and Justus. He wished he could enjoy prayer intimacy with God even now as he worked on this complex puzzle.

Ev not only broke his train of thought, she derailed it. "Why did you look up my birthday?"

"I was curious. I sometimes look up things in the encyclopedia too, just for curiosity. You're not in *World Book*, incidentally."

She studied him a moment and wagged her head sadly, an "I give up" gesture. She spread out a file folder between them. "Look here. Laurel sets up one of these charts when she writes a mystery. It's a great idea, Jack! The vertical columns are the Suspects, and the horizontal ones are Means, Motive, Opportunity, Alibi, and Other. Then you fill in the blanks. Isn't this neat?"

The skepticism in his mind must have seeped out onto his face, for she became instantly defensive. "It organizes your thoughts and keeps you from missing an important detail. Also, it shows what we should be trying to find out. For instance, here. Opportunity. Who had the opportunity to do something to cause Colleen Abcoff's death? We're assuming poison, probably aconite. And who would know about such a poison? See how it works?"

"Wait a minute, Ev! This is all proprietary stuff. Strictest confidentiality. I'm not even giving it to Weineke or the law enforcement specialist. And you're spilling inside stuff to a writer! That's like blabbing it to the newspapers! In fact, it *is* blabbing it to th—"

"Stop it!" She very nearly slapped his face — she had that look in her eye. "Don't you dare think I'd be so stupid, Jack Prester!" She glanced around the room guiltily and dropped her voice. "I don't talk about the case, and she doesn't ask me anything about the case. We don't —"

"Then what's all this? Of course, you —"

"She showed me how she does it, but I filled in my own charts. And changed them a little. She isn't interested in the case. She's interested in our methods. She wants her story to be authentic, so she has to know how the chain of command goes, and how we investigate, and all that kind of thing. And then she uses her own crime and characters and everything."

Silence hung between them for a moment.

She spoke low, tight and controlled. "Let's clear this up right now. If you don't trust me, just say so, and I'll get Hal to assign me somewhere else."

He kept his voice just as low. "No. I don't want you to go."

"Do you trust me?"

"I trust you." *Mostly.* "I just don't want to see some aspect of the investigation compromised because of —" he waved a hand helplessly, knowing he was in deeper than he could get out of "— of idle conversation where either you or I said something without thinking. This is an extremely high profile case —"

"Hal explained that to me."

"— and the media are churning the waters as we speak. Press from four states, half a dozen mobile TV units in the park, and the local radio stations sent some people out. When's the last time you saw a radio reporter face to face? We can't afford to be lax in the tiniest regard. They're going to stick this case on the front page as much as they can. Millions of readers have visited this park. Shucks — millions of *reporters* have visited this park."

"Hal said all that. We're in a fishbowl with this one."

Jack drew a couple gallons of air in through his nose. "Enough said." *Get off it, Prester.* He tapped the square where

95

Andy Abcoff, vertical, crossed Means, horizontal. "Let's pretend the agent really is aconite. Abcoff doesn't have to have the slightest idea what monkshood is. All he has to do is pay someone who does know. He waves a hundred-dollar bill and says, 'Quick, effective poison,' and the unknown person supplies him. Same with Walling. She might be the one who did the supe, and the attack on her is something else altogether. Life is more complex than your little chart here suggests."

She twisted to stare at him squarely. "Abcoff? A hundred-dollar bill? A twenty, maybe. You can pooh-pooh it if you want. I think it's a very helpful idea, and I'm going to use it." Independence. "Laurel also builds character charts, but we already have the characters. So I modified it to keep track of what we learn about each person."

She whipped out another paper. This one charted the names in the horizontal column and the attributes vertically. Parents, children, income, unique needs, preferences, music — an amazingly eclectic array of traits were tracked.

Jack looked at Lovey's Parents and Other Close Relatives column. It was blank. And he wouldn't have the slightest idea how to begin to fill it in. "I'll give you this. You're fairly comprehensive about listing suspects. But again, it could be someone we don't know about yet. Or a blast from the past — an enemy from some other park and time — or someone sending in a professional hit."

She had the Carl Sandburg National Historic Site superintendent, Galen McFarland, on her list, as well as Abcoff, Lovey, Bodine, Richard Platt, Walling, Bill Weineke, and Hiram Jones.

Hiram Jones? He frowned. "Who's Hiram Jones?"

The waitress set his bacon and eggs in front of him. "Owns the hardware store downtown. If you can't find it there — sometimes he don't have it — you might try Ace Hardware up at the north end by the Stony Brook Motel." She gave Ev her oat bran muffins.

"Thank you." He said grace while Ev was extricating her eating utensils from their tightly rolled paper napkin. Were grace and other forms of routine prayer still prayer in the deepest sense? Jesus always blessed His bread. "Why Hiram Jones?"

"He's furious because he claims the park stuck him for several thousand dollars of nonreturnable insulation. They asked him to buy it for them, and he did so in good faith. Then they got it from GSA instead. He can't get his money back because the company he bought it from went into receivership. To top it off, the company claims the government caused them to go bankrupt."

"Yeah, sure." Good eggs and bacon.

"Actually, that might be legitimate, Jack. You see, the Small Business Administration helps companies get started by sending government contracts their way — business to see them though the first few years, when it's roughest. But after three years, the government quits giving the company preference. All of a sudden a major source of income dries up. If the company hasn't built a clientele apart from the government contracts, it folds. That could well be the case here. I can find out easily. I'll check on it."

Jack nodded. "That sort of thing is your bailiwick. I'll take your word for it. You know, Hiram here is an iceberg tip. If we really start to dig for everyone who has a gripe with Colleen Abcoff — or Diane Walling, for that matter — your list of suspects there is going to be eighty-seven feet long."

"All the same, I don't think we should discount people like Hiram, especially local ones."

"I agree. You might want to make the contact on that one. I think his store sells auto parts as well as hardware. You're going to have to get to know him soon in any case." He could tell without looking that she was glaring at him.

Since they were making plot charts and suspect charts, they worked out a genealogical flow chart of the Krazy Kemper sisters. It probably didn't contribute significantly to the investigation, but it was sure interesting.

9

I Think That I
Shall Never See

a poem lovely as a tree.
— Joyce Kilmer, "Trees"

" 'I think that I shall never see, a poem lovely as a tree.' "
Homer Clarence Symes, Jack reflected, looked like exactly what
he was — a paper pusher. The park's personnel officer was
probably still on this side of fifty, but his receding hair was graying already, fading to a ho-hum salt-and-pepper. *Mousy* — pejo-
rative as it may be — was the first word to come to Jack's mind.
Symes's little gold-rimmed glasses, slight paunch, and sallow
skin completed the picture of a man who spends his days among
ledgers and computer terminals.

" 'Poems are made by fools like me, but only God can
make a tree.' " Jack completed the famous lines. They stood
side by side in front of the administration building, Symes at
Jack's right and Maxx at his left. Neither Maxx nor Symes
seemed particularly smitten with each other. Maxx pretty
much ignored the personnel officer, and Symes eyed the dog
uneasily from time to time.

The overcast was thickening, and Jack wondered if Ev
knew how to get the top up on her new old MG.

Symes smiled. "That is perhaps the first poem I ever committed to memory. I couldn't have been more than six or
seven."

"Me too. Of course, when a boy six or seven memorizes a

poem about trees, there's coercion involved. I had to do it to win a recitation prize."

"You won a prize for poetry recitation at six?"

"No, I lost. A girl who recited "Paul Revere's Ride" end to end won it. Four pages, fine print. I was outclassed."

Symes chuckled and pointed off fifty feet to the granddaddy of all oak trees. Gnarly and full of character, it spread in glorious majesty across an acre of sky. "Now that one. Scarlet oak. You should see it in October when the full sun hits it." He pointed elsewhere out across the asphalt. "Over there, just beyond the admin officer's parking space, that tulip tree. Most visitors don't know what tulip trees are. If they notice it at all they think it's a maple."

"Similar leaves, sort of."

"The similarity is slight. People really don't care, and they probably have a tulip tree growing within a quarter mile of them, if they live in most areas of the East."

Jack looked at the little man. "*You* care."

"Botany is an interest of mine. Always has been. You had to be coerced to learn the poem. I didn't." Symes turned and started back into the building. "The young woman who works with you. Evelyn."

Jack fell in beside him and held the door. "She'll be here in an hour or so. She had some things to do in town first." Getting acquainted with Hiram, who will probably be able to retire to Florida if she wants to keep her sports car running. He and all the other auto-parts dealers in town. Maybe they can get a group rate to Miami Beach. Or Cancún.

"Good. Good. She had a problem with her insurance carrier. I took it upon myself to talk to the company and work out a solution for her. She'll have to sign some papers."

"She'll be thrilled. And relieved. She was thinking she might have to swallow the loss herself."

Symes stopped in the doorway and cleared his throat in an insipid way. "Ah . . . uh . . . there's a more or less understanding that dogs don't come into the building." He glanced again at Maxx.

"Just as well. He's not real good in an office setting. He breaks pencil points off by pressing too hard, and he tends to slobber on the paperwork. Be right back." Jack jogged out across the lot to his truck and unleashed Maxx. "Saddle up." Maxx hopped up into his steel cage, and Jack hooked the door open. "Stay." He returned to the office.

Symes was still waiting in the doorway.

Jack followed him in and back the hallway. "Do they really have assigned parking spots here?"

"Not really. Our names aren't spray-painted on the curb. But we tend to take the same slot each day. Habit."

"Like getting territorial about your pew at church."

Symes chuckled again, a feeble audible smile. "Exactly." He crossed directly to his work station, riffled through the third deck down of his in-basket, and pulled out a sheaf of papers. "Bill Weineke said you wanted personnel records for Ms. Walling and Ms. Abcoff. Particularly prior positions they held. I made hard copies for you. It's so much easier to read, I think."

"I agree. I'm grateful. I guess I'm still not of the generation who squints at computer monitors comfortably. Or microfiche, either." Jack flipped rapidly through. "Thank you. This is exactly what I want." He paused and thought a moment. "Next I'm going to ask Bill for records of all unsolved incidents similar to Abcoff — presumed poisonings, maybe — in the area in the last few years. Is he going to then dump my request off on you?"

"Quite probably. I'm considered — how shall I say this? — the mundane-tasks specialist here. Sometimes they're jobs totally unrelated to personnel management."

"Then I might as well ask you directly. Similar deaths or near deaths, in the Park Service nationally and any nearby."

"Mm. Yes. I can do that. I can hit any computer Greg can. He'd probably ask me to do it anyway, since he's so involved with the investigation." Symes stared at nothing for a few moments. "You might also talk to the state police — that is, highway patrol. They handle the bulk of drug enforcement. I can tap the records, but they might remember something that isn't in the record."

"Good idea."

"County sheriff's offices, of course. Bill can get you their phone numbers quicker and more easily than I. He's in constant commerce with them. Blount and Sevier counties would have the bulk of it, but don't forget that Monroe and Cocke counties also touch on the park in Tennessee. In Carolina, you have Swain County and Haywood to an extent. Monroe County doesn't abut the park, actually — it's across the river, but — how far will your field of inquiry extend?"

"I don't know. But since Greg and Bill are handling the routine investigation — the usual pursuits — that leaves me to look at unusual things." Jack paused. The more he thought about this . . . "You know, I'm thinking, here are two unsolved problems back to back. Not just Abcoff. Both. Are they related? Have there been others, and do they have a common thread? The Walling incidents and Abcoff could be the same thing. They could be totally unrelated. Finding similar unsolved cases — I mean, not just cases that look like these but all serious incidents — might give us some insight into the person or persons responsible."

Symes's thin eyebrows rose. "Brilliant approach. You have a psychology background, as I understand it."

"Yes. Might as well use it, since I spent all that time and money getting it."

"You were born and raised Park Service, is that correct? Rural or urban areas?"

"Rural. Remote."

"Interesting. How shall I say this? Stereotypically, people raised in rural circumstances do not earn advanced degrees."

"You put it very well. I'd probably just say, 'Country boys are no good except for milking cows and maybe driving truck.' I ran into that a lot."

Symes nodded knowingly and waved the note he had just written himself about Jack's request. "I'll work with Greg on this. If we put our heads together, we should be able to assemble the information promptly."

"Thank you." Jack good-byed the man and continued around the corner toward Richard Platt's office. He bumped into Andy Abcoff, figuratively and very nearly literally.

Instantly, the bereaved resumed the glare he had been wearing when last he left Jack's presence. "You're going to hear from my lawyer about that false arrest."

"Tell him to read up on citizen's arrest before you do, and mention that we documented the marks on Lovey Hempett's throat. Since we're unexpectedly face to face, clear up a couple little points for me if you would. You were supposed to be out of the area until Sunday. What brought you back?"

"That's none of y—"

"Official inquiry. Do you want to make it a formal sit-down discussion? I have the time."

Abcoff stared at him, and not in a friendly manner. "I finished my business there and decided to come on back and finish business here."

"Details?"

"Too numerous to mention."

Should Jack pursue or skate off elsewhere? He schussed away across the pond. "Why did you feel the need to carry a weapon for protection at a funeral?"

"The world is full of bozos — and one smart person. I hear someone tried to run you down."

"Something like that." Jack's neck hairs bristled. He knew it was mostly personality clash, but the guy irritated the willikins out of him. "Let's go sit down and discuss matters. I have —"

"Sorry, I have a plane to catch." Abcoff smirked and flashed an airline ticket sleeve, pulling it just far enough out of his inside jacket pocket to let Jack see what it was.

Jack sidestepped to block his way. He held out a hand. "May I?"

Abcoff's jaw dropped a bit, as if the man were dumbfounded that someone would doubt his veracity. It took him a long moment to remember that Jack was an official investigator and, as such, best not disregarded. He brought it out and let Jack pull it from his fingers.

The ticket was a current airfare, all right. Sevier-Gatlinburg to Hendersonville, via a local white-knuckle airline. Abcoff had just over two hours to make his flight.

"Suspicious me. You see, when I was in college, I'd carry an old bus ticket along. If someone cornered me and I didn't want to talk to them — the dean, frequently as not — I'd wave it and say I had to catch a bus. It worked an embarrassingly frequent number of times." Jack handed it back to him. "I envy your guts. I've never had the courage to fly these little puddle-jumpers."

Abcoff stared a moment longer and snickered as he stuffed his ticket back in his pocket. Was that a derisive snicker or merely a condescending snicker? Jack couldn't tell. He did notice that although he good-byed Abcoff, he got no farewell

104

in return. The big man hastened out the door. Jack continued on.

Richard Platt's little naturalist's office looked like an explosion in a van line warehouse. Open cartons cluttered the floor so thoroughly that you couldn't walk in a straight line. The papers and memorabilia of a lifetime of service were stacked all over, waiting to be crammed into boxes far too puny to hold the burgeoning memories.

From his desk chair, the rotund man who looked a little too much like Santa Claus smiled at Jack. "My last full day in uniform. If they want to fire me for spending it packing instead of naturalizing, let them."

Jack squatted down beside a box of books. He hefted the two volumes on top. "Britton and Brown's *Flora of the Eastern US*. Heavy stuff, literally and figuratively."

"I'd like to say it's my bible in the trade, but I rarely use it. I like the popular what-plant-is-that work as much as the public does."

He hated to disturb the man's packing. Moving out of an office is a surprisingly heart-wrenching act under the best of circumstances, and Platt's circumstances were far from good. Jack laid the books down and stood up. "Surely you're an expert on ecology, biology, geology, and all."

Platt removed his glasses from his little red nose. It didn't dispel the Santa effect. "My family is centered around Flat Rock, so I've lived in the central Appalachian area nearly my whole life. Yes, I can call myself an expert without being boastful."

"Extended family, you mean? Your wife is here, isn't she?"

Platt looked at him oddly. "Bill didn't put it in his reports? I would have thought he did."

"Put what?"

"I'm not married. I have what is currently termed a 'significant other' and three children. I'm pretty sure that's the major reason Colleen turned on me. She disapproved. Strongly. She broke people for less."

"When I was talking to others, they didn't mention it. The disapproval, I mean."

"Marriage." The man stared at his tangled array of boxes, and his voice slipped into the past. "I was rebellious, once upon a time. I decided marriage was not an institution I wanted to fall victim to. To be tied to a person. Living situations didn't last any more than did marriages, and divorce is always so messy.

"Our sixteen-year-old daughter is pregnant. The fifteen-year-old boy is out on street corners in Knoxville with a pager and more money than I see in a month, dealing. The twelve year old has pink hair that sticks straight up and thinks his older brother is God on the hoof." He looked up at Jack, meeting him eye to eye. "And now my lady has left me. This forced retirement was the final straw in a shaky relationship. The fruits of rebellion are slow coming sometimes, but they come."

"So you're alone."

"I'm alone. Some brothers and sisters in Flat Rock. A cousin. No wife to walk hand-in-hand with into the sunset. No children to turn to when I'm aged and doddery. I didn't think yesterday, when I was young, that this would matter. It matters so much."

Jack leaned on the doorpost. "I heard you were down in Atlanta yesterday. Trying to redress some of the injustices? Fighting for a better deal?"

"No." There was a finality to his tone of voice. "No, the damage is done. Colleen was an ogre, but she knew how to use paperwork. The documentation can't be reversed."

"If it's false —"

"Nothing false. Consider an illustration I heard once — I forget where. The captain of a ship notes in his log every fourth or fifth day, 'The first mate was sober today.' When the ship returns to home port, the owners read the log and fire the first mate, getting rid of a chronic drunk. The log is accurate. The mate was sober on those days. However, what it does not say is that the mate was sober all the rest of the time also." He spread his hands. "Documentation."

"That makes you, if not a strong suspect, at least a person of interest." Jack watched the man's hands and feet for nonverbal clues and saw none. "Vindictiveness. Let's say vengeance."

"Then I'm not alone."

"No. We have bushels of suspects. You're just going to have to wait in line. Do you know Galen McFarland, the man with whom you exchanged places?"

"Professionally and personally. For years. We first met at a training class in Harper's Ferry years ago."

Did Jack detect a twitch in Platt's hands? "When Colleen Abcoff first raised the subject of switching positions with Galen, how did you feel?"

"Dubious. I couldn't see that moving from a superintendency to this chief naturalist's position, no matter how prestigious the park, would benefit me. But it would certainly help Galen's career, so I acquiesced. Besides, there are important issues here. A strong hand at the helm could improve the park immensely."

"Issues." Jack shifted, afraid to enter and sit down for fear of disturbing the many piles of papers.

"The boar population. The red wolf reintroduction. The salamanders, and in fact many of the amphibians, are increasingly endangered. And the Fraser fir loss. How should we handle that?"

107

"What about Ms. Abcoff's development plans?"

Santa Claus hardened. "My position on that is public knowledge."

"Tell me about it anyway. I hear all these theories and rumors but nothing solid."

Platt settled back and laced his fingers across his considerable front. "Spruce-fir forests. The park is the southernmost range of red spruce, a northern species. For some reason in the last few years the trees have stopped growing. No new annual rings, poor needle retention. And the Fraser fir."

"Tiny insects are doing in the firs, right? Balsam woolly adelgids."

Santa almost smiled, albeit grimly. "Yes. They appear as a fuzzy white growth on the tree bark of Fraser firs. They attack the trees only after they mature enough that their smooth baby bark, so to speak, roughens into adult bark. It's about the same time they start producing cones. Adelgids can kill a mature fir in three years, and we can't stop it."

"A lot of dead trees and virtually no reproduction."

Platt nodded. "So what shall we do with all these destroyed forests? An introduced pest killed the firs, and pollution, we guess, is destroying the spruce. All we have left — or soon will have — are extensive stands of ghost forests. Killed not by nature but directly or indirectly by the hand of man. Colleen was going to put a considerable chunk of that destroyed wasteland to use by building an Appalachian wonderland inside the park. A sort of master Disneyland based on the local culture, complete with the equivalent of magic kingdoms. A park within a park. Her rationale was that the area was destroyed anyway by exotics and therefore no longer of use as a preserve."

"Nothing left to preserve."

"Precisely. So we might as well draw revenue off it. I'm

sure she knew better. She must have known better. But that position suited her dream for empire-building, so that was her public position. Colleen Abcoff above all was a consummate politician. She promised lots of jobs to the locals if this went through. They opposed her in public and supported her in private."

"Bodine Grubb?"

"He among them. She promised revenues to the regional lawmakers and prestige and new directions to the national leaders. Something good for everyone. She hadn't really pushed the plan publicly yet. She was lining up her power sources behind the scenes, so that when the environmentalists exploded she would have her people in place to quell the explosion."

Jack considered this a moment. "That's crazy. If she had this wild plan, and everyone here knows about it, so would all the environmental groups in the world. They'd be on her like fifty cardinals grabbing for the last sunflower seed."

"Crazy. Exactly right. The Smokies are a United Nations' International Biosphere Reserve. The holiest of holies as regards ecodiversity. I could not convince anyone that she would seriously consider a development like that within the park. It was too farfetched. No one was bothering to mount a defense because no one believed she could try it. But she could. No one as yet realizes how very, very close she came."

"Except you."

"It's a nonissue now. The developers she was lining up would need a powerful and well-positioned leader to carry the project forward. I don't see anyone of that sort on the horizon."

"So the danger is past."

"Let us hope so."

Jack could think of a dozen other things he ought to talk

about with this man, but he wanted even more to talk to Bodine. He also wanted to get started with his survey of possible suspects hidden in the rosters of the parks where Colleen used to work.

But most of all he wanted to find a rest room. Standing up like this for so long had gotten to him, not to mention three cups of coffee at breakfast. He excused himself with a few pleasantries.

A yellow plastic sandwich board was set up outside the men's room warning that it was not in use because the janitor was cleaning it. Jack could see through the open door that the janitor happened to be female.

OK, so he'd use the tourist facility across the street. He walked outside into a misting drizzle and crossed the parking lot. Ev was going to have to learn how to put her top up for sure now. He was pushing in through the door on the men's side when he happened to notice a car parked on a service road out behind the developed area.

Virtually hidden by the dark and lowering forest beyond the asphalt, the trees, and the leafy rhododendron, there sat the black Lincoln.

10

The Beauty of a Rare Spring Morn

. . . greeted Sir Edmund as he stepped out.
— Richard Hillyard Allen, *The Vicar's Secret*

Ah, what a beautiful morning this day was turning out to be! Jack's heart, muddled just a few moments before, burst into song. He yanked his radio off his belt and keyed it. "Six-oh-one, six-oh-three, six-ninety-eight. I have our black Lincoln, visual. He's in the service road fifty feet off the pavement, here at — he's moving!" Jack sprinted for his truck.

Blending to near invisibility in the darkness and the forest, the black car glided forward. It rolled out onto the pavement.

Jack paused long enough to see which way it turned and ran the last fifty feet to the truck. He pointed at Maxx back in the cage. "Stay!" He flopped into the seat and cranked the ignition, backed out of his space at twenty-five miles an hour and slammed it up into first. The truck leaped forward at thirty and out onto the highway. He was doing fifty by the time he got his seatbelt hauled around and hooked.

He got on the horn again. "Six-oh-three, six-oh-one, anybody! He's proceeding west on Little River Road. I'm on his tail. Who's out there?"

"Six-ninety-eight, six-oh-two. That's Greg Vosniak to you, Jack. I'm just leaving the parking lot at Sugarlands. I'm right behind you. Six-ten, six-oh-two."

Six-ten answered, so crackly Jack knew he couldn't be

anywhere near. Apparently 610 was out at Cades Cove. Between them, they decided 610 should set a roadblock where the Cades Cove road left Little River Road. Then they called a maintenance man at Tremont and told him to hurry down the road and close the gate at Metcalf Bottoms.

It was raining hard enough now to require windshield wipers.

Jack saw red taillights flash ahead. It was a tourist car that had just been passed. Horn blaring and emergency flashers blinking away, Jack came up behind him. The driver pressed right, and Jack swung out left, praying that no one was coming eastbound on this narrow, winding road.

Greg Vosniak was trying in vain to raise a ranger at Elkmont up ahead. A couple of other voices joined in the radio chatter, but no one was near enough or in the right place to do any good. Greg told dispatch to send a sheriff's department unit down 321 and south on the Wear Cove road, in case the Lincoln turned north.

He and everyone else were getting into the spirit of the chase. Jack was certain, and the others probably knew too, that the Lincoln was listening in on the radio chatter. Otherwise he would not have taken off like that when Jack radioed that he saw him.

Jack laid the radio on the seat. He hated to lose the seconds it would take, but he slowed enough to grope around underneath and find his red roof light. He pulled his ashtray open — the handful of parking-meter change rattled in it — and plugged the light into the cigarette lighter. He cranked down his window, licked the suction cup on the bottom, and slammed the flashing light against the roof.

He took a left-hand turn too fast. The radio slid sideways across the vinyl seat and disappeared over the side. It fell with a clunk between the seat and the right-hand door. Beyond reach. Of course it immediately proceeded to say, "Six-ninety-eight, six-oh-two."

Should he stop at the roadside to retrieve the radio and answer 602, or should he press the chase? Probably if he were in a proper attitude of prayerful communion with God, not just on a casual on-demand basis but all the time, he'd have a clearer idea of what to do. He hated having to admit he failed so miserably in that area. He needed help now. Guidance.

He glimpsed the Lincoln ahead. He was closing! The Lincoln had no options but to follow this road to the next roadblock. A couple of service lanes providing access to borrow pits and maintenance yards left the paved road, but they dead-ended. The Elkmont turnoff just ahead dead-ended.

Six-oh-two declared himself out of the race. Either he blew a tire or an engine — Jack couldn't tell which. Someone was about ten minutes behind 602, which would put that person twelve minutes behind Jack.

They zipped past the Elkmont side road. Now, as the road followed closely along the gorge and the riverbank, the way became tortuous. Jack made a couple of nasty passes around tourist cars that he never should have made.

And there remained the danger that he would round a tight curve and find a two-car head-on collision, the Lincoln and a poor innocent who happened to be eastbound at the wrong moment. Jack would never be able to stop in time to avoid making it a three-car wreck.

The radio chatter intensified as others got caught up in the chase. The comm center finally raised someone from the sheriff's department. Jack was close enough now that the Lincoln ought to be able to feel the heat from his headlights.

They were coming up on Metcalf Bottoms. If the maintenance fellow had made it there in time to close the gate, they had this joker. Jack came out of a right turn to see the Lincoln scant yards ahead of him. Yes!

Beyond the short straightaway, a flashing yellow light marked a parked maintenance pickup with an aluminum boat in its truck bed. Yes! Yes!

A portly man out in the roadway was rapidly swinging a big iron-pipe gate closed. *Yes! Yes! Yes!*

No! He wasn't going to get the gate locked in time. If he didn't run right now he'd be crushed.

He ran and dived down flat onto the grassy berm.

The Lincoln hit the unlatched pipe barrier with a clang. The Lincoln's back end wagged. The iron pipe swung out wide. The Lincoln recovered and rolled on down the road.

Now here came the pipe swinging wildly back again, right at Jack. It clunked against him at an angle as he passed, about headlight level. His whole truck shuddered and lost traction. He counter-steered against the fishtail and accelerated.

The road turned seriously snaky now, hugging the riverside. Radio chatter speculated on why Jack wasn't answering. *Because my radio's out of reach, and I'm going to have this guy shortly.* Jack's Dodge was much more maneuverable on this tightly sinuous stretch than was the Lincoln.

He adjusted the windshield wipers to high as the rain came in earnest.

The Lincoln nearly missed the double curve ahead. Its back end swung out too far to the right, skidded, sprayed roadside gravel across the pavement as it swung wide left. Its brake lights flared on, brilliant in the dull, rainswept gray.

Jack hit the curves too fast for conditions. Like ball bearings, the wet, loose gravel unhooked all four wheels. He went into a frenetic skid. As the back end came around, his front wheels dug into the mushy berm. The cab tipped left, flinging him sideways.

For the second time in seventy-two hours he was riding

out a rollover. Bouncy little trees and cushioning bushes had caught Ev's vehicle and brought it to a soft, safe stop. Great, solid, unforgiving creekbed boulders reached out to catch his.

Cold water.

Maxx squirmed.

Rushing water.

Shove head up out of the water.

Cage upside down, half in water, half out.

Jack will tell him what to do.

Cage door open. Don't wait. Scramble out. Get out.

Truck upside down.

Maxx leaped out into the tumbling stream. The swift current carried him abreast the half-submerged cab.

Clamber ashore.

Smell gas. Smell blood. Smell Jack. Jack's blood. Maxx's blood.

Wait for orders. No orders.

The big black car pulled up, screeched to a stop. Maxx knew the scent of the person.

Coming this way. Help coming.

No. No help. Gun.

Jack? No orders.

Hostile. Danger. Gun.

Maxx felt the person's attitude. *Anger. Intent to kill.*

Jack? No orders. Defend Jack! Defend the truck!

Snarling, Maxx leaped forward.

The person screamed. The gun roared and hurt his ears. The person turned, ran back to the car, jumped in. The back wheels spun, throwing gravel. It stung Maxx's face, his eye. He bit at the spinning wheel. Missed.

Take the perp down! No orders.

Same smell as other time. Same person.

Jack ran with Maxx then, chasing this very perp.

Chase!

Maxx ran down the road after the car.

Scent fresh and clear. Rubber smell fresh. This way.

Squirrel smell. Chipmunk. Keep running.

No other cars passed this way.

Strange scent. Omnivore. Very fresh. Like pig but not quite pig. Like javelina but not quite javelina. They crossed here. Forget it. Chase.

Deer. Also deer. Not recently.

Dogs crossed here. Not dogs. Wild. Wolves.

Maxx slowed, limping.

Have to walk. Shoulder hurts. Won't work right. Blood smell still strong. Ribs hurt.

Walk. Catch the perp.

Tired. Pause. Lick.

Twist around tight, just barely reach blood on shoulder. Lick. Nibble it. Bite it. Try to stop the pain.

Chase perp.

Walk.

Tired.

Squirrel chirrs in tree overhead.

Wolf smell strong here. Fresh. Nearby.

Shoulder hurts. Ribs hurt.

Tired. Rest. Sit. Lick blood.

Bear smell. Dogs. Both here recently. Very fresh.

Chase perp.

Can't.

Try.

Can't. Shoulder won't work.

Lie down. Shoulder hurts. Ribs hurt.

Rest.

11

"John," said I, as we stood
looking at each other across the boat,

"This Rain Is Wet"

— W. H. H. Murray, *Crossing the Carry*

"This rain is wet!" Bill Weineke looked as if he were about to stand up in the boat. Tied to the shore, the rowboat was none too stable anyway. The current tugged at it. Its stern bumped against the right wheel of Jack's upside-down truck.

Jack glared at him. "If you think that's wet, try standing here in the river." With a deep breath, he doubled over and ducked below the surface again. This water was cold enough to freeze Brazil. Jack pulled himself along under the over-turned truck bed, groping. He was certain Maxx's crushed cage was empty. Now he was trying to find a furry body wedged somewhere in the jump box or the rocks, pinned beneath the truck. Nothing. His lungs howled at him, protesting mightily against the lack of oxygen and the relentless cold.

He wormed his way back out and popped to the surface. Icy water poured out of his hair and down his face as he gulped air. He would have pulled himself ashore, hand-over-handing along the safety rope around his waist, but his hands were too cold to grip it.

Greg Vosniak hauled him in by his rope like a catfish on a line. Jack flopped to sitting on the weedy bank.

Weineke carefully maneuvered himself ashore without falling in.

The maintenance man was wearing his rain gear, rubberized pants and a rubberized hooded jacket. His clothes were in his hand. "Here. My shirt and pants are still pretty dry. Take them there wet clothes off and put these on."

Weineke didn't wait for Jack to acquiesce. He knelt in front of him and unbuttoned his shirt. "I realize you were soaked because your cab is underwater, but you didn't have to go and dunk yourself twice more."

"Yes, I did. If Maxx was under there I had to find him before we winch the truck out. The current could have washed him away when the truck was lifted." The rain in his face felt warm.

Bill looked at him hard. "It might have anyway."

"I know."

I know, Bill, and I can't stand it.

He struggled to his feet, shivering uncontrollably, and let them strip him. He let them put the dry clothes on him. He let Greg slip his own body-warm jacket on him. It felt good. He let them try to cajole him into seeking medical attention. On that he remained adamant. No. He was all right. You don't need an ambulance ride for a bloody nose, and it wasn't even bleeding anymore. He had to find Maxx.

Why, oh, why did that stupid mutt run off, if that's what he did? Was Maxx wedged in the rocks downstream somewhere, drowned, or was he halfway back to Townsend already? Jack couldn't picture Maxx leaving him and the truck. If Maxx were alive he'd be here. Labs don't drown. They're born and bred to swim comfortably in frigid water. They retrieve ducks, for pete's sake. He couldn't have drowned.

Unless he was injured.

His cage was crushed.

"That Lincoln oughta be at the Cades Cove road by now."

Weineke keyed his radio. "Six-ten, six-oh-one."

Silence.

Repeat.

"Comm, try to raise six-ten for me."

The disembodied comm center voice called the Cades Cove ranger, apparently switched frequencies, and tried again.

Greg and Bill looked at each other. As one, they broke and ran for Bill's car. Jack ought to jump in and go along. He couldn't. He couldn't bear the thought of another high-speed ride along a winding road.

He was scared.

Four bells, the prowl car spewed roadside gravel as it sped away.

The maintenance man stared at the flashing lights that were gone instantly. "This ain't real. Want to take my truck?"

Jack shook his head. "I'll help you put your fishing skiff back in your truck. We're not going out into the water anymore, are we?"

"Let's leave it. The tow truck'll be here shortly. He might want to use it to hook onto you."

"Yeah, that's true." He wished he could think better. He wished he could think at all. He watched the crystal water tumble and roil down through the rocky riverbed. He rubbed his face. "I'm too addled to be any good to anyone. I'm going to work my way downstream a ways and see if I come across Maxx."

"You sure you shouldn't wait for the tow truck? And Bill said —"

"I'm sure. And I know what Bill said. I was here when he said it." Jack coiled the rope they'd used to belay him and slipped it over his shoulder.

Life was too heavy to carry. He ought to head out for

119

Cades Cove and help the rangers. He ought to get on the radio in the maintenance pickup and tell Ev he was all right. She'd worry. He had to find Maxx. Maxx might be hurt. Bleeding.

He walked down to the river and began working his way along the rocks and brush streamside.

He wouldn't whistle. If the dog was swept downstream and made it ashore on the far side, he might hear the whistle and try to swim back across. He might get into trouble with the current. Jack would have to depend upon visual contact, then assess the situation before calling the dog to him.

What if someone out along the road found his dog? There was no way he would hear about it. Maxx might be all safe and warm this minute while Jack scrambled through rank weeds and slippery rocks. Why did the stupid mutt not stay put? Jack should not have been so lax about obedience. He stopped every few feet, trying to peer through the churning water, scanning both banks.

The rain abated before it soaked through this jacket. The exercise, dry clothes, and windbreaker were doing their job — he didn't shiver anymore — but he was still wearing his soaking-wet running shoes. His feet were blocks of ice. His toes ached.

Very shortly his calculated concern gave way to uncool terror. He began whistling periodically, hoping the dog was anywhere within earshot, not caring on which side of the stream the pooch might be.

A helicopter came *bam-bam-bamming* along Little River Road. It wouldn't be seeking a dog impossible to see from the air. It would be looking for the Lincoln. A nice gesture, but futile. A big black Lincoln that wanted to stay lost need only park beneath a fir tree. His hair dried out around three. A little before five he realized he had followed the river right out of the park. Townsend lay ahead only a couple of miles. The river had flattened down, though the water still ran fast. He stood on the empty bank and watched the empty stream rush by. His empty heart sighed. He whistled the piercing whistle that could call Maxx in from Canada. It echoed off the steep hillside beyond. Crows cawed somewhere. A flock of chickadees came peeping through behind him. Otherwise, silence.

He walked along the river another half mile, occasionally climbing over a fallen tree or ancient wire fence, and essentially gave up. Had Maxx been captured by the current and lived to tell the tale, he would have found him by now. There was no way the dog could have ridden the river this far. No way, in fact, would the river have carried his lifeless body this far.

A quarter mile across this pasture, a little red sports car was sitting on the shoulder. Jack gaped a moment. Then he cut away from the river and slogged across the low, soggy field. He crawled over an old horse-wire fence and up the berm to Ev and her MG.

He climbed in without invitation, folding his legs up one by one and stuffing them in sideways. "Do you know what happened out by the Cades Cove road? Bill and Greg were afraid something was amiss."

"Nothing. I talked to Bill a couple hours ago. He said you'd probably turn up downstream here eventually, so I came out and watched for you. The reason the ranger didn't answer was because he was away from his car too far to hear the radio. The black car didn't show up there. It just disappeared." She touched it off and drove toward Townsend.

She didn't say anything more. He was grateful. Another mile or so and they arrived at his motel. She parked in front of his room. He stared at his door without moving.

"Be right back." With far too much energy and enthusiasm, she trotted off to the lobby. She returned moments later, unlocked his motel door, and stepped down to the curb. She handed him a key. "I told the desk clerk your motel key is in your wet clothes yet, but he doesn't believe me. He thinks this is an assignation. I didn't bother to argue."

"Thanks." Time to move. He extricated himself with no small degree of difficulty. Sitting in this bucket seat, even for so short a time, was making him stiff. He'd be a fireplace poker by tomorrow morning.

She preceded him inside and marched directly across to close the far window. He was grateful for that too. He felt cold again, now that he'd quit walking.

She turned and looked at him. "You probably don't feel like eating. You ought to anyway. I assume you want a hot shower first. I'll go make reservations at that café across the parking lot."

"They don't take reservations. But yeah. That's a good place." He paused as he dug a pair of jeans and underwear out of his drawer. "How'd you know my clothes are wet?" He pulled his wet shoes off and left them lying.

"Overturned in the creek? It's all over the park, not to mention the evening news, with pictures. Incidentally, I took pictures of your truck too. They'll be ready tomorrow. And those pants you're wearing are big enough on you to fit two people into."

He pulled a shirt off the hanger in the closet with the water heater. "Find my uniform shoes, will you? I'll be right out."

The hot water felt so good he stretched his famous thirty-seven-second shower out to maybe two or three minutes. As he was drying off, he heard the closet door click. Why was she nosing around in his closet? Admiring the water heater maybe?

He stuffed his shirttail in as he came out into the room. His uniform shoes were sitting on the bed. So was a pair of socks.

She turned away from the window. "You have a beautiful view. I see why you like this area. I saw three different kinds of birds besides robins and English sparrows, and I've only been watching a minute or so. I put your running shoes upside down on the water heater. That should dry them as quickly as anything."

"Thanks." He sat down on the bed to put on his shoes and socks. He glanced over where Maxx's food and water dishes sat. They were gone. His eyes flitted to Ev.

"I put them in the closet. Now you don't have to look at them unless you want to." She sat in the chair by the window. "As soon as I heard Maxx was missing, I called Hiram Jones. The hardware store? He sells weapons and ammunition, and he knows all the hunters in this area. I guess the bear hunters hang out there. He'll spread the word. He put up a missing-dog notice in his store for me. There's a bulletin board. And Laurel ran off some bills that we stuck up on phone poles. She has this little laser-jet printer that isn't any bigger than her laptop. Graphics and everything. It does a marvelous job."

Jack grimaced. "You do all the organized, sensible stuff while I stagger around in the woods accomplishing nothing."

"Accomplishing a great deal." Her voice purred, cloud soft. "I'm so glad you didn't find him in the river, Jack."

"So'm I. Hiram still open?"

"Till six."

He got up and retrieved the phone book from the desk drawer. She recited the number from memory. He put the book away and dialed.

A voice that made Andy Devine sound like Luciano

Pavarotti snarled a surly greeting.

"Jack Prester. I lost a big black Lab today."

"Your girlfriend already has the notices up. Find him?"

"Not yet. Ev says you know everyone in the area. Where do I get a horse? I want to go out early tomorrow along trails and back roads, cover a lot of territory, and some of it is places a vehicle can't go."

"Ride much?" The voice sounded like marbles in a hubcap.

"Much."

"Not the commercial stables. They're expensive, and they won't let you go out unescorted. I assume you want to."

"Yes."

"Where do you want it and when?"

Jack had to think a moment. "Dawn at Metcalf Bottoms, in the park. Know where that is?"

"Yep. Forty dollars a day plus ten dollars to trailer it?"

"Sounds good."

"Sunup at Metcalf Bottoms. It'll be waiting for you." Click. Dial tone.

Jack hung up absently. He realized he was staring at Ev, and he dropped his eyes. "He's either extremely businesslike, or he has the manners of a Norwegian troll."

She giggled. "Both. Jack? Can I go along, please?"

"No, and not for the reason you think. You haven't ridden much, and you'd get extremely sore. I mean extremely. It's literally not worth the pain. Let's go eat." He dug a pair of travelers' checks out of his underwear drawer because his cash was soaking in a soggy pants pocket somewhere. "I better cash these at the front desk, since I don't have any ID with me."

The desk clerk tonight was a young man with one of those haircuts that's shaved around the sides and thatched on top like a hut roof in Pago Pago. He leered at Jack and Ev most unprofessionally.

Jack laid a check on the counter. "May I?"

"Certainly, Mr. Prester. You're in room four, right? I . . . uh . . . don't see your truck."

"Rolled it today." Jack countersigned and counted his cash twice to make sure.

"So sorry, sir."

As Jack and Ev headed for the door, the kid grabbed a phone and punched in an extension. Jack heard him say breathlessly, "I was right, Bertha! It *was* him!"

It was drizzling again, so Jack helped Ev put her top up. The latch system was designed by a Neanderthal. It took both of them leaning on various bars and handles to get it closed. They strolled on over to the restaurant.

Jack still felt numb. He let Ev hold the door. He let Ev talk to the hostess. He practically let Ev hold his chair for him. He stared at his menu without anything registering. He might as well let Ev order for him.

"Jack, look!" Grinning, Ev stood up, waved, and sat down again.

Laurel Clum came sweeping through the dining room, with long, silken jacket tails flowing out around her. The last person in the world Jack wanted to see . . . no, the last person he wanted to see was Saddam Hussein, but Laurel Clum came in a close second. He stood up stiffly.

They greeted all around, some more enthusiastically than others, and Jack let Ev invite Laurel to join them. Laurel accepted.

He sat down stiffly. The waitress came, and he let the women order first. When the waitress looked pointedly at him he waved a hand. "Whatever. I don't know," and Ev interpreted that as "He likes patty melts. And bring him a small

125

salad, please. He hasn't had his greens yet today." Salad? Maybe letting a health-food freak order for you isn't the best thing.

Laurel was hitting on all cylinders, a ball of energy. "I put up some flyers in Wear Cove and Townsend. I stopped by because I had an idea you two would be here sooner or later." She whipped a small leather-bound notebook folder out of her purse. "Technical question. What's the difference between a national park and a national monument?"

"They're spelled differently." Jack wasn't hitting on any cylinders to speak of. "You'll notice none of the letters in *park* is found in *monument*. But they have the same first name."

Ev sighed. "A national park is established by an act of Congress, and a national monument by presidential proclamation. That's the easiest difference. There are other details, mostly administrative."

"That'll do fine. It'll sound authoritative. That's what I'm looking for." Laurel jotted herself a note. "The theme of this book I'm working on now is the urgency of protecting biodiversity. Usually in —"

Jack frowned. "In a mystery novel?"

Laurel's brown eyes crinkled in the most charming way when she smiled. "Oh, yes. If I were to preach to you — write my message in a nonfiction format, that is — you'd put your guard up. You'd analyze everything I said and agree or disagree and perhaps reject the message. So if I really want to convince you of something, I'll frame it in a fiction context. Your guard's not up when you read fiction. You're too busy enjoying the story. The message soaks right in, with little or no critical analysis."

"So that's why Jesus told all those parables."

The eyes sparkled. "Bingo. Do you read mysteries?"

126

"My bank statement's pretty much a mystery to me. Other than that, no."

"Ev says you grew up in New Mexico. You really should try Tony Hillerman. You'd love him. His protagonists are Navajo tribal policemen. Try *Coyote Waits*. And *People of Darkness* is truly unique. As I was saying, usually in ecology stories the villains are the developers. I don't want to go that route."

"What other villains are there?"

"Plenty. White collar crime. Embezzlement and then murder to cover it up." She paused as the waitress deposited salads in various places.

Jack's was one of the places, thanks to Ev's misguided faith in the virtues of eating live plants.

"At the funeral I talked to that Andy Abcoff. He, and several other people as well, told me about an idea to build a theme park inside the national park. So I'll take that idea and twist it a little."

"It's already pretty twisted." Jack stabbed morosely at his lettuce.

"I agree. But I want to change it somewhat. It's been around a while, and I need a fresh approach. New and zingy." Laurel tackled her salad with gusto.

It was probably Jack's luck that he was trapped in this restaurant with not one healthy-eating fanatic but two.

Ev frowned. "Around a while. What do you mean?"

"They've been working on this for three or four years at least, according to another source. The former superintendent got the ball rolling, and this one — Ms. Abcoff — gave the ball political momentum."

Jack looked at Ev.

"The trick is to take bits and parts of real life and reweave them into a credible story." Laurel salted her salad. Actually, that wasn't a bad idea. This iceberg lettuce was pretty insipid.

"For instance, I can just lift that little mini-mystery right out of real life, change details, and work it into my plot. Also, I hadn't thought about it until you two came along, but I see a perfect place in the story to wreck the protagonist's car."

"What mini-mystery?"

Laurel looked at him blankly. "Oh. I thought you knew." She momentarily laid her fork down. "The superintendent before this one. Gerald somebody — I'd have to look in my notes."

"Rackenberg. He died a couple years ago. Forget how." Jack added, more for Ev's benefit, "I didn't know him, but Dad did."

"Rackenberg. That's it. Right about the time he was drafting this plan for a theme park, he was killed by a hit-and-run."

128

12

Out on the Mountain, Sad and Forsaken

lost in its mazes, no light canst thou see.
— Fanny Crosby, "Jesus Is Calling"

"Out on the mountain, sad and forsaken, lost . . ." Jack couldn't remember the rest of the verse. He remembered the tune but not the lyrics of the poem-made-hymn. And he fit it to a T.

He sat on a fallen log the diameter of a bathtub as his horse ripped at grass here and there beside him. It was a good old horse, though it had taken Jack and him a couple hours to really mesh and get working together. The bulky gelding, strawberry roan with a white blaze and white stockings extending above his knees, looked as if he had some percheron in him. His streaked gray-and-honey mane wasn't any more than six or seven inches long, a mere fringe on the thick, crested neck.

Riding that wide a horse without having ridden at all for a while made Jack ache excruciatingly. To ride for nearly fifteen hours straight was to twist the cruel knife. His body hurt almost as much as his heart.

A few leftover clouds remained from the afternoon's buildup, but they were flattening out, shrinking. By the time the moon came up, the sky would be nearly clear. The orange of the day deepened to the blue-gray of afterdark.

And Jack was as lost as a mouse in a cornfield.

The horse showed no inclination to make a beeline for the

barn when given his head. Once you got into the woods you couldn't even make out cardinal directions, particularly with the overcast that had persisted most of the day. The simplest trail wound circuitously, never pointed exactly where you were going. And now here he sat on one hillside among hundreds and no way to guess which.

He was accustomed to the sweeping, open world of ponderosa and junipers out West, where you could ride a horse between trees practically without detouring or ducking. The country here, almost none of it horizontal, was too rank with growth to negotiate on foot, let alone on a horse. The trees themselves were spaced too close. Adding insult to injury, thickets of brambles, of rhododendron, of thorn shrubs and saplings rendered the forest understory nearly impenetrable.

He wondered if Ev had gotten her car running yet. Laurel showed up at his door half an hour before daybreak this morning, clad in sweat suit and slippers. Ev had called her when she couldn't get her MG started. Welcome to the wonderful world of British sports cars, Ev.

Laurel, the angel, aroused from a sound sleep, had immediately and cheerfully gone to fetch Jack from his motel to Metcalf Bottoms. He knew better than to think the favor was for him; Laurel had done it for her friend Ev.

Laurel dropped him off at the picnic area less than half an hour before a teenaged girl in a ponytail trailered the horse into the loop. Jack had spent that half hour trying to track either Maxx or the Lincoln. But the mélange of tracks and tire marks where the wrecker pulled his truck out had just about obliterated any telling trail, and the persistent rain yesterday completed the erasure.

He wondered where his truck languished, impounded in the park or behind the garage that had so recently accepted poor Ev's white Taurus? Were his seats in the process of mildewing this very moment, so that the interior would forever after smell like a neglected mushroom farm?

Since the Lincoln failed to show at the Cades Cove Road junction and did not double back past Bill and Greg, either it was hiding in the park, tucked away in some forgotten side track, or it had cut north over the Wear Cove road. The sheriff's deputy who drove south down that road said he saw no one. But again, once over the hill the Lincoln could have hidden in any number of leafy bowers. The sheriff's deputy could easily have missed it.

Jack had ridden the Wear Cove road end to end and back again, whistling all the way. No Maxx. He wouldn't have gotten lost if he hadn't started trying side trails. Side trails to nowhere. That was the problem.

Ev drifted back into mind, and he wondered how keenly she felt Maxx's loss. She never really expressed affection toward the mutt, but she was usually affable. He liked the dumbfounded gape on her face when he told her he had looked up her birthday. He'd hauled up her complete dossier on Hal's computer when he was in DC last March. She could look him up too, if she thought of it; he wasn't going to mention that, though. Especially because his own birthday was — what? — a week away? His thirty-fifth. He had to count back to his birth date to make sure. Yeah, thirty-five. He tended to lose track of birthdays since Marcia died. He didn't feel particularly good about marking life's milestones when she didn't anymore.

As the last light of day faded, he untied his jacket from the back of his saddle and put it on. His topo map was useless. Even if he had light to read it, with a topographic map you just about have to know where you are before you can find out where you are. He rolled the map and tied it to the saddle.

Having cropped most of the grass near the log, the horse

tugged its way to the edge of the clearing and resumed eating. Jack was about ready to join him. No eatery is open to feed breakfast to a country boy leaving the house before five, and he'd been nowhere near a lunch or dinner source.

Besides a box lunch or two, he should have brought a handy-talkie — borrowed Ev's if nothing else. He wanted desperately to hear a voice.

He wanted to hear Maxx.

The moon was up high enough now. He tightened the cinch, gathered in the reins, and swung aboard. Grass sticking out both sides of its mouth, the horse picked its way across the clearing and settled to the faint trail descending the ridge.

Available light dropped instantly to near zero as they entered the woods. No one had brushed this trail since D. Boone wore half-size knickers. Branches at stirrup-height, waist-height, and head-height assailed Jack constantly.

The trail hooked around into a steep, soggy creek drainage and disappeared. The ground was torn up here, the smell of fresh-plowed earth heavy on the night air. Maybe half an acre had been ripped apart, small trees pushed aslant, bushes uprooted, ground covers torn asunder. It looked as if someone with a deep-seated psychological hatred of nature had cut loose with a rototiller. The horse, normally a placid beast immune to surprises, stuck his nose high and sidled nervously.

With piglike grunts and snuffles, animals somewhere in the woods departed rapidly. Considering how dense the forest was in this drainage, they made little noise in passage. Boars. Wild hogs. What would they do if they came upon a healthy dog? An injured one?

The horse lowered its head to drink. It pushed its nose around in the creek, but the water had been muddied too much. Jack urged it upstream fifty feet to clear water for another try. He waited until he could hear pigs no more and the horse's slurping ended, then whistled up Maxx for the millionth time. The black and brooding silence of the night would not even throw his whistle back to him.

His trail lost, he took off down a game track, probably the pigs', that he had to follow more by feel than by sight. When that melted to nothing, he let the horse maneuver its way down the tumbling streambed.

A shallow overhang chipped into the base of the ridge, a black blot in the charcoal landscape. He unsaddled and tied the horse nearby. He didn't have to dig out much dirt to build himself a level bed down under the overhang. Hungry as a barn fire, he snuggled into his crevice, rolled up in the dinky saddle blanket with 80 percent of himself still uncovered, and tried to rest. Grief had stolen nearly all his sleep last night. After a full day in the saddle, he ought to be able to catch at least a few winks tonight.

He was just drifting off when crows disturbed him back to wakefulness. Why would crows be calling so long after dark?

They weren't. The sky was barely starting to turn pink.

Stiff as a pencil, he crawled out from under his executive suite. It took him thirty seconds to unfold and stand straight enough that he could shake out the blanket and saddle up. Cold played a part. He was bone chilled — and hungry enough to eat the horse.

Somewhere, very faintly, a dog barked. He bridled the roan quickly and swung aboard. His legs howled with lusty, stabbing pain, especially where they met his torso. He ignored them. He heard the dog bark again. That way. A great distance.

He had to dismount and walk in order to fight his way through the dense bottomland growth, but at least the ground was nearly level. A split-rail fence stopped him. Beyond it, a neglected, overgrown pasture promised easier travel. His horse in tow, he waded along beside the fence like a man negotiating three feet of snow without snowshoes, trying to walk in the tangle of bracken and raspberries and ground cover. Heavy dew soaked his shoes and pantlegs through.

He whistled. No response but a wood thrush tuning up on the hill behind him.

They came to a gate, but it was so old it fell apart as he tried to open it. He dismantled it, therefore, led the horse over the bottom two rails, and wired it back together. Walking had loosened his sore muscles, but not much. He remounted and followed a game trail out across the ragged grass. The horse nipped at everything it could grab as it strode along.

The next gate swung open without disintegrating, far enough to let the horse through. He rode through a real pasture now, braided with faint cow trails and adorned with cow piles. He turned the horse toward a rusty, corrugated-iron barn roof in the distance beyond a neglected orchard. Even if the barn was abandoned, it would offer a lane out to someone's house and, if heaven smiled upon him, breakfast.

The sun would be up any minute. Robins began staking out their territories with warbling songs or hopped through the pasture grass, pausing, stretching up like picket pins.

Bristling and barking dangerously, a ragged, scrawny, gray-blue hound came roaring out of the orchard. The horse jumped, tossed its head, and settled back to the trail. The dog circled him, still barking. It feinted at the horse's legs, scooted away, ducked back in.

A girl's lilting voice called from the distance beyond the orchard. She followed it with a penetrating whistle.

The hound didn't obey whistles any better than Maxx did.

It continued to lunge and feint at the horse as Jack rode through the orchard.

The orchard gave way to a little house that city slickers would no doubt call "quaint" or "picturesque." "Small" would be another good adjective — one story, with a leanto at the back, a detached summer kitchen the size of Jack's closet at home, and a porch the width of the front. On the porch, two old rocking chairs beckoned, inviting weary bones to rest. The house's siding, laid vertically, had never seen paint. With a soft, gray dignity, it blended gracefully into the woods behind it.

Beyond the shaggy, unkempt lawn, the barn Jack had spied from afar stood with the same air of ancient graciousness. Once upon a time it had been painted red.

He urged the horse forward toward the house and stopped. A woman stepped out on the porch, a blonde woman in a floral dress and white apron, a woman with a large shotgun, not to be trifled with.

Lovey Hempett.

She squinted. "Well, I'll be . . . You." She swung the shotgun up expertly and rested it on her shoulder as she stepped down off the porch. "Bugle, here! No more. Bugle!"

Reluctantly the hound broke off the attack, leaving sudden, ringing silence.

Lovey grinned suddenly. "I know! I saw your flyer when I stopped by Hiram's Friday afternoon. You're looking for your dog. That big black dog."

"Yes." Jack glanced at Bugle and risked being devoured alive by dismounting. "And secondarily, I'm looking for breakfast. I didn't eat yesterday."

She nodded past him to the horse. "So Hiram loaned you his daughter's gelding. He didn't mention that."

"This is his?" Jack smiled. Of course. It figured. "That

part hadn't happened yet. I called him Friday evening."

"Hiram says you lost your dog when you wrecked your truck. Dumped it in Little River."

"That's true."

"Tried following the river down looking for him?"

Jack nodded, bone weary, and it was not far past sunup. "I followed it clear to Townsend. So I thought maybe he took off after the person I was pursuing, up over the Wear Cove Road."

She studied him for a long, long moment. "You a country boy or a city boy? You got a sort of accent."

"New Mexico. Country to the core."

"Mm. I gotta milk. Tell you what. You go start a fire in the cookstove while I do that, and we can both have breakfast."

"Sounds good to me."

She headed off toward the barn.

Jack stood a moment, trying to get organized and utterly lacking the capacity to. He tied the horse to the porch post, loosened the cinch, and removed the bridle. Instantly, the horse dropped its head to rip grass, stretching as far as its leadline and halter would let it. Jack hung his jacket on the saddle horn and washed his face and hands in the china basin on the front porch. He was building quite a chin-stubble, having not shaved since early Friday morning. Maybe he ought to grow a beard. Look distinguished. He had a good start on it. Hesitantly — he hated just walking into someone else's place — he stepped into the dark house.

Her house had two rooms, this one and that one, of equal size. This one was a combination parlor and workroom, rustic but tidy, with a sofa, a straightback chair, a quilt frame with a half-finished quilt, and in the corner by the window a big basket of knitting beside an armchair. Beside the basket lay some school workbooks and a practical math text. A ladder and great square hole in the ceiling no doubt led to a sleeping loft.

That one was the kitchen. He walked through the archway into the late eighteen hundreds. Her linoleum, forty years old at least, had worn out. It was clean, though. A kerosene lamp graced the unpainted table by the window. The wood stove, white porcelain with porcelain knobs and dampers, was a kind Jack had seen only in museums and at the Pioneer Yosemite History Center a continent away.

Something brushed his cheek. He wheeled. Dozens and dozens — hundreds — of bundles of plants hung from the open kitchen rafters, drying. In shades of green and gray, picked at all stages with flowers on some, fruit on others, they waited mutely to benefit mankind. None was labeled.

She didn't have any paper to start a fire with, but here beside the stove sat a box of dried moss, corncobs, and pine cones. He opened both dampers, the one in the pipe and the one on the front stove door. He arranged moss and cobs in the firebox, laid some pine cones next, and stacked some kindling on top, tepee style. Her matchbox was down to a dozen or so, so he used his butane lighter.

The moss fizzled, the cobs and cones crackled, and the kindling started to catch. As the fledgling fire grew, he added bigger sticks. He filled the teakettle too. Its bottom was blackened, so he assumed she usually put it right over the fire. He lifted a stove lid and set the kettle directly over it. On the drain board lay a well-used iron skillet, so he set that on the stove to start warming.

She came in the back door presently with bulging apron pockets and a bucket full of foamy milk. She paused to look at the wood stove. Her quick blue eyes darted to his, and the most wondrous smile spread across her face. "Know how you can tell a real country boy from one of them slickers who's faking it? A real country boy knows how to work a cookstove."

He felt vaguely flattered. "What else can I do for you?"

"Set a spell is fine. You look like road kill in a rainstorm. Spent the night on the mountain, right? Sorry you haven't found him yet."

"I'm going to have to shave with a Weed-whacker." He sat down on one of the two straightback chairs by the table and was amazed at how comfortable it felt. Or how weary he was that such a primal hardwood chair should feel comfortable.

"I took a minute with your horse. Don't have no plain oats, so I gave him a scoop of cow mash. I tied him to a laurel bush out in the yard so he can graze."

"Thanks. Sure he won't hurt it?"

"Don't matter if he rips it up. They's plenty." She waved a jar of coffee. "All I got's instant. Sorry."

"Instant's fine. Wonderful."

She slapped a hand on the kettle. "Couple minutes yet." She took half a dozen eggs out of her apron pocket. Talk about fresh. From an honest-to-goodness slab she cut rashers of bacon and arranged them in the pan.

Jack slid down on his spine and stretched his legs out. It was so nice to sit on something that didn't move. "Ever go up into the park during rhododendron season?"

She grinned. "I sure do, every year. Hit's a mighty pretty sight." She tossed a handful of flour in a bowl and stirred in other things without measuring.

"I understand the bloom is spectacular."

"I don't mean the flowers. Got them right here, all around the house. I mean the cars and the RVs. The RVs especially. Like palaces, some of them. Whole parking lots full of the latest models." She plopped her dough on a little tin and popped biscuits into the tiny oven beside the firebox.

The bacon began to sizzle. It smelled indescribably inviting.

She grated cheese on a grater like Jack's grandmother used before she discovered Cuisinart. "When the park's looking for something they sometimes send up a chopper. A helicopter. You don't rate no chopper, huh?"

"Just as well. Nothing beats being right there on the ground looking."

"That's what I always thought. But I'd love to fly in one once." She glanced at him. "You wouldn't, huh?"

He grimaced. "I get seasick."

She looked at him as if his teeth had warts.

"My dad figured out the sure cure. He signed me up for a summer to work aboard a Liberian freighter. He figured I'd be seasick for a week, and then I'd be fine forever after."

"Sounds kinda fun. How old were you?" She stirred her bucket of milk vigorously to bring the cream into suspension and commenced to pour it into glass half-gallon jugs. Apparently she sold her extra milk.

"Sixteen. A great adventure. The captain agreed with Dad. 'A week,' he said. After the week was up, he said, 'OK. Some people, it takes two weeks.' Three weeks after I shipped aboard, he put me ashore in Venezuela, drove me to the Caracas airport, and bought me a ticket home. Do you know how often Liberian ship captains buy airfares that they don't have to? That's how sorry for me he felt."

"So it didn't work."

"I got sick on the plane coming home."

She burst out laughing. He was glad she had recovered that melodious voice. He should ask her about that altercation with Abcoff, here in this nonthreatening setting. He didn't.

For one thing, his brain was mush.

"Close enough," she said of the kettle's temperature, and

she poured not-real-hot coffee. She offered him genuine sugar and cream so fresh it didn't yet know it had left the cow.

The conversation drifted, as she built two plates of biscuits, eggs, bacon, and grits delicately flavored with cheese. She scooped flatware out of a drawer and brought breakfast to the table. He swung his chair around and tucked himself in under the table properly.

She sat down beside him. "You want to say grace?"

The offer surprised and delighted him. He did so, keeping it short and to the point. More routine prayer. He had not prayed last night as he fell asleep. He tasted. Hungry as he was, he lingered to savor. "This is the best breakfast I've ever tasted."

"Sure. Lizard lips would taste good to you now. You been starving yourself for days."

"Not a factor. Trust me. This is art."

Her cheeks flushed. She refilled their coffee. "Church is at eleven. Welcome to come along with me."

"I'm starting to smell ripe, my face is hairy, and I was rolling around in a cave all night. I'll spare the congregation. Thanks, though."

She studied him, unblinking. "Is God looking at you this minute?"

"Yes." He knew where she was going with her point.

"The outside of you or the inside of you? And does He expect you to look any different inside at eleven?"

"The outside could use some spiffing up." So could the inside.

"Hit's a real caring church. My uncle got me going there. We go to worship God, not check to see if our neighbors washed behind their ears. You ain't going to offend nobody, God least of all."

Who could stand against logic like that? He agreed to go if

140

they didn't make newcomers stand up.

They arrived in a rattletrap Ford pickup fifteen years old at least. Its radio was tuned to a gospel music station, and the tuning knob was dusty. She was a one-station listener. Good music too. The truck was neither better nor worse than the other cars it joined in the unpaved church parking lot. A congregation of more than two hundred crowded into the small white frame building. They even pealed the church bell to bid the latecomers hasten.

The choir entered from the back and sang themselves down the aisle to their places behind the lectern, clapping in time. The congregation clapped gleefully along. The first thing their pastor did was make announcements, and the second was ask any visitors to stand up and introduce themselves.

Jack hated this. God knew who he was. But Lovey stood with him, dragging him to his feet, and told the congregation about his quest and about Maxx. Right then and there they all prayed for him and for Maxx. Their earnestness and grace nearly brought tears to his eyes.

One of the congregation mentioned that Harold Gaines fell off the barn and broke his pelvis and that Boy was staying with a stepfather. That occasioned more instant prayer. Jack liked this idea that you don't have to store up prayers for some special time.

They sang old-time hymns he knew and loved, hymns to which he could sing the bass line. The pastor spoke fervently and eloquently on, of all topics, the power of prayer. The service lasted an hour and ten minutes, and then a dozen different families greeted Jack, asked God's blessing upon his efforts, and invited him to lunch.

It was only then that he happened to notice with his conscious mind that he and Lovey were the only white worshipers in the church.

13

I Have a House Where I Go

when there's too many people, I have a house
where I go where no one can be.
— A. A. Milne, "Solitude," *Now We Are Six*

"I'm lucky." Lovey sat in her porch rocker, dipping back and forth as she crocheted a washcloth. "I don't do too well dealing with people. I could never be a waitress, for instance. So God's blessed me with a house here where I go when there's too many people. Way out where others don't come." She glanced at Jack. " 'Cept for some folks who go climbing all over the mountain for one reason or another."

Jack lurched his own rocker back and forth mostly to keep himself awake. The porch board beneath his left rocker creaked with every stroke. After the want of yesterday, the satiation of today felt so good. That world-class breakfast, lunch with friends of Lovey's Uncle Harold, the comfort of this rocker after those dismal sixteen or seventeen hours in the saddle, and best of all, the spiritual filling.

Plenty, and peace.

"Thanks for pushing me into going to church. You're a blessing from God. I needed it, and I was feeling too lazy and sorry for myself to get in gear and go."

"Figured so. When you need refreshment most — spiritual, I mean — is when you feel least like looking for it. Faith don't just come most times."

"Lack of faith. It's always been my short suit." Jack gazed out across the front lawn where the strawberry roan, now on a longline, was diligently mowing grass. "When I lost Marcia and Matt . . ."

"Your kids?"

"Wife and kid. Car wreck. Maxx was about two years old. I'd be sitting there crying, and he'd come over and put his head in my lap. It wasn't that irritating thing of shoving his head at me to be patted, like he does every now and then. He just laid his chin there. Commiserating."

He shrugged to underline his point. "Lack of faith. I was supposed to be taking comfort from my Savior, Jesus. Instead, I was getting it from a dog."

"And didn't you never think maybe that's how Jesus delivered it?"

Fortunately she gave that point a moment to sink in, because it boggled him. Thanks to the blinding power of guilt, he'd never considered that.

She rolled along in that rich voice. "I don't pay much mind to religious theories. They never fit right with real life, you know? Jesus does. He knows all about real life, more than some of these preachers do. He's practical. He understands that a body don't always do the perfect thing. Sometimes life don't let you. You just got to get from life what you can."

He waved a hand about. "Is this what you want from life?"

"No. Way no. What I want, I want lots of money. Right now, I get money any way I can. Someday though, I'll find a rich man and marry." She tossed a completed washcloth in a basket and immediately commenced another. "Marry my prince."

"I noticed you took your milk to church to sell. You make handwork like that washcloth there, right?"

She nodded, briskly crocheting away without a pause.

143

"Hit sells good in some of the tourist shops. Every now and then I take a coffle of stuff in. Some's consignment, some's wholesale. I sell vegetables in summer and cider off the orchard there. The apples aren't very good for anything else but. Cider's a big item round Halloween."

"And moonshine?"

The crochet hook flew.

Jack felt sharp as a pile of Jell-O. He wished he were better able to lead this interrogation — for that was what it was — around to what he wanted. "You know where Jesus tells us to turn the other cheek. And judge not lest you be judged. Practically everything he said in that passage goes against what a police officer does."

"You ain't a cop exactly."

"Yeah, I am. It just doesn't show as clearly. So how do you hold Scripture inerrant and inviolable while you're holding a gun and somebody's in front of it? Especially when you have to move aggressively. I think I have it worked out, but it makes me uneasy."

He kept his eyes adrift, watching the horse. "Maybe you can help me here, Lovey. When real life gets in the way of theological theory, you might say, how do you reconcile the two? For instance, moonshine and Jesus."

"Ain't no word against 'shine in the Bible. Jesus made wine at Cana."

"OK, then pick something else. You make money any way you can — how do you draw a line?" He looked at her, and she, studying him, had folded her busy hands into her lap. Was she resisting the question with her silence or marshaling her thoughts? "You ever see a movie called *Pretty Woman*?"

"Yeah."

"I musta seen it a dozen times. I'm gonna be like that. I'm gonna marry myself a rich man like that. I figure it'll happen if you just work at it hard enough. She made her way the best she could, and got her wish."

"They didn't marry, at least not in the movie. Besides, the girl was hooking — making her money illegally and immorally when she found her prince. That's what I'm talking about. For example — in theory — would adultery be justified to achieve the end of snaring a wealthy husband?" What he was really asking was, What about the relationship between you and Abcoff?

And that was the question she answered. "You asking the wrong person that. Hit bothers me a whole lot. I was thinking of doing just that once. Adultery. You know Andy Abcoff, the feller who tried to rough me up after the funeral. Him."

"I didn't know he has any money."

"He don't, but he told me he did. Told me lots of things. Promises. And I believed him till I found out. You know how some people spend all their money on punch cards, and the lottery, and horse races?"

"Compulsive gamblers."

"That's the word. Compulsive. He's a compulsive stock market whatever. He's always spending money on the stock market. When I was in there cleaning, I'd hear him and his missus arguing. They argued the livelong day. Worse'n Aunt Estelle, and she's been divorced all them times 'cause of her arguing. The missus, she'd make the money, and he'd spend it. He kept saying they was gonna be rich, but she'd say not the way his picks lost. Then he'd say she was just playing at being a ranger — nobody was taking her serious — and then she'd really get mad. Like a hog in a bear trap."

"And you'd marry an arguing man like that?"

"Takes two to argue, and he was sweet towards me. That didn't bother me none. But then I found out she put him on some sort of an allowance, and she was talking about rewriting her will and stuff. That's when I realized he has nothing. 'Twas all hers."

"So you told him forget it. Forget about you."

Her voice softened. "Just between you and me, I told him I wouldn't go off with him 'cause he was married. But the truth is, I mighta, if he was as rich as he told me he was. I ain't proud of it, and I don't reckon Jesus is very proud of me, but that's how I felt then." She took up her crochet hook again.

Guilt. Everybody's got it.

He tried to think and found himself drifting toward sleep again. He rocked faster. "Now I'm asking an official question instead of just making conversation, and I apologize to have to do it. Were you and Abcoff ever intimate? An item, so to speak?"

She hesitated. "No. Not that he didn't ask plenty. Especially I didn't intend to get into something like that with that Indian woman sneaking around, checking up on us. She was way too thick with the missus to risk something."

"Diane Walling?"

"Yeah, that's her name. She works at the park. She was always over at the house talking business with Mrs. Abcoff. Was there the day she died even, though of course we didn't know it at the time that hit was her last hours."

"How do you know that? Were you there?"

"I cleaned for them on Friday. Didn't go this Friday though. Just as soon stay away from there now." Her eyes narrowed. "Was that question official too?"

"Actually, yes."

"Well, quit it." She crocheted in silence a few minutes. When she spoke again she seemed to be talking more to herself than to him. "Hit's like the moonshine. Because of my pappy, everybody thinks my still is over against the hills there somewheres. They're always trucking around back there

146

looking for it. I get a kick out of watching them be frustrated. But then sometimes I figure I got the name, I might as well have the game, you know? Like with Mr. Abcoff. Everyone says you're doing it, so why not do it? But then I think different of it."

She lapsed into silence again. Jack pondered how to ask official questions without sounding official. His cheeks and chin itched. Maybe he wouldn't grow a beard after all.

He woke up with a crook in his neck, all scrunched in the rocker. The roan was tethered in a different part of the yard, asleep in a newly mown, beaten-down ring, one foot cocked. The sun had slipped down below porch-roof level. Golden late-afternoon light poured over him from the west. Lovey's rocker sat empty. Sometime during his nap she had tucked a well-used blanket over him.

Embarrassed, he stood up and stretched. It wasn't all that often that he fell asleep in the middle of an interrogation, but once was once too many. He folded the blanket and carried it into the house. He heard her in the kitchen.

She turned and grinned as he entered the archway between the rooms. "There you are! And you look a dozen times better. Dinner ain't much. Frying a chicken, making some potatoes. Just throw that blanket on the sofa. I'll take it up later."

He did so and returned to the kitchen. "What can I help with?"

"Not a thing. Water's hot. Coffee?"

"Sure." He built his own, just to have something to do. "Thank you for the nap and the blanket. I appreciate it. As beautiful as your unfinished quilt is in the other room there, I would think you use nothing but quilts."

She giggled. "I make a quilt or comforter and hit'll sell for a hundred and fifty dollars. Sometimes more. Then I go

147

down to Wal-Mart and buy me an eight-ninety-nine blanket that's just as warm."

"Practical." Money any way you can.

She built salads of dandelion greens and garnished them with crumbled bacon. He set the table for her and noted that the small round vase holding a great mound of fresh nasturtiums was new since breakfast.

"Like them fancy restaurants do." She giggled and, plucking two of the nasturtium blossoms, decorated their plates of chicken, creamy mushroom-rich gravy, and mashed potatoes.

Jack grinned as he sat again at her bountiful table. "In the restaurant trade, they call that 'the presentation.' "

"I call it being fussy, but I do it sometimes just for fun." She offered grace, simply and eloquently, and dug in. "Do you like to play Monopoly?"

"Good grief, it's been years. Yeah. When I was a kid, we'd get these marathon Monopoly games going. Frank Harrold and Ernie Morales and I. We'd loan each other money and get exorbitant loans from the bank just to keep the game going. The worst thing that could happen to a Monopoly game was for someone to go bankrupt and lose."

Her eyes danced. "I try to get Jess and Boy playing, but they usually ain't interested. How 'bout after dinner we play a game?"

He had intended to saddle up and hit the road after dinner. But he said yes because he couldn't refuse and because the moon, nearly full, would offer sufficient light to travel by later.

Immediately after eating, they cleared the table, and she brought out her Monopoly game. He tried not to gawk. Her game, obviously long used, had the very old-style nonslippery money, stained turned-wood figures instead of the pot-metal ship and iron and all, stained red wooden hotels and stained green wooden houses. She kept calling the hotels barns, and that is indeed what they most resembled.

"Now the rules." She set up the bank on an unused side of the board. "We usually play that instead of somebody being the bank you just do your own banking. And you get four five-hundred-dollar bills to start with instead of all that change."

"Sounds good. And we always played that if you landed right on Go you got five hundred instead of two hundred."

"Us too. And we usually round up or down to the nearest five so's you don't have to mess around with ones." Her ones did indeed look virtually unused.

Jack bobbed his head. "Is Mediterranean free or five?"

"Five." Deftly she dealt them each four $500 bills.

The lovely Lovey Hempett played cutthroat Monopoly that made Al Capone's dreams of owning Chicago pale in comparison. Jack thought of Ernie Morales's tactics of old. Lovey could teach Ernie a thing or two, and that was going some.

By george, Jack could play cutthroat too. Twenty minutes into the game she eyed him suspiciously. "That's cheating."

"I don't cheat. I make advantageous mistakes." Ernie's line. "And besides, I notice the Community Chest bugger card hasn't come up yet. You know — 'Pay forty for every house and a hundred fifteen for every hotel.' "

She grinned. "Hit's an old game. Got wore out, I guess."

"Worn out indeed. We hid ours too. That one can wreck a fellow quicker'n anything."

They finished the game by kerosene light because she usually used the generator only when she was washing clothes. He left her place an hour after dark, the agony of Monopoly defeat stinging his psyche, his stomach still content from the excellent food.

She had sketched him a very good detailed map, with the distances quite well proportioned. When he came out onto the state route and saw a phone booth beside the corner gas station, he called Ev to ask about Maxx. She didn't get mad at him for waking her up at past 1:00 A.M., though she had every right to.

No word yet. She would check in again with Hiram in the morning. His truck was at the same place her Taurus had been. He declined to ask her if the MG was running yet, lest she take it wrongly.

He arrived at his room somewhere around 4:00 A.M. He unsaddled and tethered the horse in the grass behind the motel, showered, and flopped into bed, a very sad and lonely man.

14

Petronius Woke
Only About Midday

and as usual greatly wearied.
— Henryk Sienkiewicz, *Quo Vadis*

Jack woke up around noon, still dog-tired. Maybe he was just wearied by so much of life happening to him so quickly. Two-and-some days in the saddle didn't help, probably, nor did the highly irregular hours. He called Hiram, shaved his incipient beard, showered, ate at the restaurant across the parking lot, and was reading his Bible when Hiram's cap-backward employee arrived with the trailer.

They loaded the roan and headed for Gatlinburg. The young man, Billy Somebody, dropped Jack off at the garage/used-car lot. Jack paid the bill plus a generous tip specifically for Hiram's daughter — a thank-you for giving up use of her horse all weekend — and Billy continued down the road to take the horse home.

Cosmetically, Jack's gray Ram didn't look too bad, considering that at almost fifty miles an hour it got rolled, then was dumped upside down onto a pile of partially submerged boulders. Sure, the roof was caved, and the windshield was gone, and the grill and right fender were ripped off, and the right door was crushed shut forever, and the driver's side wasn't much better, and the engine had been torn loose and soaked in the river for a couple of hours. Shucks, anyone can have a bad-hair day, so to speak. The twisted frame, though

— now that was something else.

Incredibly weary, he prowled through the collection of used trucks here on the lot while the cap-backward mechanic explained how great each was. Jack pictured good old boys driving each of them on back roads that would make a goat think twice, up dirt tracks crooked enough to give a snake motion sickness. He had bought the Ram new and kept it in near perfect shape right to the last moment. It was time to buy new again.

Reluctantly, very reluctantly, he called Laurel Clum's motel because he knew Ev was out investigating somewhere and it wasn't worth trying to find her. Besides, her car sometimes ran and sometimes didn't.

Laurel was in. With a good cheer that utterly depressed him, she dropped what she was doing and drove him up to Sevierville. With the top down.

That evening he wrote a check to his money market account well in excess of $10,000. Talk about wearying.

Driving his new truck, he picked up Ev at her place Tuesday morning at seven. She settled into the plush-upholstered seat and belted herself in. "It's beautiful. This year's model or last?"

"This." He pulled out onto Parkway easily. Few were the folk out at this early hour.

She squirmed around to look at the generous space behind the seat. "Is this what they call a crew cab?"

"Extended cab. Not a full seat in back. Just those little fold-down jump seats at either end."

"It's a neat idea. You can still take a couple extra people along if you have to. What did they name this color?"

"Electric red."

"It's . . .uh . . . it's certainly colorful."

"It is that. That homestead place we ate at before? What do they call it?"

152

"Sure, that's fine. Uncle Gene's, I think. You know, Jack, technically speaking it's not red exactly. It's more carmine. That pinkish cast. I like it. Nice seats too. Comfortable. I like this console between the seats. You even have that beverage holder there built right in. Pretty snazzy!"

"Yeah."

Ev watched him a moment. "You should be delighted to have a brand-new truck. It's a guy thing." She paused a moment more. "You're embarrassed, aren't you! You have —"

"That's not true!"

"You have this fancy truck that's twice as upholstered and appointed as anything else you've ever driven, and you're embarrassed! Jack, it's not all that ostentatious by today's standards. There's not a thing wrong with fabric instead of vinyl. You should see the car my father drives. It talks to you, and it shows your exact speed electronically. It even gives you the outside temperature. This a very nice truck, but it's not a limousine. It's not supposed to be."

"It's not a truck I want. It was the only four-by they had on the lot that would carry my stuff and I could take immediate delivery. I was looking at their little one, their Ranger SL, and there's no room behind the seat. I needed someplace to put my camping stuff, and —"

"I remember behind your seat. You literally had the kitchen sink back there. Or something that would pass for it in a campground. Jack, you don't have to apologize for this."

"I'm not apologizing. Anyway, all my stuff will fit back there and even room for Maxx."

And the conversation froze, dead in the water.

He pulled into the parking lot behind the restaurant and escorted Ev inside. As a constant stream of regulars filed in and out, rather like ants between the sink and the sugar bowl, Jack and Ev ordered, ate, and swapped information. He had precious little for her. She had bundles of it for him.

Three different local people stopped by the booth to express their concern about Maxx and assure him they'd keep an eye out. And he was a stranger in town. He realized belatedly that the waitress was pointing him out to everybody, as one would a national celebrity. He remembered Hal's emphasis that this case would be high profile. Maybe he was.

And he realized also that these were people who genuinely cared about dogs.

He asked how her MG was doing, and she told him the mechanic was installing a new starter free of charge. He drove her down to park headquarters. Bill Weineke, bless him, had gathered all Jack's stuff out of his truck, even the parking-meter-and-toll-booth change in the ashtray, and stored it in the ranger cache.

Still, it took Jack almost two hours to retrieve his things and sort through them. The jump box was both the wrong size for his new truck and ruined. The envelope with registration, warranties, insurance, and owner's manual was soaked. So were his sleeping bag and other camping gear. Here were his waterlogged clothes. He retrieved his wallet. With more than one heavy sigh, he spread the wet stuff out to dry and stowed the dry stuff in the back of his, speaking euphemistically, supercab.

Word must have spread. Bill checked out Jack's new rig. So did Greg Vosniak and Leonard Walker. Jasmine Inge, the finance clerk, and Trish Casey in Procurement both came out to admire it, but Jack suspected it was so they could smoke a cigarette, since they lit up before they got there. Even the quiet little Homer Symes, who probably drove only ten-year-old Volvos, showed up to look it over.

Over a cup of coffee in the lunchroom, Jack studied the sheaf of goodies Ev had given him and weighed the relative

154

merits of reading all day or getting out somewhere. Not a difficult choice.

Near noon he headed up the hill on his way to Carl Sandburg Home National Historic Site.

The Newfound Gap Road, known to the world as US 441, roughly bisects the long oval of the park. At the top, as the road clambers up over the Smokies and descends the other side, a spur road takes you out along a ridge to the highest point in the park, Clingman's Dome.

Visitors can climb higher than the highest point by ascending a ramp, one of the world's great circular nonstaircases. It begins as a paved trail at the parking lot, leaves the ground like a freeway off-ramp, and spirals up until the visitor emerges above the trees. From that lofty perch, the visitor enjoys 360 degrees of superb view.

Jack had heard about the spiral ramp at Clingman's Dome and seen its picture in a multitude of Park Service books. He turned aside now and drove out to see it in person. Maybe half a dozen cars studded a parking lot built to handle hundreds. Damp, cool air reminded him he was a couple thousand feet higher now than he had been an hour ago.

He found himself waiting beside his open door and realized he was expecting Maxx to come bounding out of the cab behind him. He slammed it and walked across the parking lot to the trail head.

A short way along the trail, another path plunged down over the side, a well-used hiking track. If you weren't carefully looking for trail markers, you'd probably miss it. He passed sturdy brick rest rooms that seemed out of place here, however welcome they must be for many.

Finally the trail left the bare, scraggy flat rock of the ridgetop and began a smooth, gentle glide upward. It looped out past the mid-sections of trees. Densely spaced evergreens crowded around it. Still it spiraled upward. He walked out to the nethermost top, a circular viewing platform hanging upon nothing above the forest. The cold, biting wind whipping across this unprotected aerie reminded him he'd left his jacket in the truck.

He perused the engraved plaques telling which mountain and fire lookout was sticking up where. As he looked out across dead fir forest, he thought about all the florid "God's magnificent creation" writing he'd read. He couldn't think of any that didn't assume that God's magnificent creation was serene and pure and somehow above man's sins. He recalled reading the word *majestic* frequently.

Maybe someday he'd write about what God's magnificent creation really is like: a vibrant, frenetic, ever-changing, struggling, overcoming, exuberant, living thing, rich in its inscrutability, and infinitely more complex, for good and for bad, than religious nature writers ever suggested. He descended the spiral, back to real life.

He would have arrived at Flat Rock, North Carolina, a lot sooner if he hadn't dawdled along the way. He stopped in at Oconaluftee, down at the south end of the park, and listened to the district ranger tell war stories about Colleen Abcoff. Jack summarized the tales as "Colleen used Diane Walling the way parents use a teen-age son." Wash the car. Mow the lawn. Enjoy your date. Keep up on your homework. Run to the store for me. Watch your little sister a few hours while I'm gone. Write 0 in the dependents' box so that they withhold more, or you'll have to pay tax in April. Be independent, be servile, all on command.

Grinning, two different people whipped out Saturday newspapers and showed Jack a photo of his spectacularly wrecked truck. He was indeed a media darling. He shuddered at the thought.

In Cherokee he shuddered again — lurid commercialism perpetuated false stereotypes of Indians from two generations ago. He compared this against the respect and dignity most Western tribes were working for, and he yearned to get West again.

He stopped at a drugstore and bought a toothbrush. This trip was going to take longer than he had anticipated.

He arrived in Hendersonville in late afternoon and found a cheap motel room. Very cheap. After all, when eventually he listed expenses, he would ask the United States Government to pay for two motel rooms on the same night. Bean-counters in Washington sometimes question stuff like that. He left a message on the superintendent's voice mail and settled in for the evening with Ev's pile of material.

He was impressed with how far she had come in the half year he'd known her. Nothing in these folders was brilliance. Rather, it was a giant step better than brilliance — thorough. She noted everything chronologically, documented everything, then wove everything together into a cogent half-page summary of how it all might relate.

Ev.

The loss of Maxx had driven a wedge between them, a wedge that should never be there. She sympathized. She did the best for him she could. He should not be shoving her away the way he did. This very trip was more escapism than business.

How many caring people did he wall away from himself when he lost Marcia and Matthew? He recognized for the first time, now that he was doing it again, that he had built a tight box then and climbed into it, pulling the flaps down. He sat in one right now, feeling sorry for himself, protected by the kind of impenetrable shell that he, as a psychologist, tried to talk other people out of.

Ev.

She put up with his nonsense, and yet she never ever really gave way to him. She was her own person. When he hid inside his shell she waited outside it, not breaking in, letting him be his own person. That was respect.

Ev.

He thought about her a long time, her huge, dark waif eyes, her elfin hair that floated when she moved.

And for the first time since Marcia he thought about marriage.

15

The Fog Comes on Little Cat Feet

— Carl Sandburg, "Fog"

Sometime during the night the fog had tiptoed in on silent feet, sifting itself through the trees, masking the buildings. By habit, Jack took the dog for an early morning walk, even though he no longer had a dog. He could walk briskly this morning for a change, not having to wait for lengthy inspections of fire hydrants and power poles, for the constant pauses and snuffles that rendered walks with Maxx so maddening.

As he walked through the thick moisture, water beaded on his hair and eyebrows. Too many thoughts churned in his mind for him to sort them successfully. He needed Ev's prodigious ability to organize. She was a hefty portion of those thoughts.

He passed a restaurant with gingham café-style curtains and half a dozen local pickup trucks in the lot. So he ate there. On the way back to his room, he weighed waiting for Galen McFarland to call against just going out to Carl Sandburg and taking potluck. Potluck won, hands down.

Flat Rock, North Carolina, possesses a stately, reserved dignity that only age and wealth can give a community. Perfectly landscaped homes, large and uncrowded, loll about on quiet streets. Jack enjoyed driving through the place. He also appreciated that an excellent sign system led him gently by the hand directly to Carl Sandburg's door. Not every sign system delivers you where you want to be.

The great, white Sandburg home sat picturesquely on a hill above an expanse of open meadows. Trees generations old stood along the fence rows, marking pasture limits in broad vertical strokes of charcoal gray. With languid fingers, the fog erased some features and gently veiled others.

The Visitor Center stood apart at the base of the hill. Jack liked that too. Too often park facilities get in the way of the thing they're trying to protect.

The girl at the desk smiled well. She looked efficient and warm simultaneously. He introduced himself and asked to talk to the superintendent.

She got on the phone with his request and returned to him moments later. "Brenda says he's available. Go on up the hill, and instead of taking the walkway to the front porch, go right. His office is in the little white frame house beyond. Brenda will be keeping an eye out for you." She seemed to hesitate, as if uncertain whether she should speak. "Are you the one who rolled the truck into the river?"

"My hour of fame. Why couldn't it be for ending world hunger or something?"

She giggled and turned to help a gray-haired woman inquiring about rest rooms.

As he walked the path up the hill to the house, he saw a purple finch, two goldfinches, and a happy little indigo bunting. He was liking this place better by the minute. He emerged from under a bower of trees into the front yard. The fog here was condensing to coarse mist, almost a fine rain.

Once upon a time a fountain and lily pool graced the front lawn of Sandburg's home. The concrete pool enclosure lay dry and forlorn now, and the fountain had been removed. Pity. It would make an elegant statement.

Off to the right, down a side path, a portly woman with un-

160

naturally blonde hair waved and yoo-hooed.

Jack turned aside and walked down to her. "You must be Brenda."

She looked blank. "How did you know?" The blankness evaporated. "Galen's secretary. Please come in." She led the way to a small, white frame building, just as the interpreter on the desk had promised. What the girl had failed to mention was that almost all the buildings here were white frame. "A woman named Evelyn Brant called yesterday and said you'd be coming. Galen was expecting you then."

"Evelyn thinks I simply drive from point A to point B. I'm really not that disciplined."

McFarland was not in his office. Brenda frowned at his empty chair and at the unoccupied rest room in the hall, its door standing open. "The man is never where you want him. Gone all last month to Florida, gone all last weekend, gone yesterday, here this morning and gone again." She flopped her hands helplessly.

"Where was he last weekend?"

"Gatlinburg. And he was up in Asheville yesterday. Oh, well. He can't be too far — his station wagon's outside. Have a seat there and make yourself at home, Mr. Prester. I'll go call around."

"Thank you." He sat. The moment she left he hopped back up to look at the walls up close.

Most people, by the time they make superintendent somewhere, have collected a lot of miscellaneous memorabilia. Galen McFarland not only collected it, he elevated its display to a higher form of art. His office walls held a wealth of eclectic mementos — purloined trail signs (Hoh River 5.2 mi), bumper stickers (Support Search and Rescue — Get Lost), certificates (Volunteer Fire Fighter, Jackson Co. FPD 23), his Horace M. Albright training center diploma, framed letters from President Reagan and Jesse Helms, and a dozen landscape photos of national park scenes, Clingman's Dome among them. Interspersed wherever there was room, those souvenir decals you can buy from places you visit — Luray Caverns, Seal Rocks, Sarasota, Busch Gardens, Everglades, Big Sky Country — were thumbtacked to the wall.

The letter from Reagan was a form letter of thanks to a generic superintendent. Jack's dad, a lifelong Democrat, had received one just like it. The letter from Jesse Helms, arch conservative, was not a form letter. It expressed shock and disappointment that McFarland should deliberately try to undercut the efforts of men of vision (by implication, women of vision were fair game for undercutting, however) to bring stability and better jobs to the region. The honorable Mr. Helms strongly suggested, in effect, that McFarland quit opposing and get with the program.

Six and a half feet tall, sporting a moustache that could strain krill, Galen McFarland walked in. He looked strong enough to rip the shoes off a horse. Not an ounce of his seventh of a ton or so was fat. He extended a hand.

Jack shook, thereby rendering his right hand numb. His fingers incapacitated, he resorted to pointing by dipping his head toward the framed letter. "I like you already. What was the occasion?"

"Have a seat. A little political skirmish that I managed to win. That doesn't happen very often." Galen tossed himself in the general direction of his oversized Naugahyde chair and let it catch him.

"Not with Senator Helms." Jack wondered if the chair ever missed. "You have quite an array of trophies. What about that hard hat there?" He pointed to an extremely battered and smudged tin hat on McFarland's bookcase as he took the visitor's chair.

"The Garden Wall Fire mean anything to you?" McFarland talked with the slow, smooth speech of the Southern aristocrat.

"My dad was called in on the tail end of it. Flew into Kalispell nine days before the snow came and they sent everyone home."

"I was eighteen, one of the first on the fire." McFarland leaned back and laced his burly hands across his middle. The chair groaned. "I'd never been to Glacier National Park. I thought I knew what mountains are, growing up here. They assigned my buddy and me to that fire, and we're being brought through the park in this rickety old bus, and all I can think is, *Wow!* The country astounded me."

"Yeah. 'Astounded' is a good word." Jack remembered his family's trip to Glacier a few years after the fires, and his father pointing out the Garden Wall and the site of the fire near West Glacier that burned at the same time.

"Fifteen hours later, four of us got trapped on that northwest ridge. The fire went right over us. Three of us soaked ourselves with our canteens and bellied down under a fallen log. My buddy panicked and ran. We were messed up some, but we survived. He didn't."

"And that's your hard hat."

"His."

Jack pondered all this a moment. "The first people in, besides hotshot crews and rangers from nearby parks, were convicts and straying juveniles from correction facilities."

"That's right. I was a camper. If I'd kept going the way I started out, I'd be in a federal prison now instead of a federal park. That experience at Glacier turned me clear around." He shifted. His chair creaked. "I called your motel this morning, but you'd already checked out. Why'd you pick such a cheap one? We have better ones, you know."

"Administratitabulatrophobia." Jack paused a moment. "A debilitating fear of government accountants. I don't remember seeing you at Colleen Abcoff's funeral."

He shook his massive head. "If I'd gone, I might've started laughing and singing in the middle of it."

"That happy, huh?"

"Which makes me a suspect, right?" McFarland glanced at his watch.

"You were a suspect anyway. Don't think a thing about it. Why so happy?"

"She tried her level best to ruin me."

"By helping you become a superintendent?"

"It looks good, doesn't it, that she got me in here even though chief naturalists rarely ever get superintendencies."

Jack nodded. "Or maintenance supervisors. If someone comes up from the ranks, it's usually a chief ranger. So what was the real story?"

"She was a virago, Prester. Know what a virago is?"

"I try to avoid them."

McFarland smirked. "A self-righteous virago, the worst kind. I made the mistake of not realizing what she was like when she first came to the park."

"Came in behind Gerry Rackenberg."

"Right. You knew him?"

"My father did. Gerry had plans to develop portions of the park, is that right?"

"And I opposed them, though a chief naturalist can't mount much opposition against a supe. Wrote some letters. When he died, we thought that was the end of it."

"We?" Jack frowned.

"Bodine, Rich Platt, Leonard Walker, myself. The three musketeers. Bodine was D'Artagnan, the odd man out. Not Park Service but one of us anyway. In comes Colleen, seemingly sweet and not at all like her reputation, and saying she wanted to get to know the staff so we could function together as a unit. Like a droop, I mentioned how hard I'd worked to come home to the Smokies. She used that knowledge to nullify that by getting me out of the Smokies."

Jack shifted in his chair. His body still wasn't completely over those days on horseback. "In other words, you grew up near Gatlinburg and after a lengthy career at Olympic, Russell Cave, the 'Glades, and elsewhere as indicated by the pictures on your wall there, you wangled a position back home in the Smokies, your Park Service dream. You intended to just homestead here. She perceived your dream and thwarted it."

"Homestead, right. Settle in and spend the rest of my career peaceably messing around in the Smokies. I already owned a house on the east side of town. And we had the red-wolf reintroduction program cooking. Then Colleen convinced me that staying in one place that long wouldn't be in my best interests and I ought to come over here a while. Then she'd bring me back there, maybe as assistant supe. She also said Platt needed the change, even though his family are all over here in Carolina."

"So she appealed to your altruism. Did you get it in writing?"

McFarland just grunted.

"Why did she do it?"

"Vindictiveness. Also, I think, to get to Platt, who was superintendent here. Why she wanted to flay him, I don't know. Me, I'm sure she wanted to punish because although I had a felony record, I got into the Park Service anyway."

"You mentioned 'self-righteous.' "

"In spades." He glanced at his watch again. "She considered me a common criminal."

"So does Jesse Helms."

McFarland exploded into wild and rollicking laughter. It took him a while to recover. He settled into a fairly pensive, docile mood. "It hasn't all been negative. I mean, I'm not that far from home. Couple hours. It was just the dream she shattered. And I've developed a lot better sensibility about small areas. This one for instance. Smokies is the most visited park in the system."

Jack nodded. "Ev and I were talking about that." She brushed briefly across his mind again.

"By comparison, we get very, very few visitors, and we're just over the hill from them, literally. People simply don't take advantage of their park system the way they should. We're a great one-day destination. Sure you have super-park over there, but you have an instructive, pleasant, mini-park right here. It's significant. Important."

"My father was always saying that, especially at Hovenweep. Mesa Verde gets 'em all. Standing in line. Nobody bothers with the Weep, but it's a highly significant area."

McFarland shifted in his chair. It made a prolonged, pained, grunting sound. "Interesting. You're second generation Park Service, right?"

"Third."

"My father was bitterly opposed to the Park Service. There's a lot — a whole lot — of local opposition to the Park Service around Smokies, I suppose you know. He was disappointed with me for my run-ins with the law, and he let me know it. But when I joined the Park Service, he disowned me."

Jack wagged his head. "That's rough. Any estrangement in a family is bad, but father-and-son relationships are worst. I'm going to have to tell my dad about my truck one of these days, and it's going to cause some serious pain between us. Nothing like yours though."

"You mean that you rolled it?"

"No, he doesn't care beans about that old truck. I mean the new one. My father's a Chevy man. He's sworn by General Motors his whole life. How am I ever going to break the news to him that I just bought a Ford?"

McFarland roared. If ever there had been ice it was thoroughly broken now. Still grinning, he stood up. "I have an appointment with the architect. We're building a lab out behind here, for artifact restoration. Special curatorial needs. It's going to be national resource. I'm sorry I have to break this off. I'll be back as soon as I can. An hour, hour and a half tops. Hang around, and we'll talk some more."

"Certainly."

McFarland launched himself toward the door and paused. "Sorry. I suggest you go down to the barn and see the goats. I'll be happy to answer questions and take you on a tour of the house then."

"Thanks." By the time Jack stood up, McFarland was out the door.

Goats?

He requested a park folder of Brenda, and she cheerfully complied. He was beginning to think she did everything cheerfully. Relentlessly cheerful people depressed him.

The folder explained the goats. Carl Sandburg's wife, Lilian, nicknamed Paula, raised world champion goats. He paused at the front door, reading the folder. The air and all it touched were fairly generally wet, but it wasn't actually raining. Broken fog still masked distances.

A smarmy-looking young man, wearing the gray and green but too young and callow to be a ranger, came jogging down the walk. "Mr. McFarland said you're interested in a tour of the grounds. Happy to." They were entering the Service younger every year.

167

Jack fell in beside him, and they walked beneath giant, brooding trees. They shook and exchanged names — Prester. Brian Bell. Hello. Hello. Jack asked, "He said he's building a lab?"

The boy rattled off a lengthy explanation of the facility and how it would be a center Servicewide for restoration and stabilization of historically significant artifacts. It was essentially the same thing McFarland said, but it took the kid three times as long.

Jack asked about the fountain and pool out front.

No, they were going to leave it like that because Sandburg himself had taken out the fountain, objecting to its ostentation. It was the same objection Jack made to his own truck. Brian showed Jack the actual fountain the antebellum owners had installed and Sandburg had removed, displayed in a shed along with some of the farm's implements.

They strolled down to a big red barn. Jack the country boy was beginning to feel more and more at home here. Great as he was, having won several Pulitzers, Sandburg was a simple man, a plain man. Jack could relate comfortably to the simplicity if not the greatness.

Bell took him through the milk house attached to the barn and showed him where lightning had struck some years ago, blowing up concrete, drilling holes, and frying equipment. And then the fellow's radio on his belt squawked something unintelligible.

"Excuse me. Sorry." He waved a hand. "Wander around. Enjoy." Away he went up toward the house.

Jack strolled out to a wooden gate opening onto an inner paddock. Beyond, a steel gate opened in turn out into a goat pasture. Sure enough, there were goats — goats with floppy ears and goats with deerlike ears. The goats shared their pasture with a pile of construction materials — cinder block, boards, and bags beneath plastic tarps. Jack guessed the stuff was for the lab.

One of the goats bleated plaintively. It had climbed up onto the pile, as goats are wont to do. Now it seemed to be struggling, as if its foot were trapped in the stack of cinder block. That was likely. One of the big reasons Jack despised goats was their gift for constantly getting into trouble. This was totally apart from their destructiveness, which extended to eating the bark off trees. In fact, here in this pasture, great collars of wire-mesh fencing protected all the trees, and an electric fence kept the goats in their field. You didn't need electric fence and wire mesh if you pastured horses, the only decent use of meadows.

He looked around. No visitors, no employees except for some women digging in a patch some distance away. The goat bleated again and shook its head.

Jack might detest goats, but he knew them all too intimately from his FFA days in high school. He opened the wooden gate into the paddock and carefully latched it behind him. He had, his junior year, been enamored of a classmate named Michelle, who took goats to the fair every fall. Puppy love does strange things. Had he not been so smitten, he would surely never have bothered to learn how to handle goats, let alone milk them. The romance faded rapidly; the skill of milking lingered to this day.

He waded through the wet grass, soaking his running shoes. And here he'd just gotten them dried out from the last soaking. He grasped the latch on the steel gate.

With a roar and a flash, the world exploded.

16

I Was Sick —

— Edgar Allen Poe, "The Pit and the Pendulum"

He was sick. In fact, he was sufficiently sick that he lost his stomach. Warm, firm hands helped him roll to his side and held his head. His ears rang, his teeth buzzed, his heart trilled, his toes ached, his fingers tingled, his face vibrated. Voices chattered in the ether all around.

A rich, rough contralto purred, "There now, you see? He's doing much better. Good strong pulse now."

That was heartening.

He took deep breaths. His chest and lungs ached. Actually, as he assayed this moment, everything on him ached. Mildly embarrassed and without the least notion why he should be, he rolled to his back and snapped himself to sitting on only the second try.

A very large black woman in coveralls hovered kneeling beside him. "You lie down! Don't go ramming 'round." She was probably in her fifties somewhere.

"With all respect, ma'am, this is not ramming." He pulled his knees up and draped his arms over them. He sat three-cornered and tried to figure out what the world had done to him when he wasn't looking. "This is sitting very, very still, and I will try to continue so for a while." He had trouble controlling speech.

She sniggered in that charming, rumbly voice. "I think they got nine-one-one on the way. Least, I told 'em to."

Jack flexed his fingers. His right hand was slow to function. "I don't know what happened. Do you know?"

"We been speculating 'bout that. We think they's a short in the fence."

"We?"

The woman waved a hand. "There's Stelle Pritchard, and Jessie Mayo, and Norma Middendorf. I'm Sally Lee Buxton."

Jack twisted to see. Three gray-haired white women about Ms. Buxton's age knelt watching him closely. They all wore coveralls. He how-do-you-doed them without knowing which was which exactly. "Jack Prester, with the Park Service." He held out his tingly hand.

The women shook feebly as befits true ladies, with the open graciousness and aplomb of people who scrape strange men up off the wet grass daily.

Probable-Stelle smiled. "We're with the Dogwood Garden Club. Most of the grounds work and landscaping here in the park is done by garden clubs as a public service. We happened to be working over there in the vegetable gardens when you . . . er . . . your accident occurred. We're going to put in a full vegetable garden this year much the way Mrs. Sandburg did."

"Accident?"

Ms. Buxton wagged her head. "Just by chance, mind you, I looked up as you were going through the gates. Mostly I wanted to make sure you weren't gonna be careless and let the goats out. You reached toward the inner gate and *wham!* You popped right up off the ground and sailed backward."

Probable-Jessie picked up the narrative, speaking in excited staccato. "Naturally we hurried to your aid. We sent Milly up to the office to fetch help. She's the youngest, so she can still run." She frowned. "She really ought to have come back by now, I should think."

171

A short in the fence. Typically, a lightning strike or strong electrical jolt leaves very little mark on the outside of a person — just a charred little hole or two — even as it zips all over inside, cooking any flesh and bone it travels through. How badly was Jack fried internally? He couldn't see any electrical burns on his hand and everything seemed to function, however reluctantly. That was hopeful.

He heard an electric vehicle of some sort — a golf cart or utility three-wheeler — coming down the hill.

"Ms. Buxton, I promise I won't go ramming." Another violent spasm of effort brought him to his feet.

Ms. Buxton cackled even as she wagged her head again. "You shouldn't ought to be doing that."

"I know it." He doddered over to the fence with measured, unsteady steps.

The golf cart pulled up beside him, and the callow Brian Bell leaped out. "Better lie down. Brenda said you had a seizure."

Jack raised both hands and fibbed. "I'm fine."

Ms. Buxton snorted. "You're lying, young man."

He smiled at her. "Yes, ma'am. Actually, I was just speaking prematurely. An electric fence doesn't put out enough voltage to really nail you. I will be fine in a few minutes."

She hooted. "When it picks a man your size clear up off the ground, you can consider yourself nailed."

"Good point." Jack moved in close to the steel gate and followed by eye around it. On the side next to the barn, the electric fence wire extended beyond its orange plastic insulator to wrap around the gate frame. Jack pointed to it silently.

Bell stepped in close and bent over to peer at it. He muttered an expletive not at all appropriate for the delicate ears of these Southern ladies. Ms. Buxton leaned in right beside him and pronounced a startlingly similar word.

With some trepidation — he was still shaky — Jack walked along this inner paddock following the wire back to the transformer attached to the barn. Someone armed with both a screwdriver and a murderous intent had bypassed the transformer. The fence wire was twisted onto the cut-and-stripped end of an extension cord that was plugged directly into an outside outlet.

The gate was juiced with 110 undiluted volts.

His uniform shoes thundering, McFarland came running down the hill. He slammed in the wooden gate with an angry, "What in thunder's going on here?!" Suddenly the strangest transformation seized Jack. Many was the time he had seen it in others, and now, unexpectedly, almost like an outside observer, he was seeing it in himself. The self-pity, the grief, the sadness all melted away, coalesced into pure, delicious, white-hot, ferocious, excruciating fury. And he loved that fury! It felt so much more satisfying than did grief. Grief enervated. This fury enlivened.

He wheeled on the superintendent. "I was set up, McFarland!"

"Hey, now wait a minute —"

"And I'm going to find out who!" Jack raised both arms and shoved, palms out, at the air between him and everyone else. "Everyone back." He looked at McFarland and Bell. "You too. Back outside the paddock beyond that gate. Minimal impact. Go."

McFarland roared, "I'm in charge here!"

"And I'm pulling rank. You got a problem, you talk to my boss." He yanked one of Hal's cards out of his wallet and stuffed it inside McFarland's uniform shirt between buttons.

McFarland took one step forward toward that wiring job. Jack stiff-armed him to an instant halt. Were Jack not so furious, he probably would never dream of getting in this sumo wrestler's face — McFarland outweighed him by at least a hundred pounds — but it didn't matter this time. Whether McFarland recognized Jack's enforcement authority or his fury, he backed off.

Brian Bell was so confused he stammered. "W-We have to unplug the fence. One of the goats could get electrocuted."

"The goats will just have to take their chances along with the rest of us." Jack motioned to Bell. "I hear the siren up by the house. Turn the aid van around and replace it with a forensics team. I want the whole ball of wax — full fur and fiber."

"What?" Bell looked like someone dealing with a person who speaks Tagalog.

"Gimme the radio." Black as a summer thunderstorm, McFarland snatched the handy-talkie out of the ranger's hand and strode off to talk to people. One thing about anger, it spreads quickly.

Blathering, Perhaps-Stelle suggested the ladies had better get back to work if they planned to finish today. They fell all over themselves agreeing with her.

Jack mastered his fury enough to thank them profusely for their intervention. They beat a hasty exit, which was wise. Who would want to stand around in the middle of an internecine war between Park Service professionals?

Millie, whoever Millie was, certainly could run. In the full coverall uniform of the garden club volunteer she came dashing down the road with the big, white, boxy aid van hard behind her. Its emergency lights all flashed wildly — multicolored lightning bugs on amphetamines. Jack knew she was leading them directly down here, but it looked for all the world as if they were chasing her.

The gardeners collared Millie and took her with them

back across the road and up to what must be the garden patches.

The van driver killed the lights even before they parked by the barnyard, fifty feet from Jack. Obviously, dispatch had called them off at McFarland's behest. Equally obviously, they didn't want to go home. McFarland stepped up to the driver's side window. They talked a moment. The driver handed out a cellular phone. McFarland punched buttons.

Up on the pile of construction materials, the goat bleated.

The callow Bell stood blinking, with no idea in the world what to do.

Jack pointed to the kid. "You commissioned?"

"No, sir."

Jack softened up. Fury is lovely, but he had to control it. He pulled his ID and held it up at reading level for the kid to see. "Jack Prester, engaged in a special investigation of the Colleen Abcoff death over in Smokies."

The kid stared at his badge a moment. "You rolled that truck, right? It was on the eleven o'clock news last week."

Jack sighed. "Right. You know what a tape is. Yellow plastic ribbon with 'Police Line Do Not Cross' printed on it. Fetch some down here and tape off this whole area. Then stand guard until I call for you. Nobody in or out, and I mean nobody, until the forensics crew gets here. Above all, don't talk to anyone whatever about any events of the last hour. Understand?"

His head nodded yes. His blank expression said Huh? Then he hopped on his electric utility vehicle and hummed up to the house.

McFarland waved toward Jack, a "Come hither."

Jack walked out across the barnyard to the road, feeling a bit better with each step. His teeth didn't buzz anymore.

McFarland thrust the phone receiver at him. "State Patrol

lab. Asheville says they're too busy."

"Thank you. Prester."

McFarland strolled away to the barn, but he didn't try to enter the wooden gate.

A pleasant female voice identified herself as Patti Dennison, emphasizing that it was an *I,* not a *Y,* and explained her job as if Jack were a Basque sheepherder with a limited command of English and totally unacquainted with police procedures.

Here came Bell with the tape. Together he and McFarland secured the scene as Jack watched from afar and Patti Dennison ran up the aid van's cellular minutes.

"Now, Mr. Prester," she concluded. "We have two options. If I bring my regular crew, you won't get results back for maybe three weeks. We're really swamped. But —"

"Not even hair and fiber comparisons?"

"When I say swamped, I mean swamped. However, I've been using starving college students on a freelance basis. They're mostly chemistry majors looking at forensics as a career, and they can use the experience in their résumés. It's been working well. But a couple defense lawyers have been causing ripples. Inexperienced help and all that. You can get results fast with the students, but I can't guarantee it'll hold up."

"How fast is fast?"

"Inside a week."

"Let's go with the students." *Help me find out who is trying to wipe out the upper echelons of the Park Service, me included. I have to get to this creep before one of the little traps he lays for me works.*

"We'll be over within the hour."

Jack thanked her, hung up, and got the paramedic to dial the State Highway Patrol barracks. They could not see fit to send someone out to a federal facility to baby-sit a latent forensics scene. Thin on manpower; you know how it is. Jack tried the Flat Rock police department. Well . . . uh . . . the dispatcher hemmed and hawed.

"Remember the picture in the paper Saturday of the truck that got rolled over in Great Smokies?"

"Yes. Right into the river. It was a high-speed chase."

"That's the one. It was my truck. We believe this is related to that case."

Oh. That was different. They'd send someone right out.

Jack thanked the paramedics for the use of their phone and spent a couple minutes talking them out of talking him into going to the emergency room. They drove away disappointed and the poorer by several bucks.

As he walked over to McFarland and Bell, the superintendent was handing Bell his radio. "Go on back up there. I'll see —"

"Stay here." Jack held Bell's eye.

Intimidated, the kid moved back twenty feet into what seemed like a safe limbo beyond two men, both better paid than he, who were locked in a power struggle.

"You're getting on my nerves." McFarland glared at him.

Jack glared back. The delicious anger had not abated in the least. "Explain to your nerves, if you would, that it's not their synapses that got rattled by house current, and they should be a little tolerant. Where were you as I was arriving?"

"Down on the building site, checking out the things I was going to discuss with the architect when he arrived. You're paranoid, Prester. You don't know that rig was for you."

Jack turned to Bell. "And where were you?"

"I don't come on till nine. Nine to six."

"That doesn't answer the question."

"Oh. I was coming here. I left the house at a quarter till."

"Corroboration?"

"Uh . . . my wife . . . that's all."

Wife? The kid didn't look old enough to be going steady.

McFarland lurched into motion. "I'm going back up to —"

"I'd like you to stay here, please."

"Prester, who do you think you're —"

"Please." Jack tried to lower his voice. It wasn't behaving well at all. The fury kept leaking out. "You called Hal from the paramedic's cellular first thing — I saw you pull his card out of your shirt. He asked you to cooperate and probably also informed you that I get testy now and then, but you should just put up with me. That I'm brilliant but temperamental. I know what I need here, and what I need is for you two to help out by staying with me." There. That was about as civil as he could manage just now.

McFarland gave in and cooperated because he didn't really have much choice. The goat's bleating was getting to Jack big time.

He covered a few other bases and learned that radio communications here were neither monitored nor taped. Mostly he was hoping and praying that the forensics crew could perform their dog-and-pony act before goats or rain or interlopers messed up even more the chances of finding something.

Praying. He ought to be handling that differently. As it was, he wasn't handling it at all. And he'd just been spared death too.

Jack briefed the two uniformed Flat Rock officers the moment they arrived, turned the scene over to them, and flopped down on the passenger seat of the electric utility cart.

Brian watched his boss for the moves, hesitated, and climbed into the driver's seat.

Grumpy as a bat at noon, McFarland sat down behind with his legs hanging out the back.

The trapped goat was still bleating piteously. Jack wished he could explain in goat-ese that the forensics crew would free it just as soon as they swept the pile.

And here Jack found a downside to his compelling fury. It robbed him of rational thought. He should be planning what to do next. Or even whom to suspect. McFarland was right. The trap might not have been meant for him. It could even have been one of the garden club ladies out to fry the supe, for all he knew — or a disgruntled goatkeeper intending to deliver an object lesson to the next goat who butted the gate.

They rolled up to the house with the tires whispering, the electric motor doing its thing soundlessly, and somewhere up in these magnificent old trees, a robin singing its heart out.

17

The Morning Fog Had Lifted

giving way to a clear day.
— Marguerite Henry, *King of the Wind*

The morning fog had lifted, giving way to a clear day. Jack stood a few moments at the coffee-room window with his hands in his pockets, letting his mind relax a bit, watching sun-dapples dance on the lawn outside. He wished Ev were here. He had to keep the principals from comparing notes before he could quiz them. Ev could have taken Brian while Jack tackled McFarland, preventing McFarland from preparing either Brian or Brenda. In that he was only partly successful. He thought he had kept them apart, but there were three of them and only one of him.

More than anything else, he needed Ev's beautiful gift of being able to get chummy instantly with other women, so that he could turn her loose on Brenda. Brenda was certainly as helpful as she knew how toward Jack. She didn't seem to be withholding anything. But Ev brought out things that women didn't know they knew.

Ev. No, that was not what he needed more than anything else. The very most of all, he yearned for a comforting hug.

Fury drains you so rapidly.

He drew in a deep, deep breath. Sadness was back, diluting his fury and dragging self-pity back along with it. He tried without success to banish them.

Brenda came into the coffee room and plopped a paper

bag on the round Formica table. "If I promise I won't poison you, do you want to share my lunch?" She fetched a Diet Coke out of the fridge and sat down.

Jack smiled. "Thanks. I'll probably eat later." He checked out the fridge himself. Any Pepsi? No. He ended up with root beer. He popped his can and sat down across from her. "That's very nice of you after the grilling I put you through."

"You were very polite and considerate."

"But not pleasant."

"I wouldn't expect you to be, after all that. Your colleague called — Evelyn. I left the memo on my desk — sorry. I didn't know I'd find you here. She'd like you to call her at her motel this afternoon. I suppose she's at lunch now, but she didn't say."

"I shall. Thank you." Jack sipped his root beer and sifted mentally through the notebookful of data, mostly negatives, he'd gathered this morning. "The forensics crew done yet?"

"A few minutes ago. I wanted to wait by the desk until they finished, in case they needed anything. Mrs. Dennison — I think that's her name — said the goat was tied by one foot to a cinder block. She thinks it might need veterinary attention, so I called our vet. He's coming out after lunch."

"Doctors who still make house calls." But not for gentle old Christian men who fall off barn roofs. "Tied with what, do you know?"

"Baling twine. We have a barn full of it. It cut in deeply, she said." Brenda nodded knowingly as she munched on a peanut butter and jelly sandwich. She was a lovely lady, but she tended to talk with her mouth full. "So you were right. It *was* a trap."

"And when I asked you about six different ways, you said you couldn't imagine the trap being laid for McFarland, even though he goes down to the goat pasture every morning. No threats or problems."

Jack would have quizzed the goatkeeper, but the man was off yesterday and today. He worked weekends. Had he armed the gate yesterday, someone would have sprung the trap by now. And had he armed it this morning, the Dogwood Garden Club, who knew him, would have noticed him here in the park. Jack had talked to the ladies late this morning, as much to get up and walk a little as to fill more notebook pages.

He motioned toward the battered old AT&T Merlin on the table. "FTS line?"

"Press nine."

He pressed nine and got a strange, buzzy dial tone. It sounded about the way his teeth used to feel. He went through the FTS motions. The Federal Telephone System linked parks and other federal agencies with an essentially free line. By going from this federal unit, Sandburg, to another federal unit, Smokies, the Service paid only for the local call from Sugarlands to the motel. As the connection went through, he pondered the irony of the government's finding such neat ways to save a few bucks here, only to waste billions elsewhere.

A familiar, most welcome voice answered on the first ring.

Jack sat back and stretched his legs out. "You wanted to talk to me. I want to talk to you. Then I got this brilliant idea — let's run this string between these two tin cans and see if it works."

"I tried that so often when I was a little girl, and we could never get it to work."

"Neither could we. Ernie and I even tried soaking it in an electrolyte. Salt water. *Nada.* What's up? Any response on the flyers?"

Ev was talking with her mouth full too. Jack could tell. "Not yet. Diane Walling has been home for a couple days

182

now. This morning I invited myself over to her place, and we talked for three solid hours."

"Good. How's Mulligrubs?"

"That cat is so strange, Jack! I fed it and took care of it for four days, and it accepted me. Not extremely affectionate, but tolerant. Disdain, I suppose, is the word. Now that Diane's home, it hisses at me. She must think I was terrible to it."

Jack never did trust cats. This just confirmed it. "How's Diane doing?"

"She has to go back in tomorrow morning for some repair surgery of some sort. I'll be taking care of the cat again for a couple days. Yesterday afternoon, Homer Symes gave me all sorts of good stuff. I have all of Colleen Abcoff's prior duty tours, along with who her superintendent and immediate supervisor were. Homer is working on getting complete duty rosters so that we know who was working under her in those places. Someone who would have a grudge. I'm just now sifting through it. So far, two of the people she used to work for were here for the funeral."

"Good. Good." Jack glanced at Brenda. The lady was popping open a bag of corn chips — not the little lunch-box size, either. "Anyone she especially locked horns with?"

"I'm going to tackle that next, but I want to talk to them from the park so I can get on FTS. Oh, and speaking of phones, I got one of those phone pagers. You dial its number, and it not only beeps, it tells me what number I'm supposed to call back. It's kind of neat. Hiram sells them."

"Hiram!" Boy, those corn chips looked good.

"I was talking to him quite a bit too. He gave me more details about some of the raw deals the Abcoffs pulled on people, but it's nothing especially revealing. No surprises. Also, he said you really know horses. He was pleased that you took good care of his roan. But then, he said, he figured you would if a horse was the first thing you thought of to go out looking with. Got a pencil?"

Jack pulled out his notebook. It was full. He flipped it over to write on the back. "Shoot." Poor choice of words, when you think about the last week or so. She gave him her beeper number.

For a few more minutes Ev explained how Colleen Abcoff had virtually destroyed Bodine Grubb's wife's career as a realtor. Jack had only to grunt now and then to keep her going. Nearly everyone who came to work in the Smokies bought into the favorable housing market rather than pay rent. Abcoff had promised verbally that she would shunt new park employees to Bodine's realtor wife. Here Jack's murky brain failed to catch it all. Somehow, Abcoff pulled a fast one and left Bodine's wife holding the bag some way, virtually destroying her professional reputation. Ev obviously understood the details. She would confirm with Bodine's wife tomorrow.

"Also," she concluded, "I'm working on alibis. Find out who could have slipped in some poison that evening."

"Ev, aren't you leaning too heavily on Laurel's speculation?" The aroma of corn chips caressed him like a siren's song.

"If it turns out to be natural causes, we don't have a case anyway."

Should he go into detail about the electrified gate? He decided to wait. "Ev? Don't go out interviewing tomorrow. Stay in your room until I get there. I'll be back by tomorrow morning. Work on reports or something." She related well to paperwork.

"Why?"

"I don't know why. Just do it. Please?" *Because we are both equally vulnerable to some loony. I'm feeling that more and more.*

"Jack? What happened?"

"I'll tell you all about it then."

"Jack?!"

If he didn't explain to her satisfaction, she'd call Hal for clarification. He just knew it. "Give Hal my love." He good-byed her and hung up.

Brenda swung the corn chip bag around to face him. "You're a junk food junkie too."

"Of the worst degree. Did you ever meet Colleen Abcoff?" He grabbed a handful, a sort of carpe diem reaction lest the bag be withdrawn.

"No. I didn't want to. I heard enough about her from Galen."

"Anyone here besides Galen ever work for her?"

"Not that I know of."

He mulled options, the first of which would be to buy another notebook. And maybe some corn chips.

He leafed down through his notes.

The garden clubbers had seen no one, familiar or otherwise, messing around the goat pasture, and they had arrived around a quarter to eight. They heard a goat bleating but didn't bother to check. Others took care of that sort of thing, and they had a lot of work to get done. McFarland usually visited the goats each morning, but he had not come down yet this morning that they had noticed. Zero.

Brenda did not call Bell on the radio. She had heard the call, asking Bell to come up to the house for a minute. She could not discern whose voice it might be because the transmission had been extremely fuzzy and broken. She assumed one of the maintenance men had called. It didn't sound like Mr. McFarland. Zero.

Brian did not recognize the call either. He made out his

call number and something like "house" and that was about it. He did not think about it at the time. When he arrived at the house he found no one. He had no idea who could have called him away. Zero.

There was a lot of other information as well, but it didn't seem to pertain, at least not now.

No hits, no runs, one big error somewhere — someone was lying.

Brenda graciously interrupted her lunch to get him the address for the forensics lab. He could try to work on the hostile McFarland now or give it up and call McFarland over to Gatlinburg in a couple days for further talks. He'd do it that way. Maybe let Ev work on him. She wouldn't get him feeling defensive the way Jack did. He thanked Brenda and took his leave.

He drove into Asheville to the lab, stopping only long enough to get a new notebook, some corn chips, and a two-liter of Pepsi. He finally met Patti Dennison personally. She was a pleasant woman with a harried look, no-nonsense brown hair, and a no-nonsense smile. As she explained what she'd need for comparisons, Jack filled half of his new notebook with notes of samples to obtain and things to do.

Mrs. Dennison gave him specimen containers and mailers. With prominently lettered inscriptions, the mailers emphatically reassured the postal service that nothing in them was hazardous or dangerous or the least bit worrisome. Jack considered it a bit of overkill that they'd use hazardous and dangerous in the same breath.

He filled up just west of Asheville and headed over the hill.

Gatlinburg or Townsend? If he went to his room near Townsend, he could cruise Little River Road slowly at night, maybe see a black dog waiting by the roadside.

Maybe.

Hardly. He drove on in to Gatlinburg. Back in the park, the night was dark, as night ought to be. Here in town, garish lights invited folks to stay up just a little longer, to shop and play. He pulled into Ev's motel under a brilliant battery of those obnoxious sulfur parking-lot lights that make automobile colors all look like swamp slime.

There sat the little mud-colored sports car (red in daylight), with its top up. Good. She was taking seriously his admonition to stay put. He climbed the outside stairs, knocked on her door, and stepped back a little so she could see him through the peephole.

The inside chain chattered against the door. The dead bolt ticked. She pulled her door open and moved aside.

He froze halfway to stare at her. He stepped inside far enough to slam the door and wrapped his arms around her. "What in the world happened?"

Her face was wet with tears, her eyes all red and puffy, her nose slurpy. "Oh, Jack . . ." She grabbed him, clung to him, buried her face in his shoulder. The crying cut loose. As beleaguered as her eyes looked, this had been going on for a while.

Maxx. It had to be about Maxx.

As he held her close, letting her cry it out, he realized that the reason he'd come directly here was to get some comfort and sympathy. He needed both badly just now. When she told him about Maxx, he'd need them even more. It is more blessed to give than to receive. Except this time.

She came up for air eventually and separated herself to go get a handful of tissues. Her motel wastebasket, he noticed, was full of spent ones. She flopped into an easy chair, so he took the other one. He waited while she blew.

She shuddered. "I'm sorry. I thought you'd be in tomorrow, and I'd be over this. I'd be able to talk about it calmly."

He waited.

She blew again. "My car still doesn't start right. The new starter didn't cure the problem at all. It still sounds like the battery's nearly dead."

That couldn't be the source of this misery. "Tomorrow, let's check out the electrical system. Look for a loose battery terminal, a rusty connection where the battery grounds to the frame, or loose wiring. Something like that."

She nodded, her face still a study in sadness. "Do you know a woman named Mayrene McAllister?"

"No. She's not in my notes. Does she live around here?"

She shook her head. Her hair didn't float as lightly as it usually did. "Washington. She's career Park Service — started out with park police, and now she's in the national office. Jack, what do you know about grievances? Grievance procedures?"

"Not as much as you do. I've never been involved in it. You surely bumped into it now and then in budget."

She grimaced. "And it was all so technical. Clinical. You calculate dollars and cents. Advise the Service on the cheapest way out. It was never . . . personal."

"By which, I take it, it is now."

She shuddered another sobbing sigh. "When Hal first detailed me to work on that problem in Death Valley, the position he put me in was a higher pay grade than my job in budget. So it had to be on a temporary basis."

"It was. Three-month appointment."

"Right. But if he makes my temporary position permanent and it's a grade raise, he has to advertise it."

Jack puzzled a minute. Then his heart went *thump*. "He put you on permanent, it's a pay raise, and he didn't advertise

188

it. Didn't offer it to everyone who's qualified Servicewide." Her face told him that was it. "Ev, they get around that kind of thing every day, one way or another, and Hal's the biggest conniver in the Park Service. He'll think of something to cover his tracks."

Her voice dripped acid. "Mayrene McAllister filed a formal grievance against Hal for failure to follow merit promotion procedures. He disregarded key regulations."

"That's Hal's problem, isn't it?"

"No, Jack, it's mine. As part of the process, she indicates in her grievance how to correct the situation. Recommends what she thinks ought to happen. She says Hal has to return me to my former position, and he has to offer her priority placement in the next equivalent job opening."

"Which is yours, just vacated, since so far there are only two of us."

And then she repeated it in plain, nongovernment English. "Dump me and hire her instead. And what she's asking for is standard. She'll get it, Jack."

Jack was about to protest that Hal was fair and loyal and would find some way out of it. He sat silent, a lump of dismay. Fair? Loyal? Hal? *Hah!* If dumping Ev was the easiest way for Hal to resolve the grievance, he'd do it in a minute. Jack had lateraled in with no promotion involved. Hal didn't have to advertise the new position before placing Jack in it. But if he had, and if someone had filed, Hal would have had no compunctions about dumping Jack. Jack knew it. Ev knew it.

"Hal say yet what he's going to do?"

She shook her head. "I forget how long he has to respond. Sixty days, I suppose. Maybe thirty. Anyway, we might be able to clear this case before I'm ousted. And if we can, maybe it will help prove that I'm effective and I shouldn't have been removed — you know, if I can protest the firing and get a hearing or something. I don't know." A shuddering sob caught her unawares. "But that's not likely. She has a valid grievance, Jack. You could even say airtight."

Yes, you could. Jack knew enough about administrative procedures to realize that much. "You might want to talk to a lawyer of your own. Not Hal's lawyer. He or she might have some suggestions."

But that was merely a wild, last grasp at straws. Jack knew that. He harbored no fond illusions.

Ev, as the saying goes, was history.

18

There Is a Perennial Nobleness . . . in Work

— Thomas Carlyle, *Labor*

"Sometimes people tend to worship work like it was holy or something, don't you think?" Lovey Hempett stood in the middle of Gatlinburg's busiest street, her feet on the dashed yellow line, philosophizing.

Jack admired philosophers who could work under adverse conditions, but this was tempting fate a bit much.

"I mean," she concluded, "if work gets you what you want, fine. But if it takes less work to get something, that's not bad, is it?"

Jack's truck's position was just as dangerous, parked on the inside lane with his flashers on and his window rolled down. "Not if it's ethical, it's not bad. But mental work is just as much work as physical labor is. Just as valuable. Hey, Ev and I are going to breakfast. Want to join us?" In other words, *Lovey, do you want to get out of the middle of the street?*

She shook her head. She'd apparently just washed her hair, and a lot of wispies hadn't made it all the way back to the rubber band in her ponytail. "I dropped Bugle off at Hiram's. Now I'm on my way to go clean Weinekes' this morning."

"Sounds like hard work to me."

"Nah. I love cleaning fancy homes. Thanks anyway. Bless you!" And she trundled on, completing her crossing of Parkway.

191

Jack started his bright new truck forward again. Actually, when you thought about it, standing in the middle of the street on a Thursday at 7:00 A.M. wasn't that big a danger, the traffic being minimal. "When does Laurel leave town?"

"She was going to go tomorrow, but she changed her plans. Next week maybe, at least not until the lab tests come back. She's hoping to be here when we get him. She's certain it's murder."

"She would be. She's a mystery writer. She probably has the hostess taste the soup before she'll touch it too."

"I don't know. She doesn't seem particularly suspicious of people." Ev stared absently out the windshield. "Lovey's in love with you, did you notice that?"

Jack looked at her. "Oh, come on."

"She never saw this truck before, right? And yet she spotted you instantly at an odd time of day and ran out into the middle of the street to talk to you. She was polite, but she pretty much snubbed me. She was talking to you. Nothing to say, no news. But she found something to talk 'bout."

"She just happened to see us. That conversation was an extension of one we had while we were playing Monopoly. I think you're overstating it." He pulled into the lot at Uncle Gene's.

Ev shrugged and slid out. He watched her a moment before he climbed out and locked up. She wasn't crushed exactly. He wouldn't call it that. But the bounce was gone. Her dream had been shattered. McFarland's dream had been shattered also. And Platt's. And, apparently, Bodine's wife's. Dreams have such an uncertain life expectancy.

Jack draped a hand across her shoulder as they went in. "Tell you what. We'll lay the rap on Leonard Walker, and then you can transfer in as Sugarlands District ranger."

She grimaced. "I suppose that's one solution."

192

He had enjoyed that brief time when they traded banter. No banter now. He missed it.

They took what had become their usual booth by the window. "What was all that about work? I missed most of it." Ev laid her purse on the seat.

"A couple years ago she started working on her GED and got bogged down. She feels guilty about giving up on it, I think, and she's trying to justify it."

"What's a jeedee?"

"General equivalency diploma. If you don't complete high school, but you need a high school diploma, you can earn a GED. Same kinds of credits, and accepted by universities and employers in lieu of high school. I saw a math workbook by her chair at her house. It was dusty." He righted their overturned coffee mugs.

"Mm." She gazed at empty distance.

"Ev? If you don't want to gather those hair samples today, that's all right. I can do it."

She snapped back to reality, more or less. "No, I want to. It's different and interesting. I'll take care of it." She straightened and pointed out the window. "There's Laurel coming across the street." But she didn't sound as enthusiastic as she normally did.

The novelist spotted them, waved, and headed for the door.

As Laurel came sweeping over to them, Jack half stood. It was all the tight booth would allow of him.

Ev invited the lady, and she instantly accepted. Ev shifted her purse as Laurel slid in beside her.

The waitress came sweeping over right behind her. Actually, the waitress didn't sweep. More accurately, she slogged. Deftly she turned Laurel's mug over and filled all three. "The usual?"

"Sure." Three times.

The waitress slogged off.

Laurel set a big raffia bag beside the seat and dug through it. "I'm glad I found you." She handed Jack a book with a Southwest design on the cover. "Here's one of Tony Hillerman's better ones. Try it."

"Thanks. The cover looks interesting." He had six inches of reports to absorb. When did she expect him to read fluff?

"Ev, you were talking about how you liked dolphins and your father was involved in the Navy dolphin program for a while. Here." She handed Ev a thin paperback in teal and pink. "Highly recommended. It's not fluff. Neither of them is. They raise some excellent points."

"*Silent Witness*. Pat Rushford. Thank you, Laurel." Ev flipped the book to read the flap copy. "Sounds interesting. Do you suppose this Pat Rushford went down to Florida to research it the way you've come to the Smokies?"

Laurel's eyes sparkled, but then they always sparkled. "She sure did. Including a cruise. It's a YA. Young Adult. But it has excellent appeal for adult adults just as much. You'll enjoy it. Pat was up for an Edgar for that one."

This led to the academy awards of the mystery writers, the Edgar, and the early works of Poe, for whom it was named.

Jack got a little bored with the whole discussion. Despite Laurel's protestations, he still thought such stuff was fluff as opposed to, for instance, anything relevant to Scripture, or Aldo Leopold, or Sig Olson. When his bacon and eggs arrived, he lost interest in the conversation altogether. But he noticed Ev perked up somewhat. He was all for anything that perked Ev up.

Ev asked, "Is there a mystery for every topic and interest?"

"Just about. And every region of the country." Laurel's

usual was eggs Benedict. "Say, I'm on chapter fifteen, and I made myself another chart. Then I thought, maybe you can use something like this."

Ev encouraged her meddling by asking, "Let me see it."

Jack would not have encouraged her.

Laurel dug down into her bag. "I was having trouble placing my characters — what person was where when. So I built this." She laid out more charts on the table between the bran muffins and the eggs Benedict. She pointed to this entry and that, explaining to Ev how she solved some problem. She gave Ev a couple of blank copies of the chart with a cheery "See if that helps."

"Thank you." Ev seemed genuinely grateful. "It happens I'm working on alibis now anyway."

"I did some more research on aconitum poison, since I'm going to use it to bump off my grandmother," Laurel babbled cheerily. Heads were surreptitiously starting to turn their way. "I'm thinking of introducing it in a mixed drink. It would muddy something clear like scotch and water. The drink has to be densely translucent or opaque. Margaritas would be good, for example. Since my grandmother is a vodka drinker, I'm going to use a white Russian. It will work perfectly."

She might as well have said, "My broker is E. F. Hutton, and E. F. Hutton says . . ." All conversation had ceased. Everyone in the room was leaning toward them, straining to listen.

It was too good an opportunity to pass up. Jack couldn't help himself. He modulated his voice between too low to hear and so loud as to be obvious. "That's kind of chancy, isn't it? It could make her so sick she loses it before it gets a chance to work. Why don't you just put a rattlesnake in her bed?"

In all seriousness, Laurel puckered her brow. "Aren't

rattlesnakes endangered?"

"Some are."

She shook her head. "I don't want to use them then. Besides, you don't always die from rattlesnake bite. I need something that's certain to do the job. It's a nice idea, though. It has the advantage of being creepy. You want skin to crawl."

Jack was going to say, "Absolutely. The creepier the better." But he didn't get the chance.

Ev was looking frantically around the room as all the silent heads ducked away from her gaze. "Jack, you jerk!"

That instant, Jack was saved from the blistering of his young life by her brand-new pager. The size and shape of a fat fountain pen, the thing was clipped to the outside of her purse. It beeped insistently.

Scowling at him, she pulled it and glanced at its readout. She excused herself brusquely and headed out to the public phone by the door.

Laurel slid back into her seat, frowning. "What's wrong with Ev? She's not her usual self."

"Private matters. She'll explain them, I'm sure. Also, her car doesn't start." He tried to put an accusing edge to his voice. It was Laurel who talked her into buying that junker.

"Automotive problems are so irritating. She really seems down." Laurel returned to her eggs Benedict, and they ate in silence for a few minutes. Then Laurel said, "I took Bodine Grubb and his wife out for a drink last night. An interesting man. He hunts. That surprised me."

"A lot of people around here do. Big industry, hunting."

"I know, I know. Part of the 'bubba' image. He went on about that for half an hour. About unfavorable stereotyping of rural Southerners. He also gave me a lot of excellent material on bear hunters. Poaching bears is also a big industry.

There's a lucrative international market for claws, paws —
and gall bladders, of all things. It's going to be a major feature
in my book."

"Along with poisoning your grandmother?" Jack finished
off the last of his grits.

"That's just the presenting situation — the crime that gets
it started. Did you ever go hunting with dogs?"

Maxx. His heart wrenched. He'd been trying not to think
about Maxx so much. "Now and then."

"Local hunters don't go out like hunters in Ohio and
Pennsylvania, where I grew up. They don't put on their orange hunting caps and walk through the woods with a shotgun, hoping to scare something up. They build a campfire
and turn their dogs loose. Then they sit around the fire and
follow the dogs by ear. They can tell by the kind of barking
what's happening. If the dogs find a bear or raccoon or whatever they're after, they chase it up a tree. Then the hunters get
up and home in on the sounds."

"So the right dog is very valuable around here."

"Exactly. He says that a lot of local hunters fit radio collars
on their lead dogs and follow the pack electronically. The
dogs might give voice beyond earshot, but the hunters can tell
what's happening with the tracking device. He drew me a
sketch of how it works. Even worse on bear populations than
poaching, though, is habitat loss. I'll slip something in on that
too."

"Good." What should he say?

"I'd love to go along on a coon hunt, but they don't do it in
spring. The raccoons are molting, and the fur isn't market
quality." She stood up and stepped back. Obviously, Ev was
returning.

Ev scooted in, appearing neither happier nor sadder than
she had when she left.

Laurel filled the awkward silence. "So it was a highly profitable evening for me. He's interested in politics also. He tried to run for legislature a couple times, but the Abcoffs were too powerful with the State Democratic Committee. Politics usually doesn't read well unless you're someone like John Grisham or LeCarré. Particularly in YA. So I'll probably stay away from that."

Jack sat back, his plate empty. "How are his political plans coming? There's a primary coming up."

Laurel smiled. "He just grimaced and said, 'Don't ask.' " She seemed to be finished with her eggs Benedict, although a few bites remained. "A very complex man. And dark."

"I got that impression also." Jack looked at Ev.

She gathered up the charts Laurel had given her. "That was one of our interviews. He had to move it up. We ought to go soon. Laurel, thanks again for these."

Laurel took the cue and stood up. "You're welcome. I'm going to buy a paper and enjoy another cup of coffee. Jack, let me get the check today."

"That's OK. I think she wrote them up separately anyway. Thanks." He ushered Ev to the door, paid their bill, and left.

He waited until they were in the truck and he was backing out of his slot. "So who was it really?"

"Homer Symes. The park personnel officer. He seems to be so good at finding loopholes and little details, like with that insurance business, I confided my problem to him yesterday afternoon. He said he'd work on it and see what he could find. Apparently he's handled a number of grievance procedures on both sides of the fence — park and individual."

"That was a smart move. Diane Walling's first?"

She nodded. "Get Mulligrubs squared away for the day. Mr. Symes was nice enough to come into the office very early this morning — so he could 'fish around on the computer a little before work,' is the way he put it. He called just now to tell me he hasn't found anything so far, but he has some other things to try tomorrow."

The traffic was getting thicker with people going to work and the tourists going to breakfast. *It must be a churning morass of cars here in the summer at the height of the season,* Jack thought.

He angled right onto Cherokee Orchard Road. "Where do you want to go after we get the cat taken care of?"

"Back to my motel. Where are you going?"

"The park. Talk to the people who are doing the toxicology on Abcoff. See if Symes and Vosniak finished a list of unsolved crimes I asked for. Shall I come get you for lunch? We can compare notes."

She nodded. She sure wasn't chipper, and her sadness hurt him.

The Siamese was sleeping on a satin sofa pillow, curled up like royalty. It twitched an ear and watched them with half-closed eyes, but heaven forfend any overtures of politeness or friendliness. Jack got the cat box while Ev changed the water and scooped the cat food. They did a quick check through the house, making sure everything was in order, and left.

Jack let Ev off at her place and drove on in to the park. He found Homer Symes at his work station. Symes had the list of unsolved crimes waiting for him, though he informed Jack that Vosniak had not been involved in its compilation. He apologized again that he could find no little loophole to help Ev.

Jack asked him about Galen McFarland's rap sheet. Homer looked blank. Criminal record. *Ah.* Within five minutes, Homer handed Jack a complete dossier on McFarland, everything the Park Service knew about him.

Age eleven, vandalism.

Age twelve, burglary.

Age fifteen, joy riding.

Age sixteen, grand theft auto.

Age eighteen, assault, the charge reduced from attempted murder.

19

Call Me Ishmael

— Herman Melville, *Moby Dick*

"Just call me Ishmael. That means wanderer, doesn't it? I put two hundred miles a day on my vehicle." Sheriff's Deputy Tom Baumgardner, whose signature looked not in the least like his name, drew an acre of air in through his nose and sat back in the booth at Uncle Gene's.

Across from him, Jack leaned both elbows on the table. "As I recall, it means 'God is listening' or 'God is hearing.' It's been a while since I studied Genesis in detail. Have you had any major accidents?"

"Not yet. Knock on wood." And the sheriff's deputy did so.

"Thousand miles a week and no problems? I'd say God is hearing you."

Tom chuckled. "Hadn't thought of it that way. This list you got here from the park — it isn't up to date." He rapped a finger on Jack's printout. "These arsons two years ago? We had the perp. He just never went to trial."

Jack swung the sheet around to see it better. Five deliberately set fires in three weeks, a pause of a month, and three more. Then nothing. "The firebug went to jail for thirty days on an unrelated offense."

"Exactly." Tom paused to shoot up on caffeine. How he could drink coffee this hot escaped Jack. "That's how we were sure it was him. We just couldn't prove it. Then he did us the favor of checking out on booze and pills."

Jack swirled his own coffee, hoping it would cool faster. "Remember any details?"

"I investigated it. I'll send you the written stuff." Tom jotted himself a note. "The guy was a derelict. He'd pick up work here and there posing as a mountain man or hillbilly. He had a beard like you wouldn't believe. A couple weeks after we began noticing him — loitering, an indecent exposure here in town in Mynatt Park, things like that — the fires started. Lost a major tourist attraction, a museum. That's when we really got interested. He was always nearby, you know, as the fire fighters were putting 'em out. The city jailed him for habitual drunkenness just to see what would happen."

"No fires."

"No fires. Until he got out. Then he set two in town and one in the park, and that got Bill Weineke torqued at him. The same day that we were all in a meeting trying to figure out how to nail him, he consumed too much vodka and valium."

Jack sat back. "Convenient."

"It went down as an OD, but Hiram Jones wanted to call it an act of God." Tom smiled. "Frankly, I don't think God's too interested in arson when there's no loss of life, but the merchants do get upset."

Jack's patty melt and Tom's burger arrived. Jack paused to say grace. "How about Gerry Rackenberg's death?"

"I wasn't in on that one, but I got scuttlebutt from the investigating officer. That one was big. National attention for a minute or two. Rackenberg was walking across the street a couple blocks from here — jaywalking, but it was real early. No traffic."

And there stood Lovey in the street this morning.

Tom crooned on between mouthfuls. "Along came a big

202

white van and flattened him. Massive head injuries. No witnesses, though everyone saw it five seconds later. We fingered the van. Guess whose."

"The president of the Sierra Club. Gerry was proposing some unpopular ideas."

"Close but no cigar. Leonard Walker's. The Sugarlands District ranger. He left his front porch to drive to work and found out that he'd be walking that day. He reported the theft within five minutes of when the hit-run occurred."

"By phone from home?"

"I don't know. I'll find out." Tom made himself another note.

They did make good patty melts here. "The vehicle was found ditched a couple miles away," Jack hazarded. "The driver was never identified."

"Yep. Perfect textbook hit-run, just like they teach you in policeman school." Tom popped a french fry. "Two witnesses who saw the van speed up and leave the scene said the driver was black. Here. This one's interesting." He poked his finger at an entry halfway down.

"Vehicle vs. Tree," it said. Jack would read the fine print later.

"I investigated that one. Just last year." Tom became cheerily animated. "You know the temporary reflector strips they lay down on new asphalt?"

"No."

"Let's say they're resurfacing 321. They put new blacktop down eastbound, covering the center striping."

"Because the resurfacing has to seam in the middle."

"Right. They can't stripe it yet because they have to resurface westbound first. So they lay down sticky plastic reflecting strips, a temporary dashed centerline, so that a guide line will be there until they get the rest of the paving done. Then they peel up the reflective strips and paint the permanent stripes."

"OK." It's a poor day you don't learn something. Jack finished off his sandwich.

"Now picture this. Three o'clock in the morning, this guy is driving sixty miles an hour down the back road to his house, heading home. He comes around a curve and *splat!* Head-on into a fir tree three-feet wide. Completely wrapped around it. His motor was in the backseat. I'm not exaggerating."

"Left the road at high speed."

"Yeah, but he didn't leave his lane! It was diabolical. Something Hitchcock would dream up. Somebody spray-painted the centerline black on a wide curve of that back road, and then laid down temporary reflector strips to lead him off the road into the tree. The road kept on curving, but the false centerline straightened out. He thought he was in his lane right up to the end."

Jack frowned. "You mean the blacked-out lines didn't show?"

"Sure they did. Wouldn't have worked if he wasn't under the influence. Way under."

"No idea who?" Jack popped his last fry.

"Not a clue. At first, they said a kids' prank gone sour. But not even kids would be that stupid. Right into a tree? It had to be deliberate. So then they tried to pin it on his estranged wife, but she was in jail all that week for refusing to tell the court where their kids were. Said he molested them. Abused them."

"Did he?"

"Yeah, probably. Soon as he was dead, the wife told Child Protective Services where to find the kids. The CP investigation said they still had marks and stories to tell. We kept the trick out of the papers — the reflector strip part. We were

204

afraid kids or a copycat would steal the idea." Tom craned his neck to look again at the printout. "There's lots more uncleareds on the books than just these. Burglaries and stuff."

"I asked for the biggies. I'll be hard-pressed to check these out, let alone a full list."

"Aah, we don't get that much crime around here. I'll send you a complete list. If you had, for instance, an attempted hit-run that didn't draw blood, it might not show up here."

"That's true. Sure. Dump it all on me."

Tom snorted. "The recruits coming into the department picture an exciting life for themselves — getting into fire fights every day and car chases." He blew a raspberry. "Paperwork. Nobody ever tells them ninety-five percent of their day will be paperwork. A simple car stop, the paperwork takes three times as long as the actual contact. On the phone, write it down; scroll the computer screen, write it down. Write something down, you have to write down that you wrote it down."

"Remember when they promised us computers were going to eliminate paperwork?"

Tom made a highly realistic gagging sound.

Jack gave him a fax number, that Tom might send him the written reports on the arsonist's and child molester's deaths. They bade adieu, and Jack drove over to Ev's motel.

He pondered how to check out her electrical system when he didn't have the foggiest idea how an MG operates. He didn't even know whether a car that old had a generator or an alternator. He anticipated that he was about to make an utter non-macho fool of himself. Men are supposed to know about cars. He did, sort of. He could take a CJ 5 apart and stick it back together with only minimal use of baling wire. He had gotten pretty good at keeping his Ram running. But he was entering alien country with this stupid little British sports car.

The slot lay empty where once Ev's MG had been parked. Only a dark smudge remained; something in the front end leaked oil. She was not in her room. She must have gotten it running. He drove on down to park headquarters.

At headquarters, Ev's MG had usurped the administrative officer's parking spot under the tulip tree. Ah, well. Served the admin officer right. If they wanted to claim spots, they should spray their names on the curb.

Jack went inside without having to tell a dog to "stay." Maxx came to his memory at the most unusual times.

Ev was in the coffee/conference room. The place seemed typical of such rooms. The refrigerator snored. The kitchen sink faucet dripped. Safety posters were stuck up here and there, because the law says you have to post them and nobody wants those big, ugly propaganda posters messing up the decor around *his* part of the building.

Ev had spread out an assortment of charts and reports across two tables. Eagerly, she zipped Magic Marker highlights on this entry and that. She turned to him with a dazzling smile as he walked in.

He grinned. "Ev, I remember a day when I couldn't get you to smile to save me."

The smile softened. "Death Valley. I was such an uptight jerk. So uncertain. Here — let me show you something."

He joined her. She did some minor shuffling of paper and laid out a double-width chart. "Bill and Greg are working almost exclusively on Diane's incidents now."

"Sure. It's not for certain yet that Abcoff is murder."

"They're investigating it like a murder though. They got alibis for everyone for the preceding twenty-four hours in her life, and alibis for the two Walling things — the shooting and the hit-and-run."

206

"Standard operating procedures."

"Right. And then I turned the tables and asked where they were. To make the record complete, I said. Then I took all their reports and filled in these charts of Laurel's."

"Rats. I left the stuff Tom gave me out in the truck. Oh, well. We'll get it later." Jack had to give the charts their due — they laid all the information out where you could see it instantly. "The Walling things here. Abcoff has no alibi for the hit-run after the funeral — he left moments before — but he can prove he was out of town during the drive-by. Am I reading this right?"

"Right. Green — well, chartreuse — highlight means proven and documented. Blue means proven indirectly. For instance, here's Bill Weineke. He returned some books to the night deposit bin at the library. They were his books, but someone else could have done it. Yellow is shaky — hearsay or something. And red means they don't have any way of proving where they were. That's why Abcoff is red during the hit-and-run and green during the shooting."

Bummer. Nobody was red in all cases, and nobody all green. No clear fingers pointing. Mixed bag.

"Ev, you don't have Lovey here."

"I guess she is a suspect, isn't she?"

"Sure. She worked for Abcoffs, was privy to their private lives, knows a lot of people. Shucks, she's related to a lot of people. Andy came on to her. And you don't have Hiram."

"Hiram's in his store all day. Or going to it. But I'll put him down too." She penciled Hiram and Lovey at the bottom. "Bodine Grubb I talked to mostly on the phone, so I couldn't get face-to-face impressions of nonverbal signals."

"Wow. You're learning the lingo." Jack picked up still another of Laurel's charts. "This one. The half hour prior to Abcoff's death."

"That one's not alibi. That's opportunity. I built that assuming it was poisoning. Laurel talked to a local doctor, researching for the fictional murder. She suggests it would've been administered within a half hour or so of the potluck. So I was trying to figure out who could have slipped something into her."

The phone extension rang, and Ev answered it. "Just a moment." She flopped to sitting, tucked the receiver against her ear with her shoulder, and began writing vigorously.

Opportunity. Apparently Abcoffs' living room was a freeway. In the two hours before the potluck, Bodine stopped by with an editorial he was going to run and then quickly pulled when she died, but he swore he didn't go inside. Walling was there getting instructions for some new project. Andy Abcoff lived there, of course. And Bill Weineke brought Symes by with a feasibility study for an in-house job-restructuring that Abcoff planned. She chased Weineke out moments later; apparently she didn't like the study. Jack penciled in that Lovey was cleaning that evening — she always cleaned Abcoffs' on Fridays.

"Here," Ev was telling the phone, "talk to Dr. Prester." She extended the receiver. "Toxicologist, about Abcoff."

Jack took the receiver and introduced himself.

"Dr. Prester, as I just told your assistant —" The man spoke with an extremely heavy Southern accent.

"Colleague."

"Colleague. We're certain it's poisoning. No signs of infection or disease, no cardiac or cerebrovascular events, no bacterial agents that would cause food poisoning. The E. coli in her was all hers. According to her husband, she usually preferred whiskey, but that evening she was using vodka. Our tests confirm that. Several mixed drinks, blood alcohol rising but not at intoxication levels. It appears a poison was administered through one or more of the drinks. Definitely poisoning, but we haven't pinpointed the exact substance."

Jack hated to say this. He really hated it. "Try aconite. Monkshood."

"That wouldn't do it unless there were a massive dose."

"What mixed drink?"

"Yes."

Huh? Jack looked at Ev. She was beaming victoriously.

Jack tried again. "The specific drink was what?"

"Right." It came across as "Rat."

Jack was talking to an extraterrestrial. Try again. "Spell it, please."

"Spell what?"

"Right."

"What?"

"The kind of drink."

"W H ah T E R U S S ah A N. What Russian."

"Of course."

Ev had gotten all the particulars, so Jack had no questions. The person on the other end promised to test for aconite and fax the complete results. End of weird conversation.

Ev, bless her, refrained from crowing, "I told you so," aloud, but then she didn't have to. Her triumphant grin said it just fine.

He changed the subject. "I see you got your car running. Or did you get a jump?"

She sobered, paused, licked her lips. "You'll laugh."

"I won't laugh."

"Bill Weineke did."

"Then he's on your list. OK." Jack amended it. "I'll try not to."

She made a derisive half-a-raspberry noise. "You mentioned about electrical connections, so I checked them all.

They were all tight. There was only one little gizmo between the battery and the starter. I didn't know what it was, but it looked pretty old. So I took it off and took it down to Hiram."

"The solenoid?"

"That's what he called it. He sold me a new one, I put it on, and it starts just fine. Eight dollars solved the problem."

"So why would I laugh? Why did Weineke?"

She looked saddened, perhaps angered, by the thought. "I suppose because I didn't know what the part was called. That chauvinist. I got it fixed, didn't I?"

"Now, now, Ev. We guys have it worse than you realize. We have a whole culture to change, all by ourselves. We grew up being chivalrous to women and assuming they know zilch about guy stuff. Automotive and such. It takes us a while to shift gears. Attitudes don't get altered that easily, you know."

"Yes, but common sense . . ." She stopped. "Never mind."

"Excuse me." Symes appeared in the doorway, looking for all the world as if he didn't want to be even a messenger behind the lines in the war between the sexes. "Some faxes just arrived for you from the sheriff's office." He handed Jack a sheaf of papers and beat a hasty retreat.

"There, you see how nervous we get just thinking about it?" Jack nodded toward the vacant doorway. He spread Tom Baumgardner's reports out on top of her charts. Penciled at the bottom of one of them was a note that he was compiling that extended list of uncleareds and would send it tomorrow. Good.

They fiddled around for an hour with the additional details, and Ev built a new column, Questions to Answer, just so that she could fill in a couple of blanks.

Jack thought of a host of questions too: For instance, why was the man zipping down the road at 3:00 A.M. anyway? He worked days. And where did a derelict get prescription Valium? And why was he drinking a pricey distillation — an empty Absolut bottle was found beside him — instead of the cheap vodka you would expect of a relatively impecunious drifter?

In other words, for all their papers and charts and graphs, they didn't know a thing.

20

The Shades of Night
Were Falling Fast

— Henry Wadsworth Longfellow, *Excelsior*

The shades of night were falling fast. Of course, being in the shadow of a major mountain range didn't hurt, either. *Anyway,* Jack mused, *it's getting dark.* He felt comfortable. Almost, but not quite, at peace. "Ev, you're brilliant."

Across the picnic table from him, Ev sipped at her coffee as she gestured toward her brand-new picnic basket. "Lucky. I just happened to see this hamper in the window of one of those craft shops when Laurel and I were browsing last week. I've always wanted one like this, with a hinged cover. It's made out of ash. These thin strips are wood. They pound on a certain kind of ash wood, and it splits into strips. I didn't know that before. The thermos I got at Hiram's, and the sandwiches and fruit are from that deli in the Baskins Creek Mall." She shrugged. "Voilà. Dinner."

"Delicious dinner, and the atmosphere is matchless. What do they call it? Ambience?"

They sat at ease in the Collins Creek picnic area. Above them the road wound up through the pass of Newfound Gap. Below them it continued down the steep valley following the Oconaluftee River — and everywhere was the sound of spring runoff and rushing creeks and birds. The sky had cleared. Its limpid blue was mellowing out into indigo as the sun got lost somewhere beyond the mountains. Whispering trees crowded in close around to protect them from the cold and savage sky.

"We'd probably better start back, I suppose." Ev commenced packing up the orange peels and sandwich wrappers. "It smells fresh and damp here, did you notice? Clean." She paused. "Why are you staring at me?"

"Why not? That's what scenery's made for."

"Oh, honestly." But, by cracky, she blushed.

He got up and carried her new picnic hamper down to her new MG. He secured it on the luggage rack with her new bungee cords. He had to admit, much as he'd hated to, that this stupid little foreign car was a kick to ride in, particularly here in the park. Particularly with the top down.

They had decided the cases were too confusing to bother with anymore, or else they needed a break. The notion of a break prevailed. While he made some calls, she drove back to her place, changed from heels to sweats, and outfitted their picnic supper. By the time she returned he had completed business and was calling around to his motel, to Wear Cove, to Hiram, making certain Maxx hadn't turned up yet.

Like any other tourists, they had paused at the Chimney Tops overlook so Ev could take a picture. They drove out to Clingman's Dome and enjoyed a clear view from the top of that strange, coiling observation ramp. They had continued southeast on the North Carolina side until supper-time hunger and the picnic area joined voices to bid them halt.

Now he went back to the table briefly to doublecheck that they were leaving nothing behind accidentally — an old habit of his that he saw no reason to break — and inserted himself into the passenger side by folding himself up like a frog on a lily pad with his knees splayed.

She slipped gracefully behind the wheel.

He watched her maneuver back onto the road and head north. "You're getting better with shifting. You don't have to thumb through the owner's manual for advice anymore, every time you want to change gears."

She almost giggled. The chuckle sort of died before it reached the surface. "Thank you. This is all very new. My father thinks stick shift is primitive. We never had a manual transmission when I was growing up. I dated a few boys who did."

"You father probably thought they were primitive too."

And she laughed aloud. She sobered by degrees into a quiet thoughtfulness. "You know, I didn't date much. I've told you all this before, I think. I was too busy with school, and being the first female president of the math club, and making great grades. Lots of A's. Same in college."

"You mentioned. You've always seemed kind of disappointed with yourself. I'm sorry you're not prouder of your accomplishments. There's great value in all that."

She glanced at him and back to the road. "I suppose so." She frowned as they hooked around the hairpin. "Third?"

"I would."

Cautiously, she went through all the clutch-and-shift maneuvering to get it from fourth to third.

"See?" Jack waved a hand. "You can do anything you set out to. You can have it all."

"That's the problem, Jack. No woman can have it all. There's just too much to have. If I have a husband and family, other doors are closed to me. Doors I want open. If I go through them, I won't have time for a man and kids."

"Lots of women combine two lives."

"And lose some out of both lives and feel guilty for it. My friends get married, and either their career founders or they stick their babies in day care. Sometimes both." She shook

214

her head. "I don't know what to do. I guess that's why I stayed pretty much away from dating."

"That was then. What about now?" He tried to make it sound casual. It wasn't. His voice tightened up like a baby's fist around a lollipop.

She stared at him so long that he pointed out the windshield, reminding her who was driving. "I don't know. It's even worse now than it used to be — the decision, I mean. I don't know."

He hadn't really thought about that before. When he fell in love and married Marcia, there was no question that he'd combine marriage and career. Men did. She hadn't really launched a career as such. She was day manager at a hotel. On second thought, that's pretty much a career move, getting into management. At that moment, Jack realized for the first time that Marcia had given up her own career goals to marry him. Forget a career in hotel management. Become a housewife, a mother. She'd never hinted at it, but it must have been the death of dreams.

Was it easier for Australian girls to do that than for Americans? Why should it be? Dreams are dreams. She had followed him so eagerly, away from homeland and away from what might have been.

What right did he have to step in and mess up Ev's career? On the other hand, Hal was probably going to do just that — Hal and that Mayrene cookie with the formal grievance. And Jack began to see, at least a little, how torn and indecisive Ev might feel.

They topped out at Newfound Gap — the air was chilled by both night and altitude — and headed down toward Sugarlands. Jack felt cold; Ev probably felt colder. He twisted what looked like the heater knob. He groped around, trying to feel whether anything was coming out the vents — metal

215

flaps to be opened manually. He popped his; warm air flowed. *Ah ha!*

"Nothing personal." Groping around under the dash on her side, he found her vent and pulled it open. The warm air rushing out from under the foot wells made riding in the clear, crisp night quite pleasant.

They wound down the gray-black road beneath lowering trees. They passed spring peepers chirping in the ditches.

She looked up now and then at the stars. "It's a glorious night."

"It is." His confused, even tormented, brain finally sifted out the right words. "Ev? Do me a favor?"

She looked at him. "Sure."

"Give marriage some thought."

He was ready for her this time. When she forgot to drive, he reached out and gripped the wheel until she should get back to it.

She drove a while in silence. Suddenly she hit the brakes and dipped into a gravel wayside. She parked as close against the right edge as she could. A white-flowering tree branch, probably a chokecherry, hung close beside Jack's ear, gray in the gloom.

She turned off the engine and lights and twisted in her seat as much as her seatbelt would permit. "Is that a proposal?"

"I don't know. I'm not any more certain about anything than you are. An overture to one maybe. I don't know."

"Aren't you supposed to be on bended knee or something?"

"Whaddaya mean, bended? My knees are bended like a carpenter's rule in this little tin can. There's not enough room in here to breathe deeply, let alone propose."

He regretted now that he'd said anything about marriage, and yet he didn't. What a muddle. "It's an unsettled time for both of us, Ev, and it's going to be for a while yet. I'm not suggesting decisions. I haven't made any either. But we ought to think about it."

"Sort of a strange variation on the classic romance-novel plot, isn't it? Boy meets girl. Boy loses dog. Boy marries girl."

"That's not it!"

"It could be. Certainly it could be. Or how about, girl meets boy. Girl loses job. Girl marries boy."

He felt exasperated. "I said, 'Think about it.' We can talk about it later."

"A rational decision made after careful consideration and discussion." Those great brown eyes almost glowed in the dark.

"Yeah. You sound wearied by the very thought."

"I suppose we modern women asked for it." She shrugged, straightened to face front, and twisted the ignition. "Laurel says romance novels are making a strong comeback. Fantasy, because true romance is so rare in real life. I'll drink to that." She flicked on her lights and pulled out onto the road.

He sighed and closed his eyes. No matter what he tried to do, it came out wrong. Sometimes tragically wrong. He was clinically trained about the importance of romance in women's lives. As part of his internship he counseled men on how to build a more romantic relationship with their wives, to repair damaged marriages and improve healthy ones. His head knew all the theory. Ph.D. with honors. His heart behaved like a caveman with a room-temperature IQ.

And it's the heart that counts.

His truck sat alone in the lot at headquarters. She pulled in beside it. She did not turn off her engine. He sat there a moment staring at the dashboard. Dashboard? This little car didn't even have a glove box. Just as well. A normal dash would leave no room for his knees at all.

He unpopped his seatbelt. Every time he thought carefully about what to say, it blew up on him. So he'd speak off the top, as he so often did. "It was a great afternoon, Ev. I appreciate all you did to make it happen. Thank you."

"I'm glad you enjoyed it. I did too. Very much." Even the ugly off-yellow of these ghastly parking-lot lights couldn't louse up the color of her big chocolate eyes.

He crawled out. The two things guaranteed to rob you of every shred of dignity are hospital gowns and climbing out of an MG. He closed the door. "Great idea, that picnic basket."

"Glad you like it. I do." She dipped her head toward her trunkful of papers. "Lot to do, but I won't do it tonight. I'll get an early start on it tomorrow."

He nodded. "Breakfast around nine or so too early for you?"

"Sounds good."

Here it came. "I've been thinking about marriage lately. I'll try to think about romance too." He leaned across the seats, balancing on the windshield. It wasn't all that big a stretch. Considering he'd been electrocuted yesterday, his muscles didn't even complain much. He kissed her and tried to make it romantic, whatever that was.

He climbed into his truck and just sat a moment, staring at the airbag cover, wishing life were simple. She pulled out and left. He heard the gears grind a bit before she got the engage-shift-release rhythm right. He drove a quarter mile down the Little River Road before he realized that he had been planning to give her this pile of papers on his seat. Nuts.

He'd give them to her tomorrow morning. Soon enough. But she said she was getting an early start on this stuff.

A couple hours wouldn't matter, and they'd already said good night.

But she'd want to at least look them over, probably. He'd take the time and effort to go back to her place.

No headlights were coming in either direction. Just to see if he could do it with this rig, he tried a moonshiner's turn on a long straight stretch. You're tooling down the road, and if you work accelerator, brake, and hand brake just right, you can break traction and swing the back around. Your vehicle swaps ends, and you're instantly tooling back the way you came.

He did it, but it sure wasn't flawless. You really need a hand brake rather than a foot-pedal emergency in order to do it right. His back wheels hooked up prematurely, and he just about went in the ditch. He stepped on it heading back toward Sugarlands. He'd arrive in Gatlinburg only a few minutes after Ev, give her the papers before she went to bed, and take 321 back to his motel. The route was longer but a lot straighter and therefore just about as fast.

As he pulled into the motel, he looked up at her second-floor window, third from the end. The light inside made her draperies glow faintly. Good. The picnic basket was gone, the top up. She'd have had to make two trips — her wad of papers and briefcase on one and the basket on the other — and it took time to get that stupid top up and latched. She must have just now locked her door for the night, so he wouldn't be disturbing her. He parked way down at the end because that was the closest slot left.

The only thing his imperfect experimental moonshiner's turn really accomplished was to send his papers off the far end of the seat. He got out, walked to the other side, and opened the passenger door very carefully, lest papers fall out. They did anyway. He stomped on some to prevent their walking off on the gentle breeze. He should buy some file folders or accordion files.

A window crashed. It was definitely the sound of a window breaking. As he snapped up straight, a ball of flame, brilliant in the darkness, boiled out of a second-floor window.

The third from the end.

His stunned brain disconnected, leaving his body to do what it wished. One instant he stood by his truck, and the next instant he was bolting up the outside stairs.

Her picture window was shattered. The draperies fluttered wildly, tossed by wind and flame and the billowing black smoke.

Alarm bells clanged.

"Ev!" He repeated it, wishing for an answer, knowing he probably couldn't hear it above the noise of smoke alarms and fire. He grabbed one of the draperies and yanked, ripping it away.

If the motel had installed overhead sprinklers, he might survive this. If it did not, he'd be dead in a minute, but that didn't matter anymore. He wrapped himself in the drapery.

"Ev!"

Either a distant voice responded above the roar of the fire, or he was imagining it. In these next moments God would either kill him or spare him, and just now he didn't care which. He begged God's mercy on Ev. He begged. He begged.

He kicked in a shard of remaining glass, took his last deep breath of clear air for a while, and stepped through the broken window with the drapery gathered close around him.

He aimed for where he remembered Ev's bathroom to be and ran, hunched over, through total roaring, hissing blackness. He mustn't breathe — fires kill with smoke inhalation rather than flame. Every fire fighter knows that. He slammed at an angle into a wall. He kept his eyes squeezed shut; they couldn't see anything in here anyway. He groped, found a door, pounded on it. "Ev!"

From inside, "Jack!"

Yes! Yes, God! Mercy on Ev! Yes!

His lungs empty, he leaned on the door and fumbled for the knob. It would be stove-hot now. He must force himself to grab it anyway.

The door flew open, and he staggered inside.

"Jack!" She clung to him.

The shower was running. He could hear it in the blackness. He slammed the door, but the bathroom was filling rapidly with smoke anyway. He pried her loose and shed the drapery. She was dripping wet. Smart move, to soak down in the shower.

He found the toilet tank and pulled off the cover. He used it as a battering ram to smash out the bathroom window. It broke in two, and he pounded on the shattered points of broken glass remaining. Ev beat on the shards with her shoe.

He couldn't remember what lay beneath them two floors down. The swimming pool was somewhere in this patio compound. So were shrubs and grass and flower beds and trees and lots of sidewalks. He boosted Ev. She clambered into the window opening, scrunched herself together, and leaped out into black nothing.

He crawled up onto the sink. He was coughing now — the air was too poisonous to breathe. From below, Ev's voice was screaming, "Way out! Sidewalk! Jump way out! Way out!"

With a muffled whoop, the bathroom door burst into flame. Smoke and heat roared against him and rushed ahead of him out the window.

He didn't fit in this little window. He couldn't launch himself well. Smoke swirled past him. He braced one foot squarely on the sill and used it to propel himself as hard as he could out into emptiness. Into the invisible hands of God.

He knew all the theory of how to land safely from a height. He didn't have time to put any of it into practice. He hung suspended. Before he could gather himself he slammed with freight-train intensity into the ground.

Grass. He was lying on grass, and coughing. He rolled to kneeling. Ev . . .

She attacked him, falling upon him, clinging and sobbing.

He clung to her — Ev alive! — and wrapped his arms around her tightly. Her hair smelled of smoke and melted plastic. *Thank you, God!* She settled, asprawl on the grass, curled up inside his embrace.

Fire engines, glorious with their clanging bells and flashing lights and hooting sirens, converged. People were beginning to pour out the motel doors. Once upon a time Jack was in a hotel when the fire alarm sounded. He and two other people were the only ones who believed the bell and left. People were believing this one. Fire fighters in turnouts hovered over a hydrant.

Ev was coughing as well as sobbing. "It blew the bathroom door open. I was in the bathroom, but the door wasn't clear shut, and it blew open." She shuddered. "It was all fire, Jack. All fire. And the lights went out. I shut the door and turned on the shower. I was sure the firemen would come. And then I was afraid they wouldn't, not in time. Jack . . ."

He purred soothing platitudes and pressed her head, her wonderful alive head, against his shoulder.

She coughed some more. "It was . . . I don't understand, but . . . I mean the timing was wrong, but . . ." She squirmed around and arched back to look at him face to face. Her beautiful alive face. "Jack? I was terrified. We got fire-prevention stuff in grade school, but that's different. And I couldn't think. I couldn't get out."

"You did well with the shower. You would've thought of the toilet tank next."

"Jack? I knew you were halfway to Townsend. I asked God to bring you to me, because I didn't know what to do. I begged Him, because I needed you. Because I was sure I would die. Jack. I don't even believe in God."

21

How Do I Love Thee? Let Me Count the Ways

— Elizabeth Barrett Browning, *Sonnets from the Portuguese*

How many different ways does a man love a woman — or a woman love a man — and how many of them do you have to have to qualify?

Jack, at Ev's right, sat back from the bank of microphones and watched her lean forward slightly to answer a reporter's question. Apparently she never did quite convince herself that she didn't have to stick her face right in the mikes in order to be heard. He ended up in press conferences every now and then, but he knew, because she'd told him, that this was her first. She didn't seem put off by the dozens of faces, few of them accepting of simple law enforcement folk, arrayed before them. Why did press people so consistently take an adversarial position, as if a press op were arranged so that the interviewees could lie?

Usually, the interviewees stand at a podium to get grilled. Some presidential press person probably set that up in the distant past, and the primal pattern stuck. Ev and Jack, and the Gatlinburg chief of police to Ev's left, though, sat at a table in a motel conference room to answer questions.

Ev had requested that the table be skirted. Jack and the chief suggested that the white plaster cast on her right leg would engender sympathy and they not hide it.

Love. Was that love last night when Jack deliberately

climbed into a burning room, or was it the overweening desire to be heroic? Or stupid? Was it love when he prayed to God for her safety, or was it faith in action? Was it love when he turned around on Little River Road and drove back to Gatlinburg, or was it professional expedience? Did he love her as in "I love you and want to marry you," or was it "I love you as a person, gender immaterial, because we work in close association and I admire you immensely"? Was there a difference? Would either lead to a lifetime of happiness together? Would both? Would neither?

A reporter from the *Charlotte Observer* was asking him a question, and Ev was looking at him.

"I'm sorry. Would you repeat that?"

She jacked her voice ten decibels. "Mr. Prester, do you personally have ties with any environmental groups?"

"I'd like to think of the National Park Service as a dedicated environmental group." He hastened to add, "However, I understand what you're asking. No. I'm not a member of any environmental group as such."

"Then," the woman pressed, "you have no personal ax to grind, is that right? You're neutral about this proposed development in the park."

No, he was not neutral. He hesitated a moment to get the wording right in his mind. "The proposed development you're talking about has nothing to do with law enforcement efforts to find the person or persons behind the Abcoff poisoning, or the drive-by shooting, or the firebomb last night, or any other incidents."

"But it might be a motive."

"Certainly it might, for the perpetrator. We're considering that. I doubt —"

"And don't you think you might go a little easy on someone who stopped Abcoff and her plans if you strongly oppose those plans? Or maybe search for the poisoner a little less vigorously?"

Ev leaned forward. "You enjoy your job, don't you? I can tell. It shows."

The reporter frowned. "Yes, I do."

"So do we. I do especially. There's a lot of routine digging, and a lot of paperwork, that would be boring if I didn't enjoy the hunt so much. I'm speaking for all of us here. I'm speaking for you. You focus on a goal and go after it, and nothing can distract you. We're focused on finding out what happened and who did it. Jack's opinion, or mine, or Chief Didicoff's here, can't shift the focus. Nothing will. We're going to find this person. I like the word you used. 'Vigorously.' We're going after him — him or her — vigorously, because we love our work, the way you do."

The *Observer* observer looked at Ev, at Jack. "Thank you."

Three more questions made it under the one-hour time limit wire, but they were repetitive of what had already been said. The chief pointed to his watch, insincerely thanked them all for coming, and closed it down. He obviously hated press conferences worse than Jack did.

Ev rolled her wheelchair back a foot and gestured toward her cast. "Incidentally, everyone, I'm accepting signatures."

What a brilliant move! Instantly, the mood in the room brightened from skeptical, if not downright hostile, to giggly and open. Ev wheeled out around the table to make her foot accessible. Cheerily, joking, the reporters gathered around to pen their names and an occasional verse. But Jack's, put there last night, was first.

The TV cameras and mini-cams folded their tents like Arabs and silently stole away.

It was going on eleven when Jack pushed her out into the lobby. "Lunch at Uncle Gene's?"

"He's not handicapped accessible. Remember those porch steps?"

"Not until you mentioned it."

"In the budget office we constantly dealt with accessibility studies and projects. You start noticing that kind of thing." Ev raised her voice. "She's with me, Chief."

Only then did Jack observe that Didicoff had been shooing Laurel Clum away as if she were a reporter. Laurel brushed past the chief to join Ev and Jack.

Bubbling like freshly poured soda, she grinned. "I was in the back watching. I'd never been to a press conference before. Great experience! I'm going to use one in my book. How are you feeling?"

Ev smiled. "Fine. It could be a lot worse, the doctor said. I hit the sidewalk when I jumped, but I rolled into grass. I broke one of the little bones in my foot. I forget whether it was tarsal or carpal. I can never remember which word is hands and which is feet."

"Remember the fish." Jack wiggled his hand where she could see it. "Carp don't walk."

Laurel looked at Jack. "You went out that window too."

"I'm fine, but only because Ev told me where to jump. Which can be interpreted in various ways." He poked Ev's shoulder. "I think I can get you past the porch."

Ev bobbed her hair. With a nurse's help she had washed it in the hospital. It didn't smell smoky anymore. "Early lunch, Laurel. Will you join us?"

"I can't. I have an appointment with the reference librarian to dig out some historical info."

Thank you, God! Jack didn't want Laurel tagging along. He didn't want her intrusion now.

"Maybe this afternoon." Ev smiled. "I have to go shopping. Everything in my room burned up."

"I'll love it! Here." She gave Ev a slip of paper. "My motel number. I'll check in frequently for messages. If you need a lift anywhere, or anything at all, call and it's yours."

Ev thanked her graciously, more graciously than Jack would have.

Jack told the kid on the motel desk where they'd be and rolled her out into the street. "Walk or ride?"

"Walk's fine with me."

Good. He rather enjoyed pushing her around in this wheelchair. He had often wondered why some people considered handicapped access such a big deal. Within five hundred feet, he knew. He maneuvered her down ramps and around obstructions he never would have noticed otherwise. At Uncle Gene's, he stopped.

"See?" She gestured at the front porch steps.

"I was thinking to drag your buggy in backwards." It worked, but not nearly as gracefully as he'd imagined. He managed to hold the door open with one foot until she was up the steps and on the porch landing and she could hold it. Getting her out again was going to be even more interesting. He rolled her to their usual booth.

Uncle Gene himself brought the menus over. His apron needed laundering. "Didn't think you'd be in. Feds and state have both been after me to build a wheelchair ramp. Haven't got to it yet."

"I noticed." Ev put some frost in her voice. She didn't bother with the menu. "Your liver and onions, please. Baked potato. Lite Italian."

Gene looked at Jack.

"How'd you know she was disabled?"

Gene smirked. "Your press interview was carried live on the local TV. You shoulda said you were coming over here afterwards. Give me a free plug."

228

"I thought you weren't drumming up new business until you get a cook." Jack almost said patty melt. Instead, "The pork chops with apples" came out. "Mashed potatoes. Bleu cheese."

Gene grunted. "Gotta stick around here and cook, whether hit's for four or four hundred." He wandered off.

Here came Tom Baumgardner in full sheriff uniform, sauntering over with another fistful of papers. He flopped down unbidden opposite Jack. "Photogenic is the word, right? *You*" — he jabbed a thumb toward Ev. "Not *you*" — he looked at Jack. "You looked asleep."

"Not far wrong. How come you're so chipper? You were up as late as I was." Jack wanted to sit quietly and talk to Ev. Not business, either.

The henna-haired waitress poured coffee. "You sure do look good on the TV, both of y'n." She scowled at Tom. "You eating here?"

"No. I don't break till two." He watched her leave, then pushed his wad of papers across the table. "Complete record of uncleareds." He pulled a three-and-a-half high diskette out of his shirt pocket and tossed it on top. "Also on disk."

Jack stared with dismay at the pile of paperwork. "The New York City phone directory is thinner."

Tom grinned sheepishly. "Few more than I thought. Evelyn, your room was cool enough this morning to go through it a little better. Your laptop's gone. Sorry. So's your purse." He held out his closed hand, palm down.

Puzzled, she held hers out palm up. He dropped into her open hand her warped car keys, Diane Walling's key ring, and a couple of dark, scorched coins that had partially fused. She sat there staring at them as tears filled her eyes. "Do you real-ize what a mess it is to replace your driver's license and bank card and credit cards and everything? And my car registration. And the material on my computer. The backup disks were in the room." She shuddered another of those combination sobs-and-sighs.

"They melted too. Sorry. It got pretty hot in there."

Jack watched her a moment. He glanced at Tom. "Baby-sit." He hopped up and jogged around the counter to the kitchen window. "Hey, Gene? Fix them to go, can you please? She's running on fumes. I'm taking her back to her room."

The cook nodded. "Be just a minute. Ruth," he bellowed, "get their salads."

With Tom riding shotgun, Jack had no trouble getting the wheelchair down the steps. The two of them simply picked her up, chair and all, and whisked her over obstacles. Uncharacteristically morose, Ev balanced the meals in her lap and rode in silence. On the way, Tom filled them in on the preliminary investigation of the burned-out room, but Ev probably wasn't listening.

How Jack missed Maxx! Turn Maxx loose at the scene, and let him sort out who had been there and where. Were the perp in the area watching — firebugs so often do — they'd have him now.

Tom entered her room first, so Jack waited outside with her.

She twisted to look at him. "What's going on?"

"He's checking for bombs and traps. We determined they lobbed the firebomb in from outside last night, but you never know. Did I mention I called Hal?"

"No, though I assumed you would."

Jack couldn't help looking all around, here and there and everywhere, like a secret service agent. "He's sending out a female bodyguard. She should be here an hour ago."

"That's ridiculous, Jack."

He held her eye. "No it's not."

An icy wind of fear blew across her face and faded away. She twisted back straight and stared at her open door.

Tom came out, nodded to Jack, and bade them a cheery adieu. Jack wheeled her in. She hopped a one-legged trip to the bathroom, wheeled herself across to the table, looked at her meal a moment, and decided a nap should come first. Jack helped her transfer from chair to bed and tucked her in.

He ate his lunch and spent an hour going through Tom's generous gift of dead trees and dried ink. The manager called to tell him a woman was on the way over. Ev stirred and drifted off again. He met the woman at the door before she could knock. He stepped outside and very nearly let the door swing closed before he remembered he needed a key to get back in.

Another stereotype smashed to smithereens. She didn't look like a bodyguard. She was coffee-with-cream black, maybe five-five, dressed not in severe matron-wear but a fashionable casual dress, nicely built — nothing beefy or un-feminine. Thelma Britt. She presented her ID and a letter from Hal. He invited her in and left.

Tom's bundle interested Jack. The reason there appeared to be so much was that Tom, bless him, had copied the original incident reports, all of them. Albuquerque saw more crime in a month than Gatlinburg experienced in three years, solved or otherwise.

Two items in the pack caught Jack's eye. One was a fire. Less than a year ago, someone firebombed a Planned Parenthood clinic here in town. Same kind of bomb as Ev's, same accelerant, same modus — lob a brick through a window, followed by the bomb.

The other, from about two years ago, was a purse-snatching. A woman waiting for her husband outside

Battles' Grocery laid her purse on the roof of her car while she unlocked it. A medium-sized runner in gloves and a black ski mask grabbed it. By the time the victim could yell, he or she had disappeared beyond parked cars. The black ski mask was one interesting point. Another was the value of the loss — the woman had just picked up a big prescription at the pharmacy. A third — the woman was Mrs. Homer Symes.

22

I Met a Lady
from the South Who Said

— Robert Frost, *New Hampshire*

Jack had just met a true Southern lady. She said, "Welcome," with a rich warm inflection that told him "You really *are* welcome." In moments, she had him settled in a comfortable, wicker chair on the veranda with a tumbler of lemonade in his hand.

A plump lady, she wore a simple, elegant cotton dress that minimized her width. She had pulled her salt-and-pepper hair back into a soft voluminous bun. The single strand of small pearls at her throat was strictly lagniappe. Put a hoop skirt on her and she'd fit right into *Gone with the Wind*.

The house was as close to Tara as a personnel officer is likely to get. Modest and probably forty years old, it nestled against second-growth woods. Beautiful landscaping set it off to full advantage. The veranda ran full length along the front and one side. Its chairs and small occasional table looked well kept and well used. They did a lot of living out here on the porch.

She sat down beside him in a wicker rocker at an angle conducive to conversation. "I'm delighted you called and asked to come by. Homer has said so much about you. You and Miss Brant."

Jack could not imagine this gentle lady using the honorific *Ms.* or even watching television. Hers was a more elegant world somehow. "This is a lovely home. It feels like an invit-

233

ing place to settle in and stay."

"Thank you."

He wanted to oil the gears and get her talking. Two-word responses weren't it. "Beautiful landscaping."

"Homer does love to putter about."

"Drive down in the park much? Look at the flowers?"

She sat with gentle complacency, her hands folded. "No. Almost never, except when we're crossing it to go to Carolina, of course. My family are all over in Flat Rock. Hendersonville. Have you ever been there?"

"Just last week. Lovely area."

"Yes, it is. I intend that Homer should retire and go back home, and I'm sure we will someday soon."

"From that I presume he's eligible."

"He has been for several years. But he still has things to do, he says."

"Yeah. That's what my father claims too." Jack thought a moment about what was said and what was not said and the overly casual tone of voice. She was too much the lady to identify a point of friction. Neither would she ever badmouth her man before a stranger. They probably really got into it, though, in private.

She smiled. "They have a wonderful summer season in Asheville. Opera. Homer loves opera. One of these years he'll get tired of driving clear over there every time he wants to attend an opera or concert. We even go up to New York now and then, when the Met is doing something special."

Opera. Jack changed subjects. "I was going through police reports and came across your purse snatching. There was no supplemental. I wondered if they got your purse back and if they ever found anything more about the person who grabbed it."

She lifted her graying eyebrows. "Oh, my. That seems so

long ago. Two years. A little more, perhaps. I was furious, of course, but it was over so quickly, it's almost as if it didn't happen at all. And the young man certainly didn't try to hurt me."

"Young man. How do you know that?"

"Well, a woman would never do such a thing. And he was so very quick. I saw him move, you know. Youthful agility."

"Logical." Jack nodded. "That wasn't in the report. It set the value of your loss at several hundred dollars."

"That's right. I had some cash in it, of course, and my opal ring. Just a small opal. And I had just come from the pharmacy."

"Getting a prescription filled."

"That's right."

Jack sipped at his lemonade. His body was getting tired. Apart from the stress and violence of running through a burning room and jumping out a second-story window, there was also staying up half the night investigating the scene with Tom Baumgardner and Chief Didicoff, not to mention hastening to the hospital afterward to be with Ev and bringing her back this morning. The only sleep he got was three hours in a recliner chair at her hospital bedside. He and Hal agreed she was not to spend a single moment unescorted until this case cleared.

"Mrs. Symes, you just added an interesting datum to the report. Can you add anything more? Tell me about the whole afternoon, if you can remember."

"Well, let's see." She rocked slowly, sedately. "I had a doctor's appointment in Sevierville, so Homer took the afternoon off. I don't like to drive distances, particularly when traffic is so congested. He took me in. And since we were going, Bill Weineke asked him to pick up a prescription for Christine also."

"You're saying the purse-snatcher got two prescriptions?"

"That's right."

"May I ask the nature of the appointment? Routine? An unusual problem?"

"Nerves. I have trouble with nerves now and then." Were this a prior generation, no doubt she would have said "the vapors." She continued primly, "The doctor prescribed diazepam. He's done that before, you know. I don't know what Christine's prescription was. I didn't ask. She called it in. So then we did some shopping. We usually get our groceries in Sevierville if we're in there anyway. Cheaper, you know."

"Diazepam. Valium."

"They're the same thing, just about. But the price is much different. Oh my, yes." She paused her rocking, her brow puckered. "Let's see." The rocking resumed. "Then we stopped at an auto-parts store, but I didn't go in. We stopped at CraftWorld, I think. As I recall, I needed some DMC tatting thread in shades of pink. Yes, that's it. I remember, because they didn't have any. Homer stayed in the car on that stop."

"You tat. That's making lace, isn't it?"

"That's right. Then we came back home, but as we were coming into town, Homer remembered something we forgot to get at the grocery, so we stopped at Battles'. He went in there, and I went next door to this little yarn shop to see if they had pink DMC. I didn't have much hope they would. They're not well-stocked except for yarn. They didn't either, so I used shaded crochet thread, size thirty. It worked almost as well, but of course it's not the same thing. It made a much coarser, larger doily."

"While he was still in the grocery, you returned from the shop and set your purse on the car roof to open the door."

"That's right. Oh, I remember one other thing. What Homer forgot in town was coconut milk. Apparently Bill Weineke wanted coconut milk for some sort of mixed drink, and Homer said he'd get it for him. It comes in a can." She sighed. "You know the rest."

"Mrs. Symes, I applaud your prodigious memory. You'd be a superb investigator."

"Thank you, Mr. Prester." She smiled, and he wondered whether it were a response to a compliment or a memory. "Poor, dear Homer. He's so quiet, usually. He came out of Battles', and here's all this fuss. The police talking to me and questioning everybody about what they saw. He was dumbfounded. Crime of that sort simply doesn't happen in Gatlinburg. And to have it happen to his wife — astonishing. That's how he said it — astonishing. For weeks afterward he called me his little celebrity."

"Did you show up in the newspaper?"

"Not by name, of course. Bodine didn't print my name, and I'm grateful. The police items are usually in B section around page five or six. I called the doctor's office, but they were closed, and I couldn't reach anyone until the next morning. They called in a new prescription — it was one-time-only, no refills — and Homer went in and got it for me. I was too nervous to go."

"I can imagine. You had the condition for which you made an appointment in the first place, and then the shock and excitement of the robbery on top of it. Double whammy."

"Triple. Homer was upset, of course, and that always makes me nervous because he so rarely gets upset. He was upset at the doctor as much as the thief. There's no way to reach the doctor unless he's in his office. All you get are those terrible recorded things telling you to call nine-eleven if it's an emergency. It was an emergency, of course, but not something nine-eleven would take care of. Terrible things, those recordings."

The lady was indeed of another era, and Jack couldn't agree with her more. He hated dialing in to one. On the other hand, he loved the convenience his answering machine provided.

He asked her about friends and neighbors who were victims of crime. There were none. He asked other details of her own moment in the spotlight, but she offered little additional. He finished his lemonade, praised the gracious tranquillity here, and drove away with Mrs. Symes, all smiles, standing on her veranda.

He cranked his window down. Nice day. Warm. He waited for the light and pulled out onto the main drag. He would stop by Ev's and see how she was doing, get acquainted with the bodyguard, maybe drop by . . .

Laurel Clum was coming up Parkway in the opposite direction in her convertible. Top down, of course. This was a top-down day if ever there was one.

Jack stuck his arm out the window and flapped a hand in greeting as she passed. He gawked. Lovey Hempett, of all people, was riding beside her. And there sat Wade in the backseat. Where and how would Laurel meet Lovey? Or Wade, for that matter?

Laurel yelled something unintelligible and beeped her horn as Lovey waved both arms in the air frantically. Jack dipped right and ducked into the south entry of a parking area in front of a row of shops. In a minute or two, the convertible came back and turned in at the north end of the lot. Jack drove north, Laurel drove south, and they met in the middle.

Wade popped his seatbelt and stood up on his knees on the seat. He yelled, "Wow," wide-eyed.

Lovey grinned outrageously.

Wade crowed, "Looka that!"

"Bought it with Monopoly money. Hi, Wade. Good afternoon, Laurel. Lovey."

Laurel smiled. She always smiled, but it was too intense this time to be casual. "We may have heard something about your dog."

Jack's chest tightened. "What did you hear?"

Wade lost his wondrous smile. "Promise you won't tell nobody?"

"I promise."

"If Jakey found out I told, he'd beat me to a bloody pulp. He's two years older and lots bigger."

"I won't let Jakey know anything."

Wade bobbed his head. His hair still needed washing. "He says in school today that his pa was running his dogs up on Cove Mountain above Wear Cove, over 'gainst Piney Spur. You know where that is?"

"I've seen it on a map." Right near the Wear Cove road. "What were the hounds after? Bear?"

"Yeah. That's another reason Jakey'll kill me if'n he finds out — that I'd tell a park feller they were out poaching. Anyways, they come on a big black dog that weren't from this area. He figured somebody dumped it, you know?"

"People do that sometimes."

"Yeah. Just toss your dog outta the car and keep going. Or the dog jumps out. He figured the dog must of jumped out because hit was hurt. His hounds were fixing to kill it, but he pulled them off it and took it home. Jakey says hit's a really good dog. They gonna keep it."

Jack looked at Lovey. "Can you draw a map to Jakey's place?"

Lovey dug into her jeans pocket. "Already did, in case we just had to leave it somewheres for you." She passed a wad-

239

ded-up paper to Laurel.

Laurel passed it to Jack. "I stopped by to see how Ev was doing, and if she needed anything. Lovey and Boy here were at her room trying to find you."

Lovey was grinning again. "You got yourself smeared all over the news, with that fire and all. Boy here come to me soon's school was out. Andy Abcoff is packing and moving, you know, so he hired Boy and me to help clean up behind. I do that when people move." Her smile hardened momentarily almost to guilt, then brightened again. "Soon's Boy told me hit might be your dog, we called the park, but they didn't know where you was, so we went to tell your lady friend."

Jack frowned. "Wait a minute, Lovey. How did you and Wade know to go to that motel? Did the people in the park tell you to?"

"No, but hit figures. She gets burnt outta one room, she gonna be in another. So we just went to the motel where the radio news said the fire was."

They should move Ev to another motel. Jack unfolded his map. With her usual clarity, Lovey had sketched the exact location. Jack extended the map out the window and pointed. "What's this road here?"

"Ain't no name. You just turn at the horse chestnut tree. You can't miss it. Hit's the only horse chestnut that's right along the road there."

Jack nodded. He smiled at Wade. "You know, sport, if I ever see you here in town, I'll say hello. But I haven't seen you lately."

Wade grinned and buckled himself back in. He took to riding in convertibles the way beauty queens take to smiling.

Jack said good-bye to everyone and was good-byed in return. Laurel drove away. Jack watched in his side-view mirror. Lovey turned to wave as they left the parking area.

He pulled into the first halfway decent hole in the traffic and drove north out of town, up to the Hatchertown Wear Cove turnoff. He knew there were shortcuts across these foothills on unpaved tracks, but he wasn't about to risk getting lost. He drove through Hatchertown, which is hardly a village, let alone a town, and spread the map across the airbag cover, following millimeter by millimeter. He turned at the dairy farm and again at the horse chestnut.

The road narrowed to a single lane through dark and lowering second growth. It hooked up over a small rise and snaked along a battered and rusting horse-wire fence enclosing a neglected, thistle-studded pasture. The lane led him out into an ancient farmyard and disappeared. Between the tiny house and the double-lean-to barn, a woman and a pair of children were working in a garden. Three older kids were practicing softball in the front yard. One of them, no doubt, was Jakey. A man in overalls rocked quietly on his porch.

The ball game stopped abruptly as Jack pulled in and parked. From the kennels beyond the house, a chorus of hounds announced a stranger's arrival.

As he climbed out of his truck he heard a most familiar barking among the baying. He walked directly to the fellow on the porch. "Good evening."

The man nodded to him.

"Understand you found a black Labrador retriever. I think he's mine."

"Could be. What's he like?"

"Intact male. Big, hundred and fifteen pounds. Broad anvil head. Licks."

"Could be your'n. Could be someone else'n's."

"The dog answers to Maxx."

"Nope. This'n says his name is Roff. Roff Roff."

"That's just because he's embarrassed by his real name, Hall's Maximian Luxembourg. I call him Maximum Licks and Burps."

Jack didn't hang around to trade any more witticisms. Following the sound of the barking, he walked around the side of the little three-room house to the bare, muddy backyard and the doghouses lined up beneath a row of pitch pines.

Maxx had a doghouse of his own, as did half a dozen hounds. He was tied on a six-foot rope to a stake by the doghouse door. A crockery water dish sat nearby. The hounds bayed lustily because that's one of the things they were probably getting paid for, but Maxx nearly jumped out of his skin bouncing up and down. His tail flailed wildly.

Jack dropped down to a squat and rubbed Maxx enthusiastically and let the mutt lick his face all he wanted to. Maxx. Lost and now found, dead and now alive, just as the prodigal's father said so eloquently. A fresh pink scar, not yet quite past the scab stage in spots, marked a deep gouge down his left shoulder.

Behind Jack, the farmer/poacher drawled, "That still don't mean he's your'n. He greets ever'body that way."

Jack unbuckled the bulky leather collar around Maxx's neck. "Maxx. Saddle up." He stood erect and watched the dog's movement.

Maxx was very stiff yet and probably a little sore. Without hesitating, the dog bounded off toward the truck. He stopped cold. This wasn't his truck. He sniffed around the door, put two and two together, and hopped up into the back.

Jack dug into his pocket for the bill he'd stashed. "There's a reward for his safe return. You hadn't gotten around to returning him yet, but you sure took good care of him — as good as the care you give your own dogs. He's obviously happy and well doctored and well fed. I deeply appreciate that. I'd be pleased if you'd accept this." He handed the bill to the fellow.

The man pocketed the money without glancing at it.

Jack ought to hang around a while. Talk. Be polite. Be neighborly. Learn details of Maxx's injury. Instead he shook hands, said good-bye, and left quickly. He held the cab door open. "Want to ride inside?"

Maxx jumped down over the tailgate and bolted up into the cab. Jack slid in beside him and, with a wave to the fellow, drove out the ragged little lane.

He stopped by the horse chestnut tree, where the lane met the road, because he couldn't hold it in any longer. He wrapped his arms around his goofy dog, felt that slimy, irrepressible tongue smear love all over his face, and wept.

23

This Is the Forest Primeval

The murmuring pines and the hemlocks . . .
— Henry Wadsworth Longfellow, *Evangeline*

This was the kind of forest you expected a dinosaur to come walking out of, dark, dank, and tangled. A mixed stand, pines (higher ground) and hemlocks (low, swampy ground) prevailed, with a variety of other trees scattered through and between. Little pink redbuds bloomed here and there, in counterpoint to an occasional chokecherry or dogwood.

It didn't look anything like the moonlit woods Jack rode a horse through a week ago. He had with him Lovey's map showing the way from her place to Townsend, but following it backward was something else — especially since Maxx's stupid tongue blurred a key junction when he licked at Jack's hand and missed. And then it opened out to meadows on both sides, the orchard on the right, and Lovey's familiar house and yard.

Lovey's truck wasn't around. *Phooey.* Jack was hoping she would be habitually here on Saturday, as she was last week. He called. No response. No Bugle either. The hound ought to recognize him now, but surely she would be out here announcing his arrival if she were around. He told Maxx to stay in the cab, rubbed the mutt's head through the open window, and strolled to the porch.

The front door stood open. So did the back. Maybe she

was just visiting a few minutes at a neighbor's.

Except she didn't have any, at least none close.

Jack sat in the comfortable old rocker a while. He stood leaning against a porch post a while, drinking in the peace. He sat down again. He was getting bored fast. Besides, he really ought to get back to town soon. He didn't want to be this far away from Ev for long.

He stood on the end of the porch and followed by eye. Out across the yard a tractor tire leaned at an angle against the chicken coop. Old, dried-out shakes roofed a shed attached to the north wall of the barn. A small galvanized culvert tunneled beneath the barn lane, connecting drainage ditches. Split-rail caterpillar fence zigzagged between the barn and the separate milking shed. Perfect!

He whistled and dropped his left hand to his side. "Maxx! Heel!"

Maxx jumped out the cab window, his tail flapping, and came galumphing over. He plopped to sitting at Jack's left knee, watching him, the tail tip flipping back and forth.

"Maxx, obstacle course! Let's go!" Jack took off at a run. Maxx leaped into flying motion at his side.

Jack pointed to the tractor tire. Maxx hesitated but a moment. He ducked down, squeezed through, and wiggled out between the tire and the coop. His bulk tipped the tire over flat. No matter. Jack was already on his way to the culvert.

Here came Lovey's pickup into the yard. She parked beside Jack's truck and waved. Wade tumbled out the passenger side. Bugle, the blue-tick hound, bayed wildly from the back.

Maxx woofed not at Bugle but at Jack. *Let's not dally.* Once you started an obstacle course, you finished it. One obstacle does not a course make, and Maxx knew it.

Jack pointed to the ditch. All caught up in the thrill of the chase, Maxx bellied out and stuffed himself into the culvert.

Jack heard him scratching and scuffing inside. The scuffing ceased.

Too late he realized that if Maxx got stuck, he was no-where near small enough to fit in there to rescue him. And it could happen, if Maxx's ripped shoulder gave out. Maybe Wade could . . . The scratching resumed. Maxx came squirm-ing out the other end, totally covered with slime, mud, rotten leaves, and an intense attar of aged manure.

Jack took off running toward the lean-to on the barn. He pointed to its roof. Maxx leaped up onto the two bulky posts wired together against the barn to receive the ends of the rail fence. From there he vaulted to the roof. Jack had to reach up and give him a little boost — he couldn't quite haul his heavy body all the way up. His ears back and his nose low, Maxx felt his way nervously along the sloping roof. The dry shakes rat-tled and clattered. Jack motioned him down off the far end.

After those loose shingles, the rail fence was a snap. Jack motioned him up onto the top rail, and the dog tightrope-walked the length of the fence to the milking shed. So his shoulder was not up to heavy jumping, but its muscles were healed enough to allow normal balance and coordination.

Yelling, "Come!" Jack ducked aside and ran out across the yard. Maxx caught up in six strides and ran freely beside him, his head high and ears flying. "Maxx! Sit!"

Maxx screeched to a halt and plopped to sitting. Jack ran a few strides farther and returned to the dog. "Heel." Panting, Maxx leaped up and fell in beside Jack's leg as he walked to-ward the porch. Jack waited until they reached the porch to release.

"Wow! That's amazing!" Lovey grinned wide enough to insert a beach ball.

Wade asked, "How'd you teach him all that?"

"He's been to dog school. Police training." Jack spent a

minute getting slobbered on, licked over, and bumped with a wet nose as he praised Maxx to the heavens and rubbed the dog behind the ears. Wade and Lovey got into the act and praised him too. Finally Jack dug a piece of bacon from breakfast out of his pocket and unwrapped it. The dog gobbled the bacon. Then, with a sudden feint and duck, he grabbed a bite of the waxed paper.

Bugle gave up announcing the intrusion of the truck and the big black dog. She curled around and chewed on the base of her tail a few moments, then sat watching.

Lovey looked at Jack looking at Bugle. "I'll let her down after while. Let her get used to the notion of company first. Come in and set a spell."

Jack told Maxx, "Saddle up," and watched the dog trot off across the yard toward their truck. He followed Lovey into the cool gloom. "I can't stay long. Got to get back to work."

Lovey bobbed her head. "What can I get you? I got milk and ice tea, but they's no ice. Cold tea. Mint. Hit's good."

"Some of that fresh milk would be great."

She looked at Wade. He grabbed a pitcher off the counter and ran out the back door.

"There was a reward for Maxx, you know." Jack unpopped a snap and fished two envelopes out of his shirt. "One for you and one for Wade."

She stared at them a moment without moving, so he laid them on the table.

She smiled. "You needn't do that. We're happy to."

"You were supposed to be working at Abcoff's, and that cheap bozo wasn't about to pay you if you weren't there. So you lost money trying to find me. Please accept it."

She sniggered. Hesitantly, as if a scorpion might crawl out the flap, she picked up the one with her name and peeked inside. Her eyes snapped up and locked his. "That's too much!"

"No, it's not. Maxx is a valuable dog." He watched her a moment. "It's easier to give than to receive. Jesus gave all the time. But He received too. He let other people serve him. Let me serve you."

She licked her lips, then smiled. "Now I'm gonna have to figure out what ten percent of this is. I tithe. We don't have to — I mean it isn't a rule or anything — but we all do."

"Just move the decimal over one."

She looked not only blank but ashamed. "You see? That right there's why going for a GED ain't worth it. The simplest math just boogers me up completely. My eighth-grade teacher was right. I'm too stupid for math. That and remembering dates."

Wade plunked a pitcher of milk on the table and brought two glasses and a coffee mug from the drain board.

Jack waited until he poured, then handed him his envelope. "The reward for finding Maxx."

"We would of done it without no reward."

"I know. And I'm grateful."

Wade held no compunctions about receiving. He looked inside and whistled.

Jack sipped milk and studied the worn oilcloth table cover a few moments. "You have a math workbook out there, I noticed. May I see it?"

"I'm not rightly proud of it."

"May I?"

She hesitated. "Sure." She disappeared into the other room and returned with her schoolbooks. She handed him the math workbook. "Hit's eight dollars, so you ain't supposed to write in it."

Jack leafed through the loose notebook papers that held

penciled problems and solutions. Simple problems. Basic math. Most were checked wrong. "Get out the Monopoly game, would you?"

She brightened. "Sure!" She hustled off and returned a moment later. She flopped the board open on the table.

Jack grabbed her wrist to stop her. "We just need the money." He flipped the box lid aside and pulled out the worn old bills. "Here. This problem right here. Do it with Monopoly money."

"I can't. I got it wrong. You see that."

Wade, wide-eyed, looked from face to face. His joy at suddenly being richer was fast dissolving into fear. "Shoot, Lovey," he offered. "I can do that one. Let me —"

"No! This is for Lovey to do." Jack grasped her wrist and gave it a little twist, setting her *kerplunk* on her chair. "Do it!"

She stared at him, frightened. "I can't."

"You can in Monopoly money. You've done it a million times. Do it!"

She shook her head. "I ain't no good at math."

"This isn't math. It's Monopoly." He roared, "Do it!"

She turned terror-clouded eyes to the pile of phony cash. Her hands shook as she counted out a simple problem in multiplication that a grade schooler could handle.

"That's right! Write it down."

"We ain't s'posed to write —"

"Write it down!" He handed her his pen.

"Specially in ink." But she did.

"Now this next one!"

"Don't yell at me, please," she wailed. "I can't —"

He stabbed with a finger at the problem. "You got three houses worth this much and a hotel this much. How much do you pay for them?"

Wade had shrunk back, staring, afraid to move.

And Lovey, strong, gentle Lovey, was sobbing. Her trembling hands counted it out.

"That's right. The next one."

She miscounted.

"No. Do it again!"

She got it right.

"Write it down." He watched her. She was still sobbing, so upset she couldn't write smoothly. He stabbed at another one. "Community Chest. You're playing with seven other people, and you have to pay each of them this much. How much?"

"That's over two hundred bucks!" She laid it out and counted it. Correctly.

"Count out the amount in that envelope. There are ten other people playing, and they each get their share of it. How much does each get?"

"Ten other people?" With barely a hesitation she came up with the right answer off the top of her head.

"Right. Each one got ten percent. Ten percent's a tithe. Count it out and prove to yourself you were right."

The fear-sobbing began to give way to laugh-sobbing. She kept saying, "I can't do it," as she did it. "I'm dumb." They worked another. Another.

He showed her how to keep the multiplication problems lined up in columns and add the columns. On the second page he forbade her to use Monopoly money. "Just picture the money in your head. Pretend you're using it." For twenty minutes he shoved problems at her as fast as she could do them. He translated the story problems into Monopoly situations.

Her eyes glassed over, and she started to stammer, to bobble. Time to quit.

He gripped her wrist again and rose in his chair, stretching, until they were nose to nose. "You are smart!" His voice rose. "Your teacher made a mistake, and you've been paying for it ever since. Your teacher was wrong!" He was shouting. "You are smart!" He took a deep breath, let go, and sat back. He dropped his voice to nearer normal. "Do you want to look the answers up yourself or take my word you got them all right?"

She snuffled. Tears still trickled down her cheeks.

He rubbed his face with both hands. "I suppose I ought to apologize, but I'm not going to. I got my doctorate working with kids. Kids whose teachers told them they were stupid, and they believed it. And they ended up killing somebody because they didn't think there was any hope, any use trying." He waved a hand toward the Monopoly board. "It's all based on math, and you mastered that math. All you have to do is realize you did."

She brushed her cheeks roughly and slurped her nose. "Ain't the same thing."

"It's exactly the same thing. Lovey, I want you to go back to work on your GED. Get Wade here to help you if you have to."

"I can do OK without it."

"You can do better with it. Back in seventh grade you started something you didn't finish. And then you started this adult ed and didn't finish yet. Whether you ever use it or not, you need that diploma to show yourself that you finished what you began. It's important psychologically. Take my word for it or not as you wish. It's true."

"I guess maybe —"

"Not maybe. Promise me."

"OK, I promise." She sniffed again and smiled. "I'll call you up when I get it."

"No. Write me a letter. Calling up's too easy, and then it's gone. I'd like a letter, something I can keep."

"OK."

Jack fished his wallet out and thumbed through it. He didn't have a ten, but here were two fives. He laid them on the table. "To pay for the workbook. It's the least I can do. Actually, you can get the stamp for the letter out of it too."

Wade giggled. "I'll help her. Uncle Herman and I ain't been getting on, and I'm staying here now anyway."

"Good man. The best help you can be is just to encourage her."

Wade nodded. He stared at the Monopoly board a few moments. "I'm sure glad you didn't try and hit her."

"I wouldn't have done that."

"Yeah, but it looked kinda chancy there for a while." Wade held him eye to eye, man to man, sober as only a child can be. "I really like you, but if you'd of gone and hit her, I would of got her shotgun and blowed your head off."

24

Little I Ask;
My Wants Are Few

— Oliver Wendell Holmes, "Contentment"

"Jack, I don't think I'm asking all that much out of life, do you? I mean, I really don't want much." Ev sat back in her motel armchair and stretched her cast-encrusted right leg out on the other armchair. "All I want is a decent job I like and a fair shake."

Jack sat sprawled in a third one. "I agree." He rather marveled at the big-heartedness of the motel management. Even after Ev burned out one room, they loaned her an extra armchair for this one. Motel managers are not, as a breed, a people noted for their generosity. Of course, Uncle Sugar was ultimately footing the bill.

But that would all end soon, for Hal had pulled the plug.

He stared at the plush carpet. The vacuum cleaner tracks still crisscrossed it. "Funny. I don't feel like a man without a job. He closed down the whole operation, huh? Boom. Gone."

"Gone. The task force is no more. I spent half an hour on the phone trying to talk sense into him. He says he can't afford to fight the grievance the way it's going. Apparently there are some complications raised. He says he called Mayrene McAllister into his office a couple times, trying to talk her into accepting some other position and dismissing the grievance. He says she's adamant. He says that if she forces herself into the operation she'll constantly be plaguing him with complaints and protests, and I can see that. The way we work there aren't many guidelines to follow. So he scrubbed the whole operation rather than get into that kind of tangle."

He sighed. "Thanks for trying." No more task force. No more job. They couldn't just dump Jack out of the Service completely, so they'd assign him to some other position. They'd assign Ev to something. Hal would either work out some other assignment for himself or retire. End of experiment.

Seven glorious months.

And now, zip.

Ev twisted around to stare out the window a while. "I can't believe this. Just one thing after another. Jack, how could Hal do that?"

"Easy. He was eligible to retire with full benefits five years ago. He can bow out anytime he wants to and draw seventy-five percent of what he's making now. Why should he put up with all the hassle for twenty-five percent, essentially?"

Her huge, chocolate eyes watched his. She had never looked more waiflike. "What are we going to do?"

It was probably a rhetorical question, but Jack wanted to give it an answer anyway. She was depending on him in a way, something Ev almost never did. He couldn't let her down. "When's the end of this pay period?"

"Midnight tonight."

"Mm. He wouldn't shut it down halfway through a pay period. I was hoping it was next Saturday. Give us a week to work a miracle." He studied the tops of his running shoes. He ought to get a new pair one of these days. Between the soakings and unseemly electrical activity and hard wear, these were falling apart. "How fat's your bank account?"

She watched him a long moment, digesting his question. "Stay on the case and absorb expenses ourselves?"

He nodded slowly.

"If we go it on our own and make an arrest, will it stick?"

"I'm commissioned. You're commissioned. A commission is a commission."

"Jack . . ." She looked like a puppy caught with chicken feathers in his mouth. "I guess this is pretty lousy timing, but I was thinking of going back to DC a while. At least until I can get around a little better."

"Your foot's really hurting you that badly."

"Yes." She melted into a little puddle of sadness. "No. That's not it. At least not completely it. I have sick leave coming for it. But mostly it's because of you. Thinking about marriage. I need some time out."

"For pete's sake, don't think about it if it bothers you."

"No, no, I already did. I mean, I've been thinking about it. I just didn't know that you were too." She smiled wanly. "Your timing's off, Jack. Two months ago I would have said yes instantly. Now I'm not sure."

"Because you got your commission, and a whole new world opened up."

"Exactly. But then I faced loss of my job. And now you're out in the cold without a job too. We both are. So if I just quit all this nonsense and get married, am I taking the easy way out?" She shook her head violently. "It's terrible!"

"Do you love me?"

"Yes. I think so." She licked her lips. "I'm not sure how much. Is that bad?"

"No. One of the nicest things about love is, it grows." Talk about romance. This was the perfect opportunity to get up and kiss her softly and roundly and extensively. He was halfway to his feet, on his way to do that, when the phone rang.

Romance took it on the chin.

He picked up the receiver and said, perhaps a little too roughly, "What?"

"Oh, good! It's you!" Lovey's voice. "Boy and I were talking this afternoon after you left. I wasn't going to say nothing, but he insisted I ought to. He's awfully smart for his age, you know. Don't do all that well in school, but he's smart."

"So are you."

She giggled. "I'm scairt to argue it with you. You'll start yelling at me again."

"If it'll keep you from giving up because of some teacher's stupid mistake, you bet I will. What does Wade think you ought to tell me?"

"Andy has a credenza with a bunch of *National Geographic*s and stuff in it. When Mrs. Abcoff dropped over, the cops came in and confiscated all the booze in the house, to test it."

"Right. That was routine. Pretty standard."

Maxx leaped instantly from a sound sleep in the bathroom doorway to a barking frenzy. The motel door clicked, and Jack realized his hand was on his gun, within an ace of drawing it — to blow away the bodyguard. Laurel Clum and Thelma Britt stepped inside and froze, wide-eyed. They carried a couple of plastic T-shirt bags, one of them big enough to hold Ev's MG. Jack forced a smile as Lovey babbled on, oblivious.

"Is that Maxx? Sounds like it. But they didn't get it all. All the booze. Andy has vodka and some stuff stashed in that credenza behind the magazines. Sort of surrounded by them. I happened to find it because we moved the credenza to vacuum, and the magazines shifted."

"Does he know you found it?" Jack watched the women shove Maxx's greeting away, cross to Ev, and settle their purchases down by the window with a rustle of plastic.

"I don't think so. We didn't say anything, and he was out in the garage when it happened."

"Thank you, Lovey. We'll look into it."

Thelma had plopped her purse down on the table. She handed Ev the Knoxville paper. Laurel took her jacket off and threw it on the bed.

"Lovey? One other thing. You sell different herbs in different forms, I assume. How do you prepare monkshood?"

"Depends. Hit blooms late summer. Fresh then. Rest of the year, dried."

"To whom have you sold monkshood lately?"

His question hung in silence a few moments before she answered. "Nobody. Ain't much call for it. Larkspur, plenty. Hit's a heart remedy, you know. But not monkshood."

The silence intruded. That wasn't like Lovey, to let silence ride.

Jack prodded, "Anything else?"

She murmured, "He asked me to come to Boston with him. I guess you might say he thinks I'm gonna. He says they ain't no reason why I oughtn't now. Jack, the way he was talking, I think he might of killed her. Or had a hand in it somehow."

"Do you think he might hurt you?"

"Boy thinks so. Remember this afternoon when he told you he'd protect me?"

"Blow my head off? Somehow that didn't come across to me as a schoolchild's idle threat." He gestured to Maxx to lie down.

"Hit weren't. He got my shotgun right there under the table. He wouldn't of had to go find it. He's afraid Andy might come."

"Lovey, if you're afraid of Abcoff — if you have these reservations — why did you agree to come in and clean for him during the move?"

"We didn't realize, Boy and me. Didn't have the reservations. Hit was money. But then today Andy was real dark. Sort of threatening without actually saying it, you know? So when he went out to get some deli stuff for lunch, Boy said, 'We're leaving,' and I said, 'We can't,' and he said, 'We're going.' And I let him talk me into just dropping and leaving, right there. Don't get paid, but Boy says it ain't worth it. He saw the look in Andy's eye before, and he didn't like it."

"Stay away from him, OK? Abcoff, I mean. We'll take it from here."

"Jack? Something else. We run up to Sevierville so's Boy could visit Uncle Harold a couple minutes. He's still in the hospital with his pelvis, you know. Boy only had to lie about his age a little bit to get in. And we told Uncle Harold 'bout not getting paid. So he said, 'Pray and God will take care of you,' and he laid his hands on us and we prayed."

"Good." And then Jack realized what she was saying.

"We drove home and bingo, there you was waiting, handing us that money."

"Where are you now?"

"Phone booth by the mini-mart at the Wear Cove crossroads."

Jack thought a moment. "Andy doesn't know where your Uncle Harold's place is, does he? Why don't you go there a while? The garden probably needs weeding anyway."

"I gotta go home and milk."

"Milk and do the chores at your place tomorrow. Spend the nights hidden, until Andy's out of town."

"Think so? Guess you're right, but the cow sure ain't gonna be happy. OK. I gotta go over to my place tomorrow."

He good-byed her, and she called God's blessing upon

him. That, on top of the way he ended up inadvertently answering her prayer, gave him a very funny feeling, at once both happy and frightened. As he hung up, he found himself staring at Ev. He would have to tell her how Lovey prayed for God's providence just as he was bringing her the reward money. And then he wondered how he could possibly explain that to Ev, an outsider in the faith, without sounding like a bug.

Ev frowned. "Why are you staring?"

"I'm asleep, but I forgot to tell my eyelids. Chores. What about Diane Walling's cat? Aren't we supposed to be taking care of it?"

Ev nodded. "Diane is doing well, and they'll probably release her tomorrow. Laurel and I took care of the cat this morning. She can probably last until Diane gets home."

A weird, piercing, whiny, hooting sound filled the room, like the mating call of one of those decorative howling coyotes whose neckerchief was too tight.

Ev whipped out her pen-shaped pager and studied the barrel a moment as Thelma matter-of-factly handed her the telephone. Ev punched an outside line and dialed the number on her pager. Amazing gizmo to a country boy whose party-line telephone number as he was growing up was two longs and a short.

Ev extended an arm and wiggled her fingers. Jack frowned. What? With no hesitation at all, Laurel set a note pad and pencil down where she could reach it. As Ev said things like, "Yes," and, "Got it," Jack pondered how women know what each other is saying without using any form of communication known to man.

Ev said, "Wait." She pressed the receiver against her shoulder. "Jack, this is the forensics report from Carl Sandburg. Do you want it faxed to the park?"

"Anything in it that park personnel shouldn't see?"

She shook her head. "Mostly negatives."

"Go ahead."

Ev gave them the fax number, thanked them, and cradled it. Thelma set the phone back on the bedside table.

Jack got around to amenities. "Good evening, ladies. Enjoy dinner?"

Thelma flopped into the third chair. "Yes, we did. Great restaurants here. And my simple native guide here" — she waved a hand toward Laurel — "led me through some hardcore shopping. Interesting town. Never saw one so hot on selling you stuff that's totally charming and totally useless."

Ev smiled. She looked at Jack as she told Thelma, "I don't know. Picnic baskets aren't so useless."

Laurel glowed. "We brought you a present, Ev. Get-well gift." She scooped up the sports-car-sized bag and set it by Ev's elbow.

Jack guessed what it was.

Ev peeked in the bag and hoisted a picnic hamper onto her lap.

Thelma looked at Jack questioningly.

He smiled and nodded. Just like the one that burned. Maybe he could communicate unconventionally after all. He shoved Maxx away with another admonition to go lie down.

Ev was smiling brightly. "Laurel, Thelma, this is so thoughtful! It's perfect. This is exactly it. Thank you so much!" The corners of her mouth stayed turned up, trying to fake a smile, but her eyebrows and eyes melted into sorrow. She gave up trying to keep a happy face, folded her arms across the hamper, and leaned her head on them to weep.

Thelma waved a hand. "You're the psychologist."

"Yeah, but I only function in a clinical setting. Pack her stuff, will you?"

Thelma nodded and set to work. Laurel hauled the luggage down off the shelf above the clothes pole.

Jack pulled the third chair tight against Ev's and facing the opposite way, sat down and gathered her in his arms. She leaned against him and buried her head in his shoulder. He held her and let her weep because there was nothing else to do. Laurel set the tissue box on the table within reach and put the hamper aside on the floor.

Eventually Ev muttered, "I'm sorry. I don't know what's the matter with me."

Jack didn't let go. Not yet. "For starters, there's the stress of wondering whether a firebomb's going to come through your window any moment. Go home. Rest. Monday morning, go to Hal's office for me and tell him personally that I said he's a world-class jerk. In fact, use stronger language. Get his autograph on your cast if you want. Then take a vacation somewhere besides Smoky Mountains National Park. Gettysburg is nice. Have coffee with Hillary. Tour the White House. Something."

She shuddered a sigh and raised her head. She smiled slightly and rubbed Maxx's head. It lay softly on her knee, those droopy doggy eyes turned upward toward her.

Jack let her go. "The notes you jotted there are only half legible. Anything I should know?"

She shook her head, blew her nose extensively, and read them off to him. "They found no recent readable prints. They also checked all the screwdrivers they could find on site, incidentally. Nothing suspicious. The hair and fibers came up negative. Nothing they found on site matched anything I provided, and I got hair from just about everybody. They do have one human hair sample with no match."

"In other words, someone was there, but they can't tell who."

She nodded. "Ms. Dennison said it could just be a visitor."

"You did a great job with that, Ev. You even got me."

"So they could match it against whatever they found, sure. And they took the samples from everyone there — McFarland and them — including the garden club people. The only good match was two goats. Apparently you can tell the difference between Toggenburgs and Nubians."

"Toggenburg. So that's what that squiggle is in your notes." Jack sat back to think.

Ev sagged, deflated and weighted down by life. She muttered an apology for running out on him when he needed her.

He picked up the phone, checked his notebook for the number, and called Tom Baumgardner. Jack could wind a tortuous path through the channels of justice in this county, seeking a search warrant for Andy Abcoff's place, or he could get Tom to do it. Tom knew his way around all the obstructions bureaucracies love to erect in front of people who don't speak with the right kind of accent.

He watched Thelma close the zipper on Ev's softside as Laurel flopped another bag open on the bed.

Ev shifted her leg. "I'm going back with Thelma, right? What about my car?"

"Do you want me to sell it for you at an obscene profit, or do you plan to keep it?"

She looked at him as if he had suggested she auction off her firstborn.

He shrugged amiably. "I'll exercise it now and then to keep the tires from rotting, and store it in the maintenance area when I leave. You can come back for it when you feel like it."

"Uh . . . that's not what I meant by 'what about it?' There's a problem."

"With British sports cars? Always."

"You know how the key was kind of warped from the fire? It accidentally broke off in the ignition this morning. It's the only key I had, and it's broken flush with the surface." She drew a huge gulp of air in through her nose.

"I'll take care of it."

She was going to protest. He could tell. And then she said simply, "Thank you."

"Let me have Diane Walling's keys too. Are they warped?"

She shook her flyaway hair and dug the key ring out of her deep skirt pocket. The key-chain charm, something plastic, had melted off. "Here. You might as well use this." She handed him her beeper also.

Thelma scooped up the hamper and took a load out to her car. Jack took out another load while Laurel helped Ev hip-hop to her wheelchair. Ev wheeled out into the golden evening light. Then she hip-hopped into the passenger seat of Thelma's blue Toyota, leaving the chair behind forever.

Jack promised to take care of that also.

He thoroughly kissed her good-bye and closed her door. She rolled down the window immediately so she could wave to him as Thelma tooled the Toyota out into the street. They were gone.

He watched the emptiness a few moments, a little numb.

Laurel released a huffy-puffy sigh. "Good. She really needs the rest. Is there anything I can do for you?"

Jack wagged his head.

"I guess I'll head back to my room then." They farewelled, and Laurel swept away across the parking lot to her convertible.

Where had Maxx wandered off to? Jack whistled and called his name. From inside the room, the dog barked.

Before leaving here, he would clear out the case-related

papers left behind in her room and double-check to make sure her amateur bag-packers had gotten everything. He turned back to the door.

It was locked.

The key lay inside on the table.

Inside, the phone rang.

And if he weren't already glum as an undertaker at a Healthy Living Convention, he just then suddenly, inanely, for no reason whatever, remembered: Tomorrow was his thirty-fifth birthday.

25

Happy Birthday to You

— Mildred J. Hill, celebratory ditty

Happy birthday to you. Happy birthday to you. Happy birthday, dear Jaa-ack. Happy birthday to you.

How he was going to dread hearing that miserable song! He thought about his thirtieth birthday and the wildly hilarious Over the Hill party Marcia had thrown for him. Ernie Morales flew in from Capitol Reef, and Frank Harrold happened to be stateside, so he came — both lifelong friends.

Marcia had carefully run her plans past him for his approval. They would get together with a few close park friends (Ernie and Frank were not mentioned; he had no idea they were descending upon him), see a movie — always a treat when you live that far out of town — and have dinner out. Also a treat. What she failed to mention was that those were not the plans. The surprise party struck the day before his birthday, and she really nailed him good.

The best woman in the whole world — he had traveled all the way to Australia to find her — and a small son who was nigh onto perfect.

But that was his thirtieth. Marcia was gone. The son was gone. Now even Ev was gone. And tomorrow, Sunday, May the two-dozenth, Jack would celebrate his thirty-fifth alone.

Tonight though, coming up on 8:30, he was neither celebrating nor alone. He stood beside Tom Baumgardner on Andy Abcoff's front porch amid empty cartons.

Tom rang the doorbell again and yelled, "Police. Open

up, please." He muttered, "This is dumb, Prester. If the vodka the kids think they saw is *the* vodka, he would've thrown it out the next day. Better, that night as they were hauling her out the door."

Maxx, the mutt, agreed with Tom by yawning elaborately.

"On the other hand, do you hide your vodka among magazines?"

"Actually, no. Towels. We got two kids and a no-locking liquor cabinet. So my wife hides it behind a stack of dish towels. Guaranteed, the kids won't find it there."

Tom tried the third time, as Gatlinburg's finest milled around in the yard. One of the cops by the porch conspicuously cleared his throat as, down on the street, Andy Abcoff's Chrysler LeBaron pulled to the curb. The bereaved got out and strode manfully through the array of badges to the porch. With a generous employment of expletives, he inquired regarding their presence.

Tom had obtained the warrant. Jack stood back and let him present it. Abcoff glared disdainfully at Tom, regarded Jack with the contempt gardeners normally display toward slugs, and unlocked his door. Half a dozen people followed him inside. Jack looked at Abcoff's shoes and went the other way.

"May I?" He borrowed a backup officer's flashlight, a big, steel five-cell designed to bring in airplanes. "Maxx, heel." He walked out to the LeBaron at the curb and inspected its tires by flashlight. With Maxx at his knee he went inside, then, in time to listen to Abcoff loudly berate the mental prowess of Tom, of Jack, of anyone remotely associated with law enforcement.

In the fully lighted room, Jack shined the flashlight on Abcoff's shoes. "You've been out in the mud. So's your car."

Abcoff's glare did not abate.

266

Jack turned off the light. "You know, I think I even recognize the mud. I washed it off my dog recently. Black mud, really wet stuff, with moss on it. Sticky. You've been out to Lovey Hempett's. Was she home?"

Abcoff's glare deteriorated to a perplexed *Huh?* To give him credit, he tried to build up another head of rage, but the fire wasn't there anymore. How much did Jack know, and how badly would it burn Abcoff? That had become the question. He snarled, "You're wrong. Do you know what she did to me?"

"Yes. She and her cousin worked most of Friday and all this morning for you, and you haven't paid them yet. I'll be happy to accompany you into the den, or wherever you write your checks, while you take care of that little oversight."

"They stole from me! I have things missing! I want them arrested for theft."

One of the city folk, a pleasant young woman with wavy brown hair, sneered. "Nobody's turned in any police report. No thefts today. Don't you trust us?" Jack had no idea a sweet young woman like that could perfect such an eloquent sneer.

In the midst of Abcoff's frantic diatribe about police inefficiency, Tom suggested to the woman, "Blood alcohol?"

"Thinking that very thing. We placed him behind the wheel not five minutes ago." She glanced at Jack. "You really opine he's been out to Hempett's?"

Tom bellowed, "Harrison? Hey, Harrison!"

A wiry, whiskery little fellow in uniform appeared at the dining room doorway.

"You know the old Hempett place, don't you?"

"Ought to. We go out there looking for a still 'bout every six months or so."

"Go make sure if Lovey's all right."

The wiry little fellow nodded and left.

"Wait a minute!" Abcoff squeaked, he was so excited. "I'll save you a trip. She's not there. I remember her mentioning this morning that they had to run out to some relative's today. That's probably why they left early, now that I think about it."

"So what did they steal?" the sarcastic young woman asked.

"Money. I had some money lying around."

Jack pressed, "Then why did you go out there?"

"I didn't."

Jack waved a finger, reminding him that his muddy shoes betrayed him.

Abcoff's eyes darted from face to face. "That's not from there. I took a walk in the woods. In the park."

The young woman walked away.

Another of Chief Didicoff's people, an officer in coveralls and a ball cap, came out with a bagged bottle of vodka. He gestured toward Jack with it and nodded slightly. Jack glanced at Abcoff. The man's face, pink under the mildest of circumstances, was tight and red.

Here came the young woman with the beautiful sneer. Behind her trailed a jovial-looking gray-haired fellow in civilian clothes and a wondrous handlebar mustache. He carried a large leather bag such as doctors used to take on house calls. Funny. He sure didn't look like a doctor. "Mr. Abcoff, I don't know that you ever met Jemmy here."

Jemmy extended a massive paw. "Pleezda meecha, Andy. Heerd a awful lot aboutcha." Didn't sound like one, either.

Andy recoiled.

The woman pointed. "Mud on his shoes and the wheels out front. We want to match it chemically against samples. Mr. Abcoff, it's amazing how closely they can pinpoint a location just from the composition of mud and soil. Sometimes within a hundred feet."

Abcoff stared as Jemmy yanked his black bag open and went to work. So Jemmy was the forensics tech.

Jack dropped to a squat just to watch Jemmy work. The guy was good. "When you get samples from Lovey's, make sure you take from the lane leading to the barn, by that culvert, and the puddle by a beat-down woven-wire fence on the driveway coming in."

Abcoff shifted his stare to Jack. "I want my lawyer!"

"Sure. Go call him, soon as Jemmy's done here."

Abcoff did. Hustling over to a desk in the next room, he dialed three different numbers. He showered the telephone with the same vile epithets he had previously laid on the police. How did he ever expect some nice lawyer to come out late on a Saturday night when he used that kind of language? Then he dialed a fourth, preceded by an area code.

Jack glanced at Tom.

Sure enough, Abcoff presently swiveled his chair around to them with a smug grin. "My lawyer will be here. From Boston, tomorrow afternoon."

Tom nodded amiably. "Good. So we have time to finish tossing the place without listening to flak."

"You have to wait!"

"Not to complete the action specified in the search warrant. I'm sure when we're done here, we'll have lots more questions to ask. Especially about where you've been."

Abcoff was staring not at his nemeses now but at that telltale mud on his shoes. It must be really difficult, Jack mused, to have to think — because your life or at least a jail term depends upon it — when that alcohol haze is messing you up.

Jemmy came in with his breathalyzer equipment, and Abcoff panicked anew. Jemmy looked like a rube, acted like a rube, sounded like a rube. He probably had his training instructors tearing their hair out. But, oh my, was he skilled. He got a good reading the first time, something Jack could almost never do, and he got corroborative readings, *bang bang bang*.

Abcoff certainly must have realized that, forensically, Jemmy was nailing him down with railroad spikes. But then, maybe not. Abcoff had that bias against people with Southern accents.

Jemmy ambled away with a good-ole-boy swagger, off to other pursuits.

Tom smirked. "If you plan to wear those shoes in court, you might want to wash them off first."

Little geared wheels whirred almost audibly in Abcoff's head. "I did stop by there briefly. She wasn't home, so I didn't get out of the car." He stopped and backed up. "Except to knock on the door, of course. Make sure."

Jack set his voice low and deep, keeping it on the periphery of Abcoff's hearing, giving it the authority that low pitch provides. "You went out there to punish her for running."

"Running? To get the money she stole from me."

"No, punish her for running. Possibly bring her back. She promised to go with you, and then she ran."

Abcoff was sort of making a cottage industry out of staring at Jack.

Jack capped it. "She's been spilling her heart out, Abcoff. We know everything."

"She lied to you!" Abcoff called her names he normally reserved for law enforcement personnel and lawyers.

"She has no reason to lie."

"She's in thick with Bodine. She knows her story won't stand up. She's afraid! She probably heard me coming and ran. Hopped in her beater truck and drove away."

"The lane ends at her place. She couldn't drive away without passing you coming in."

Abcoff, the Massachusetts city boy, had a little trouble with that. His face tensed, and worry lines crowded in beside his crows-feet. Suddenly he brightened. The wheels must have cranked out a goody, for he regained that supercilious air of someone who is smarter than everyone else. "Then she must have driven off before I got there. But she left her wood stove cooking away. She doesn't shut her doors. I could see through the door that it was hot."

Jack's spine chilled. "No, it wasn't." He balanced a hand on Abcoff's desk and leaned forward nose to nose with the hulking liar. "Her stove was cold early in the afternoon when I stopped by there on business. She called me not long after I got back to town, and she didn't return to her place after making the call. Her firebox is only big enough to burn unattended for an hour at most before going out." Jack stood erect.

Tom's voice behind Jack practically croaked. "He torched her! Why else would he mention the wood stove? You jacka-napes, you got mad at her and torched her!"

"That's not true!" Abcoff was rapidly developing a hunted look.

Tom frowned at Maxx. "He trained to sniff out accelerants?"

"He's trained to sniff." Jack would refrain just now from mentioning what a bum sniffer Maxx was.

"What would be an accelerant at Lovey's? Coal oil? I mean kerosene?"

"On the kitchen table."

Tom glared at Abcoff. "I hope for your sake that I'm wrong."

"My lawyer's going to tear this apart!" But Abcoff was talking to empty air. Tom disappeared into the other room. "None of this is admissible!"

"We haven't questioned you yet, Abcoff." It was all Jack could do to refrain from punching the guy as Abcoff had hauled off on Bodine that day. "Never asked a single question."

Yelling through the house, Abcoff asked what Tom was doing, got no answer, and launched into another essay on the witch hunt he perceived to be developing here. Just because Bodine didn't happen to like him . . .

Two or three minutes later, Tom marched by and out onto the porch with a rosy-cheeked, roly-poly young patrol officer behind him. Presently he came back into the living room. "OK, there was a coal-oil lamp in Abcoff's bedroom. I put a drop of it on a Q-tip and touched it to some places. Larry here has been documenting my actions. Ask the dog to find all the places where there's coal oil."

Elegant in its simplicity. Jack dipped his head toward Larry. "You're documenting this, huh?" Larry followed him into the bedroom.

Jack had never tried an experiment quite like this before. He got another Q-tip out of the back bathroom, stroked it across the shoulder of the lamp on the dresser, and held it down by the dog's nose. "Maxx, find."

Maxx headed straight to the kerosene lamp and flopped his bottom on the carpet. His tail flung itself about enthusiastically.

Jack walked to the lamp and laid his hand by it. "Good dog, Maxx. Find more."

Maxx sniffed along the painted baseboard and trotted off to the toilet seat in the back bathroom.

Larry grinned. "That's one."

"Good dog, Maxx! Maxx, find."

Maxx alerted to the underside of a bedroom stool.

"Two."

To a porch post out front. Three. To a bush. Four. To the LeBaron. To Tom's right hand.

To Abcoff's hands.

Tom got on the radio and rolled a Sevier County fire truck and an aid van, now that it was much too late.

The fury was back. Burning, delicious fury. Jack welcomed it. He pointed to Abcoff. "Sit at the table there."

"You can't browbeat me."

"Your brow is the least of it. You can sit, or you can be seated. Figure out which is going to hurt your poor little machismo least."

Abcoff sat.

Jack plunked a chair down and sat in front of him, literally in his face. "Why did you think you needed a gun for protection when I lifted that cannon off you?"

That wasn't a question Abcoff would be expecting. It caught him off guard. "My lawyer."

"Protection from your lawyer?"

"You know what I —"

"Since he's not here, your answer probably isn't going to be admissible. You don't have to worry about incriminating yourself." Jack sat back.

"Nothing incriminating about it. I've been getting threats."

"You've been getting them, or your wife?"

"I don't know about her. I've been."

"Threats of bodily harm or simply advice that you leave?" Jack heard radios crackling.

"Harm. Say, doesn't a red-blooded boy like you have something better to do on a Saturday night?"

"My date went home. I've got all night."

Tom's bulk moved in behind Jack as the wavy-haired young woman leaned beside him and murmured in his ear.

273

"I've got the fire marshal on his way out there."

"Fire m—"

"Burned to the ground. They lost the summer kitchen, but they got there in time to save the barn. They're hosing it down."

The pure fury Jack had experienced at Sandburg was nothing compared to the unbanked, roaring wrath that boiled up within him now. He would have pasted Abcoff right into the next zip code if Tom hadn't put a choke hold on him.

Deftly, the young woman cuffed Abcoff and got him out of there.

The choke hold eased and fell away. Tom, bless him, laid a hand on Jack's shoulder and just left it there.

Lovey. Jack sat a while with his elbows on his knees and his face buried in his hands. A shudder and a sigh and he stood up, ready again to face the world.

Out in the other room, another explosion of hostility erupted. Hostility seemed to follow Abcoff around as a puppy follows the latest person to slip it a bit of sausage.

Bodine Grubb, persona non grata especially in this particular living room, stood mildly at ease. He looked beyond the ranting Abcoff at Jack and Tom. "Police scanner sounded interesting, so I came on over."

Tom grunted. "Guess you'd expect that of a news reporter."

Bodine watched Abcoff walk out the door with his hands tied, literally. "A lovely sight."

Jack stopped beside him and slapped his leg. Maxx settled by his knee. "You didn't have much to say to him."

"I do my speaking in print. Any statements for the press?"

Tom didn't seem much less hostile than Abcoff. "Read it off the police blotter."

"A lot here won't show on the blotter. Like the little trick with the dog."

Tom snorted. "You've been skulking again, Bodine. I know better than to ask you to keep quiet about it until the trial."

"A good reporter is a good skulker."

"Also a good source." Tom scratched his head with both hands. Jack doubted this was his idea of an idyllic Saturday night either. "You heard everything, I suppose. Anything you can add for us?"

"Not that I know of." Bodine looked right at Jack. "Lovey wouldn't be staying with Herman. Harold's in the hospital, but somebody has to milk his cow. I'd guess that's where she is, right? Harold's place. Want me to tell her about her house? I'm going over that way — see what the fire marshal has to say."

"I'll tell her. I'm going to her church tomorrow morning." And then Jack happened to look at Bodine's feet.

His shoes had mud on them.

26

The Royal Feast Was Done

— Edward Rowland Hill, *The Jester's Prayer*

A banquet worthy of kings it was. Jack finished his pecan pie and wiped his mouth. "One thing about this town, you can eat well just about any time of day or night." He sat in a window booth of an unprepossessing cafeteria — not one of the chains.

Tom smiled. "You had some catching up to do too, it looks like. Yeah, this cafeteria is open most of the time, and they're pretty good. I usually eat here. You going back to Townsend?"

Jack nodded. "Look in on Diane Walling's cat for Ev first. Walling will probably be home tomorrow, but they could hold her another day for some reason, and I won't be back here for a while."

"I hate cats." Tom finished his mug of coffee.

"No fan of them myself. This one — not a single corpuscle of gratitude in its blood. You clean its box and fill its water bowl and food dish, and it lies on its cushion and looks at you like you're dirt. Sort of the way Abcoff regards us."

"Mm. That's bad." Tom gazed idly at his coffee mug, perhaps hoping it would spontaneously refill. "When I was growing up here, we'd be tooling along a country road at ten o'clock at night, and there'd a cat be, crossing the road."

"Cats and deer. And robins. They seem to think they have to wait until a car is coming before they can cross."

"Ain't it the truth. So we'd play 'Get the Cat.' Do our level best to hit it. Put more cars in the ditch that way. Don't think we ever did get a cat. Oh, hey. Toxicologist sent us a supplemental on Colleen. Acute depression of the cardiovascular and nervous systems due to aconitum poisoning. Delivered in a White Russian made from Absolut."

"The hidden vodka that you lifted tonight — what brand? I didn't see."

"Absolut."

"Expensive stuff. And the same as the firebug who OD'd."

Tom's eyes went wide. They narrowed to half-mast, their usual sleepy-looking position. "Lot of people drink Absolut. But interesting."

"Interesting, all right. All these jes' plain down-home kinda folks with a reputation for moonshine, drinking some pretty ritzy spirits. Get anything from Abcoff on why it was stashed in the credenza and not surrendered to the cops two weeks ago?"

Tom wrinkled his nose. "Nah. His lawyer wasn't there. So no speak English. Connie came up with another hidden bottle in the fireplace flue, tucked up on top of the chimney damper. Want my opinion? I think they were both closet alcoholics and hiding it from each other. I bet Andy didn't know about the stash in the chimney. The one in the credenza might've been hers too." Tom dipped his head, a "look there" gesture.

Jack turned as Bodine Grubb threaded between empty tables, heading this way.

To make room, Tom scooted over 1.5 millimeters. "You came to apologize for getting angry when we took samples of the mud on your shoes."

With a thunk, Bodine slid in beside him. "Nope. Still say there weren't no call for that. Told y'all where I was. Out behind the house in the flower bed. Even showed you where.

277

Are you for sure gonna ask for an indictment on that arson charge?"

"Yep." Tom studied the man's profile. "You don't look real pleased. Here I thought that news'd warm the cockles of your heart."

"Oh, hit's warmed. Hit's warmed. I have to have three days' lead time though, since we only come out once weekly and hit gets printed in Knoxville. So if I say as of Monday he's gonna be arraigned, that's accurate?"

"Talk to the prosecutor before you put it to bed."

Bodine bobbed his head. "Also I'd like a copy of the run report for the fire out at Hempetts'."

"What's the matter? Fire chief won't give it to you?"

"Not when the investigation's ongoing. But by the time they finish up hit'll be too late to get it in this week's paper."

Like a brace of cats whose tails are being trod upon simultaneously, Ev's pager cut loose. Jack jumped. It's startling when you think your wallet's screaming, because you've forgotten about the pager. In this cavernous, virtually empty room, the thing piled up decibels like building blocks. He managed to shut it off. It displayed the number of her home phone in DC.

He excused himself and jogged out to a bank of pay phones by the front door. He spent the next three or four hours, it seemed, endlessly punching numbers — her number, area code first, and then his credit card number with its numerous digits. And to think they expanded ZIP codes to nine digits too.

She answered on the first ring. "Wow. Less than three minutes from when I called the pager. That thing's great!"

"And it seemed like forever too. Got home all right, I trust."

"Smooth trip. I just wanted to let you know I'm back, and

I'm really sorry I abandoned you."

"You didn't. It's all right." *You abandoned me. On my birthday too.*

"Since Thelma was driving, I spent the time trying to reconstruct those charts with the alibis. Jack, I can't place Bodine during Diane's drive-by or that Friday when you lost Maxx."

"He's with us now. I'll poke around a little."

"Who's 'us'?"

If Jack didn't know better, he'd say she sounded jealous. The door was open for him to make a little sport here. But he was too tired for cheap shots. "Tom and I."

"Say hello to Laurel for me."

"I shall. Oh, hey. I asked the kid at the garage and called Hiram. They don't want to mess with the MG, but Hiram gave me the name of a company in California that will mail you parts for British cars if you send them your Visa number and the keys to your yacht. I ordered a new lock set — ignition, door, and trunk. Incidentally, your trunk wasn't locked, so I took out anything that kids might swipe. Ev, the cheese compartment in my refrigerator door is bigger than your trunk. Opens easier too."

"Go ahead. Dump on my cute car. You looked happy enough riding in it." Pause. "Jack? Remember, you said you got a mile or so down the road Friday night and decided to come back and give me the papers on your truck seat."

"Right."

"So when I asked God to send you, you were there. But the timing's wrong. I would've had to pray almost half an hour before I needed you if God really turned you around. Do you see what I mean?"

How do you explain this to an unbeliever? "Black holes and Einstein. You've heard of black holes. They have such terrific gravitation that they bend light — suck it in and don't let it out, which is why they're called black. They also bend time. Time stretches out practically to forever inside one."

"That's weird to even think about."

"I agree. Anyway, scientists say it does. Now, Einstein claimed that space and time are a continuum. You mess with one, it affects the other."

"Are you sure about that?"

"No, but it's close. OK. God creates the universe, however He went about it. As part of it, He also creates space and time. That means, essentially, He exists outside of time. He made it. So He sees the past, the present, the future, all fully and completely. He's not locked into time like His creation is. Like we are."

"That's even weirder, Jack."

"Hey, I'm still working on how it can be tomorrow today in Australia. So, taking that to its conclusion, you might even be able to pray for something after the fact and be able to influence it. Maybe you can, maybe you can't. That's up to God. But the mechanism is in place. It could be. And that's what it would be here. You need something at nine-oh-five, but the wheels for that something have to be put into motion at eight thirty-four. God puts the wheels in motion even though they precede the prayer by half an hour, because He operates outside of time constraints."

Here was the perfect opportunity. He told her about Lovey's burnout and his desire to provide her and Wade with the promised reward. Ev was skeptical. But then, so was he. And midnight was no time to wax eloquent, even on spiritual matters.

Ev remembered some more minor holes in her alibi chart. Her good-bye seemed drawn out, as if she didn't particularly want to say good night. To be truthful, tired as he was, he was in no hurry to say good night either.

The hands passed the twelve together, and he was now officially thirty-five. He did not mention that. They broke it off rather clumsily, and he headed back to the table.

Bodine had just finished almost a full meal, and Tom was drinking more coffee.

Jack slid into the booth. "Ev is reconstructing some of the data that burned in that motel room. She lost her notes on where you were Friday afternoon the fifteenth and Thursday night the twenty-first."

"Who, me?" Bodine shrugged. "My Daytimer's at the office. My paper brain. Call me tomorrow or Monday when I'm in the same room with it, and I'll look it up for you."

"You can't remember?"

Bodine spread his hands. "Look at me. Hit's past midnight. Some days I'm home at five, and some days it's the next day. You go where the news is, if there is any. The irregular hours mess me up completely. That's why I write it down." He nodded to Tom, to Jack. "Gentlemen, hit's been my pleasure. See you tomorrow. Or whenever." He tipped forward to maneuver himself out of the booth.

Jack nodded amiably. "Shalom."

Bodine froze in mid-tip and looked at him. It wasn't a glare, or a stare, or a gawk. He just looked.

Jack held his eye quietly.

Bodine sat back down. "Now what would make an old country boy like yourself say that?"

"Laurel Clum, the mystery writer, asked you how your political plans were coming, and you replied, 'Don't ask.' On another occasion, you phrased a rhetorical question, 'What's to see?' I take it you're not from around here."

Tom was looking from face to face. "He come out from Charleston about twenty years ago."

281

Jack kept his voice low and soothing. "I'm sorry, Bodine, that you're not proud of your heritage. It's a fine one."

"Not around here, hit ain't. Might's well be a Yankee."

"What heritage?!" Tom stared at Bodine.

"Jewish, my rednecked Southern friend." Bodine slipped effortlessly into the clipped standard English of Californians and news commentators everywhere. "I grew up in Kosher Canyon — West LA. You never met my pappy."

"No." Tom said it hesitantly, as if that might not be the correct response.

"That's right. Because his name is Eli Grubbmeyer, and he talks with a Yiddish accent, and he drives around in a big, fat, gas-guzzling luxury car. We moved to Charleston when I was in high school, and I came to Gatlinburg as soon as I completed my journalism degree. Been working on the accent ever since. You have a good ear, Prester."

"Well, I'll be diddled." Now Tom really was gawking.

"Why here?" Jack applied maybe half his brain to the conversation and the other half to ramifications. Well, maybe a third. He was getting really droopy.

"The area was just starting to explode. I could still pick up land fairly cheap, especially up around Pigeon Forge. My father bankrolled me — a silent partner — and we've been playing the real estate market ever since."

Jack nodded. It figured. "And the newspaper is as much a front for your investments and a source of inside tips as a journalistic effort."

"You might say."

Tom sat back. "You could've kept that little secret forever and a day, Bodine."

Jack agreed. "Why spill? I'm an outsider. Nobody."

"I'm impressed that you worked it out, I guess. Or maybe I'm more tired of hiding my heritage than I realize. When the

British were still chopping down trees with stone axes, my ancestors were building Jerusalem."

Two and two were beginning to look uncomfortably like four. "The Abcoffs knew."

"Why do you say that?"

"Their hatred, for one thing. Being from the Northeast, they might pick up on it more quickly than some. What I want to know now, Bodine, is whether either or both of them were blackmailing you or threatening to."

Bodine studied Jack levelly, holding him eye to eye. His face widened into a humorless smile. "G'night, Tom. Shalom, Prester."

He left.

Tom spaced out a few moments and snapped back. "And question number two would've been, 'Does Walling know?' Bedtime. My think tank's empty."

"Couldn't agree more." Jack hauled himself out of the booth.

"You still minding that cat tonight?" Tom put his uniform Stetson on.

"Yeah."

Tom led the way out into moist, spring night air. "I'll go along if I may."

"Sure." Jack didn't bother to wonder why. He climbed into his lavishly upholstered truck cab, the one with black dog hair all over the seat already. He rolled the window down, the better to enjoy a chorus of shrill frog songs surrounding the cafeteria lot. A lot of vying was going on in the swampy berm beyond the lot. Poets call spring cheery, invigorating, refreshing. Poets aren't frogs, or they'd realize how frantic the season truly is. Maxx licked Jack's ear in cheery greeting and settled to sitting.

Tom's cruiser followed Jack's truck over to the Walling

place. Jack led the way inside, threw the wall switch, and by habit checked around, looking for problems or things out of place.

Tom stepped in behind him. "I see what you mean." Like a sphinx at nap time, the cat lay curled on a sofa pillow, giving them the evil eye. Interest? Hardly. Gratitude? It is to laugh.

The red light was flashing on Walling's answering machine in the counter between kitchen and dining area. Jack flicked on the kitchen light. "Her tape is almost out. I'll write down what's here and flip it over." He picked up the pencil beside the machine and pushed the message button.

There was but one message, a nasal voice. *Beep.* "Better run, Diane. Pack and leave. Because you're next, Diane. Oh, you are so next." *Beeeep.*

They stared at the machine.

Jack played it again. Again.

He scowled. "Male or female?"

"I'd give it eighty-percent chance male." Tom shifted his stare to Jack. "It sounds kind of like Bugs Bunny." He frowned, puzzled. "Why would Bugs Bunny threaten Diane Walling?"

"Maybe it's Porky Pig after speech therapy. Tom? Remember that line 'You're so next?' "

Tom's face melted. "The Barber of Seville! That stupid Bugs Bunny cartoon that spoofed the opera. Bugs in a barber's tunic." He mimicked Bugs. " 'You are next. Yes, you're so next.' "

Jack leaned on the counter with both elbows and hoped that by studying the answering machine without blinking, it would give him some insight. "Too bad voiceprints are inadmissible. Any facilities that can do an analysis on this?"

"Matter of fact, private lab in Knoxville. They do voice and sound analysis for recording studios, and contract to private investigators. Cops don't use them much."

"The courts may not buy voice prints, but it would sure give us a person of interest to work on."

Tom grinned and started pulling plugs. "I need the whole machine as well as the tape. I probably can't get them cracking on this till Monday morning, but believe me I'll be on their doorstep then. Get funding out of Special Projects. Think the park can reimburse me then?"

"Maybe. I'll try." The outlet and phone jack were on his side of the counter. Jack accepted the phone wire and handed Tom the machine plugs. "Before you get too elated, remember that this could be a copycat or sick mind taking unsavory advantage of the situation. Not our perp at all." He jacked the phone into the wall.

"Or it could be a murderer. I'll set this up on my line tomorrow and get everyone we consider halfway a suspect to record into it. You too. I'll call you at your room in the morning."

"I'm going to church. Call me at the park in the afternoon." Jack sighed. "I remember going through this with hair samples, and we came up with zip. Except Ev did most of the routine collecting."

Ev.

Tom stood there a few moments in thought. "Gimme that pager, will you? What's its number?"

The pager? Jack unclipped it from his belt and handed it over. He had to check his notebook before he could recite the number.

Tom crossed the room to the sofa. The cat twitched an ear. Tom slipped the pager under the pillow. The cat raised its head, then settled back in snooty disregard. The disdainful eyes closed.

Tom returned to the kitchen. "Watch." With a wicked grin, he dialed the number.

27

Despite a generally held
suspicion that nature placed

Insects on This Earth

specifically to chastise the
delicate and sensitive hides of men . . .
— Stephen Dalton, *Borne on the Wind*

Jack occasionally wondered about the role of insects in the world. An inordinate number of them seemed out to bite him. He swatted ineffectually at a horn fly that was trying its level best to suck his scalp dry. He had parked off in the extreme corner of the church lot. He would never admit it to Ev, but she was right — this rig embarrassed him.

Should he lock up? *Nah.* Back in the truck bed, Maxx was being pestered by something whiny also. He shook his head. His leathern ears and big loose lips rattled like a flag in a windstorm. Jack cranked his window down and invited Maxx into the cab. The flies wouldn't bother him nearly as much here.

He was greatly disappointed to see that Lovey's truck still wasn't here. If she wasn't here or at Harold's, he had no idea where to seek her. He had talked to the pastor maybe twenty minutes. That gentleman didn't know where to find her either.

Jack joined the other worshipers streaming into the church.

He noticed that people filled up the middle of the front-

286

half pews first, the exact reverse of tendencies in every other church he'd visited. "Folks always fight for the backseats in canoes and churches" had long been his maxim. He recognized the family who had invited him and Lovey to lunch last week. He greeted them, was greeted, and settled in beside them.

Moments before the choir came singing their way down the aisle, Lovey slipped in beside him. She was smiling, but her eyes were red and puffy. She smelled of ashes and charred remains.

He leaned over and whispered, "I went over to your place early today, hoping to get there before you did — or at least to find you there." He squeezed her hand. "I'm sorry."

She smiled and squeezed back, and then they were helping the choir out with "Standing on the Promises," and conversation ended. During the final chorus, Wade appeared and squeezed in beside Lovey.

The pastor went through the announcements quickly and cleared his throat. "Let me tell you what our Lord has done. Last week we prayed for God's blessing upon Mr. Prester, who had lost his dog. Our prayers were answered. His dog was returned. In fact, you may wish to meet him — the dog, I mean; you already know Mr. Prester — after the service.

"Last night, an evil person burned Lovey Hempett out."

A collective gasp arose.

"Mr. Prester's dog is a police dog. It quickly found and identified the culprit." The pastor corrected himself. "The alleged culprit. Had we not prayed, perhaps Mr. Prester would not have found his dog in time to serve in that way."

He stepped down between the front pews. "And now, fellow servants, we have a heavy task. Especially for you, Lovey child. Together we must ask God's forgiveness upon that evil person. Remember that Jesus Christ stands among us this very moment, as He promised. Remember that He reads our hearts. Remember that He has granted us immense power through our prayers. We must be sincere in our petition.

"After services today we will all drive over to Lovey's for prayer on the site of the burnout. Then Clay, and you John, and Barley, we'll take some rough measurements and calc'late what will be needed to rebuild."

Now Jack understood why he liked this church. Following prayers, he settled back to enjoy what promised to be an excellent service of worship. A moment later he wasn't so sure he liked this church after all.

For the pastor roared, "Birthday time! We got this week and last week too to catch up on."

A little girl, dressed in frills and bows, shyly dropped ten pennies into a birthday bank. The congregation sang to her. A mother brought her baby forward and physically guided the tiny hand to slip a penny into the slot. She sang to her baby along with the rest.

"Adults? Don't hide. I know Ms. Washington ought to be up here."

Tittering, a bent and aged lady doddered forward.

A bass voice called, "Hey, Mabel! Need change for a five?"

Mrs. Washington possessed good timing. She stuffed a dollar bill into the bank as she waited for the laughter to subside. "Hush your mouth, Ephraim. This here's close enough. I was eighty-four last Tuesday."

Jack found himself rising out of his seat. He didn't want to do this. His feet carried him down to the birthday bank. He didn't want to be a center of attention here, especially not for his thirty-fifth. He pulled out his change. No pennies. A quarter and a dime did it.

Grinning, the pastor let his deep, dark eyes drill into Jack's soul. He didn't have to ask with words.

"Thirty-five today."

The congregation sang to him, as they had sung for the infant graduating from infancy, the child fast graduating from childhood, the lady about to experience the ultimate graduation. Now they sang to a lonely man who had forgotten for a moment that his Lord understands all about birthdays. Already Jack was two years older than Jesus ever got. Marcia and Matthew were gone. Ev was not here. But Jesus was, as were His servants. Jack returned to his place comforted as he would never have guessed he could be.

The pastor decided to spend another week on the topic of prayer, since God had been moving powerfully lately. After the service, well-wishers gathered around Lovey with condolences. These people who appreciated dogs so keenly trooped out to meet Maxx in person. Jack whistled him out of the truck and over to the church stoop to sit by his knee. The mutt licked three dozen kids' faces and five dozen hands, at least. Wade stayed close to his buddy Maxx, absorbing attention by osmosis.

Jack finally caught Lovey's eye. "You two want to ride with me? I'll bring you back to your truck then."

Wade literally ran to the truck. Lovey was more discreet but just as eager.

Wade buckled himself into the driver-side jump seat in back. "These things are pretty neat."

"You're the first to try them. Let me know how they work." Jack torched it off and waited until most of the others had left the lot. "I feel badly about it, Lovey. I told you not to go home. Maybe if you'd been there you could have saved your house."

"Maybe he woulda hurt me too, or kilt me. I doubt I'da saved much. The picture album. I woulda like to saved that.

Hit had all the old pictures of my kinfolks." She snorted. "Know what got saved? That stupid math book. I took it along over so's Wade and I could work on it. Everything gone but that miserable math book."

"So, Wade, you're a math tutor."

From the backseat came a smug sort of chuckle. "Know what? I decided I'm gonna be a EMT like you and Larkey. I went over to the firehouse after school and talked to Larkey 'bout it. He told me I have to finish high school with good grades. He did."

A little positive reinforcement wouldn't hurt here. "So did I. That's great. You'll make a good one! Hey, tell me. How come everyone sits in the middle of the front pews?"

Wade cackled. "Uncle Harold says hit was the first sermon Pastor preached when he took over. He said, 'Love ain't thinking pretty thoughts, hit's thinking of others.' Now you can plunk down on the aisle and make people stumble all over you sitting, or you can take the middle so they can just sit down. And you can sit in back and make all them embarrassed people who's late walk front and disturb everything, or you can fill up the front so's they can slip in the back."

"You got that memorized!" Jack felt rather like he was driving in a funeral cortege. Lovey's house lay in ruins. Why wasn't she more distraught?

Wade chattered a mile a minute. "Uncle Harold talked about it often enough. He says that speech made him a member right there."

"And I can see why. Lovey, tell me something. It's definite that Mrs. Abcoff was poisoned. Where would the poisoner get monkshood — aconite — that could be put in a mixed drink?"

"Hit'd change the color milky, likely."

"Allowing for that."

Lovey pondered the dashboard a few minutes. "If'n I was the poisoner, I'd have to grow it myself, would be easiest. There's a couple people round here I could get it from, but they'd be suspicious if they heard someone I knew died from it, you know?"

"Right. And no one bought any from you."

"Right. I didn't put up no fresh monkshood last year. But nobody asked me for none anyway."

"And how would you prepare it?"

"A decoction, leaves and flowers. Steep it and evaporate off most of the water without heating it."

Jack was following a pickup with three people in the cab and seven in the bed. All ten started singing "I Saw the Light." Lovey cranked down her window and joined in. Jack picked up the bass line, and they sang the rest of the way to the smoldering ruins, where they all sang some more.

It was late afternoon when he finally pulled into the parking lot behind park headquarters. Intense prayer and worship is wearying. He felt drained and elated, like a lottery winner. A couple of cars languished here, but few indeed are those working Sundays. Jack let Maxx and himself in through the comm center door, waved to the girl at the radio, and wandered around until he stumbled onto a computer that looked relatively user-friendly. None was friendly enough to understand and correct for his innocent mistakes. Computers are a thinly disguised scheme by the under-thirty-fives to take over the world.

He settled into a swivel chair, stuck Tom Baumgardner's diskette of unsolveds into a randomly selected drive and tap-tap-tapped a few minutes. Found it. Called it up. To his right, Maxx curled beside the chair into a languid pile of spaghetti and noisily slurped at his paws. Jack scanned, high-lighted, arranged.

That blasted beeper went off again. Jack lurched, startled. A string of errors tracked across the monitor screen. Maxx jumped almost as high as the cat, but he didn't streak away screaming into oblivion the way Mulligrubs had.

Ev's number. Jack climbed onto the FTS express pony and dialed.

She answered on the first ring. "Hi. How's Lovey?"

He knew she considered Lovey a rival in a way. Her concern pleased him. "Took it well, and her church is already making plans to rebuild. The women are even planning a pick-it shower."

"A picket shower? They're going to picket the courthouse until Abcoff is hanged?"

"Nah, he was out on bail before the arresting officer could get the paperwork done on him. Pick . . . it." Jack put lots of space between the words. "Two words. Apparently you bring a basketful of kitchen gadgets and utensils and towels and all that sort of thing. Your own stuff. And the guest of honor picks out what she needs, a little here and a little there. She keeps her choices. That's the shower gift, and you go out and buy yourself a new one. No duplication, no unneeded items. She gets exactly what she needs in good, usable condition."

"Amazing. I love it."

"How's your foot?"

"Doing well. Jack? Someone's getting away with murder. And that's not to mention the attempts on Diane and me. Whether they're related or not, they need a solution. If we have to back out now, he'll get away. I don't think Bill and Greg will ever catch him."

"I agree."

"Now that I'm home, I don't want to be here. The rest is lovely, but I don't want to lie around. I'm coming back. Find

292

it on our own, like you said. I can't let this go by."

"You can't drive."

"I'll think of something." She hesitated. "You're not at your motel packing to leave, are you?"

"No, I'm in the park office working."

"Oh, good! I'll talk to you tomorrow."

He almost said, "I love you," but it didn't come out. They said good-bye. The line went dead. The red light on the phone unit was slow to go out. Why couldn't modern technology ever make a phone system that simply did with dispatch what it should do?

Maxx bolted to sitting, alert to the door. Jack swiveled.

Staring at Maxx as if he were the hound of the Baskervilles, Homer Symes stood frozen in the doorway. He flicked his eyes briefly toward Jack. "I'm surprised to see you drive in. But since you did, I have the printouts your assistant requested."

"Ev?" He dipped his head toward Maxx. "He's safe."

With the trust of a rabbit for a lynx, Homer came sidling over. He peeked at Jack's screen. "Are you assembling the same information?"

"I don't know. What did Ev ask for?" Jack accepted a wad of paper and leafed through it. It was a listing, neatly tabulated, of all the people Colleen Abcoff had worked under during her many tours of duty, and all the people who worked under her.

"This is an expanded version of the material I gave you previously." Homer leaned over Jack's shoulder to point, taking care to stay well to the left, keeping the chair and Jack between him and Baskerville. "These entries are — how shall we say it? — to the second order of magnitude in both directions. For example, when she was chief ranger here, I listed the assistant supe and supe, of course. Also the district rangers and subdistrict rangers under her. Two steps in either direction. It was about all I could manage."

"But not the grunts and seasonals. This is brilliant. And no, it's not what I'm working on here."

Homer frowned. "That looks like the other project you requested, the tabulation of unsolved cases."

"Expanded version of that, from the sheriff's department."

With a blank expression, Homer studied the screen. "I realize I'm not in law enforcement, and your ways are not my ways."

"Not such mysterious ways. You arrange it into various scenarios, and see what you get. A lot of mind-work for not much fruit, usually. But you can come up with a good one now and then. It helps if you can get three or four people to put heads together and brainstorm. Brainstorming pulls some amazing things out of hats."

Homer looked skeptical. "But you can't make a scenario unless the data point to something. I cannot imagine how this accumulation of seemingly random and unrelated material can point to anything."

"It points to quite a bit. Look." Jack scrolled down. "Let's assume our perpetrator is responsible for at least some of them. These cases in particular."

"Why assume that?"

"No really good reason. But he's just pulled off two blatant crimes and gotten away with it. That suggests he's had practice. It's a test assumption, not a real one. A 'what if?' "

"He. It's a man then."

"He or she. But statistically, yeah. It's a man. Here. A women's clinic firebombed. If this is our perpetrator, he's pro-life. A child molester dies when he wraps his vehicle around a tree. The man who suggests the development in the park is killed, as is his successor when she revives the scheme. A strongly suspected arsonist who is about to skate —" Jack stopped and translated his jargon for the pedantic Homer "— about to go free conveniently kills himself. This is soon after a young, agile purse-snatcher grabs a hefty chunk of Valium from your wife."

"Oh, my," purred Homer. "Oh, my! My Jane. That chills my bones, to even think about it."

Jack pushed back a little and swung to be able talk face-to-face. "If the arsonist and the purse-snatcher are the same person, the arsonist grabbed the purse for money — an easy hit, because she laid it on her car roof — and found an unexpected bonanza of drugs. He used the cash to buy some good vodka, settled himself in a nice private place, and had a party. He misjudged the Valium and OD'd. It's easy to do. Alcohol and Valium are lethal in combination."

Homer nodded slowly. "Stunning."

"But there are all these other unsolveds. Abortion. Child molestation. Desecration of the park. Arson. So now let's assume that the purse-snatcher and the arsonist are *not* the same person. Now what do we see?"

"And you're also assuming one person committed them all."

"Or at least some of them, but we don't know which." Jack swiveled back to the monitor. "I arranged chronologically the cases you might call public service projects. Ridding the community of dangerous people and dangerous ideas." He scrolled to his last five and turned again.

Homer frowned. "A criminal with a conscience? Robin Hood?"

"Exactly. Now we have a caped crusader." Jack pointed. "He struck here, perhaps in desperation. It worked. The next one was a little easier. Emboldened, he picked up the pace.

Even if he was caught, he could probably wring some sympathy out of the jury by pleading moral cause."

"Maybe he did get caught."

"Quite possibly. I'd have to go through all the cleared cases and still might miss him. Look here. Two superintendents. The first dies hit-and-run. It would look suspicious for a second to die in the same way, so he switches to poison. Very effective poison, easily obtained. You can grow it yourself. The assistant supe is going to head down the same erroneous paths, so we wipe her out by a method unrelated to the others."

"Of course. To allay suspicion." Homer stood erect and stepped back, still eyeing Maxx with something akin to horror.

"There are other scenarios, but they don't satisfy the conditions as well. See how we work it?"

Homer nodded. "And I see that brainstorming could be most valuable." He smiled. "About two years ago, a representative from personnel at Region came out to explain a new accounting system to us. He was immensely proud of the detail and the work the people in the regional office had done. In about ten minutes, we humble persons at the park level had come up with a dozen cases where their new idea simply could not be applied. Everyday situations, not exotic cases. Had they brainstormed at Region, they could have found their bugs."

"Bugs." Jack smiled. "If it weren't for the bugs in the system, so many great ideas would actually fly."

Homer sniggered. "Thank heaven for bugs. I rather like the time-proven ways myself." He started backing toward the door very slowly, inconspicuously.

"I agree." Jack took the hint. "Thank you very much for these. Ev and I will work on them. I'll let you know if they turn out to be material to the investigation."

"I appreciate that. Incidentally, Jane thinks you are a wonderful and polite young man."

"Thank you. I felt I was in the presence of true Southern aristocracy."

"I'll tell her that. See you later."

Jack smiled and nodded and watched the nervous Homer beat a hasty retreat. He swiveled and dialed Ev's number. Busy. He worked on his caped crusader hypothesis ten minutes and tried again.

She must have had the telephone right at her elbow.

"Hey, I was just talking to Homer Symes. As a brainstormer he's a complete washout, but as a tabulator he's tops. You want to do something?"

"Yes!"

"You're talking to Hal in the morning, aren't you?"

She practically snarled. "You bet I am. I don't think I'm going to tell him we're staying on it though."

"Good girl. Listen. I'm going to fax you a bunch of stuff through Hal's office. See if you see anything. Maybe match names against who attended the funeral. Whatever. I'm going to fax them to my dad too. He knows all the political ins and outs. He can shed light on who might hate whom."

Her voice sounded elated. "Jack, we're going to nail that creep!"

"That we are. Later."

"Later." She hung up.

Jack fiddled with his data a little longer. He faxed Homer's material to Hal's office and both Homer's and Baumgardner's to his dad in Hawaii, with a cover sheet.

Superman. Batman. Robin Hood. No caped crusader is a normal person. Not even the Lone Ranger. The more he toyed with the hypothesis, the better he liked it. Only one small glitch remained.

Who was that masked man?

28

There Is the
Caw of a Crow

and the Hesitant Song of a Thrush
— Edgar Lee Masters, *Jonathan Houghton*

The crows were discussing nesting plans around the Chimney Tops to the right. Somewhere against the hill on the left, a thrush explained in halting phrases that the ornithologists are wrong. Birds don't just sing to set up territories. They sing for the pure, engaging joy of it, and anthropomorphism be hanged. How many robins and thrushes do you hear cutting loose like that on rainy, blustery days?

Jack troweled himself back into the MG. Getting in and out was easier now that he had applied a quart or two of WD-40 to the seat-adjustor tracks and moved the seat all the way back against the top well. He torched it off and continued up the hill toward Newfound Gap at the crest.

What a glorious day! Imagine sitting in a stuffy little cubicle crunching numbers and cases when you can be out in warmth and sun and cheer, not to mention a sports car.

He had been amazed this morning at ten when Bill Weineke stuck his head into Jack's borrowed cubicle and asked, "Did you order something from Moss Motors?" It was the lock set, delivered priority.

Jack and Bill hastened into Gatlinburg to Ev's motel, put heads together, and installed the new ignition. They would replace the door and trunk locks later. At last Jack could get the MG out from under the motel manager's feet. He drove it back down to park headquarters as Bill followed.

He tried to work. He really did. At two he hung it up, defeated by spring. With Maxx in the top well, he took off to see Clingman's Dome in the sun. Bill Weineke came within an ace of accompanying him, then begged off at the last moment. With words such as "Suit yourself" and "Drudge" and "Poor sucker" hanging in the air behind him, Jack salvaged the day, Weineke or no.

He was surprised that only a score of cars were parked in the Dome lot. At least some of them had to be hikers on the trail that took off over the side from the Dome walkway. He saw no one coming or going at the moment. Either the thrush had followed him or another like it was bubbling over about the lovely territory it could call its own, if only for the season.

He'd been here before, but the place looked completely different. Weather, time of day . . . whatever . . . it seemed a whole new and exhilarating experience.

He put Maxx on lead and walked down away from the Dome trail, just to see what lay in the other direction. Besides, he didn't want Maxx placing a land mine in areas where visitors were likely to pass. They hung around off the far downhill end of the parking lot a few minutes until Maxx had completed his business and started back up.

He was a hundred yards from the car when a familiar voice shrieked, "Look! He has it running!"

Here came Ev and Laurel in that red convertible.

Jack couldn't keep his grin from splitting his face. He jogged over to the passenger side as the car screeched to a halt in the middle of its lane. Maxx turned inside out greeting his lady friend.

"What are you doing here?" They all said it simultaneously.

They all laughed. They all answered at once. They all stopped.

Breathlessly, Ev took off on one of her monologues. "Saturday I called Hal's voice mail and told him I was in town and I was planning to talk to him first thing this morning. Then last night I decided no, I'm coming here instead. I'm feeling much better now. So I called Laurel, and she agreed to come get me, since I can't drive. And as we were coming through, we decided it's such a beautiful day we just had to come see Clingman's Dome. So here we are."

Jack couldn't have been gladder. "And I was sick of working in an office space eight feet by eight feet, and here I am. The door and trunk locks aren't changed yet. We'll do that then."

"That's great, Jack. I'm really grateful."

"Tell him!" Laurel jabbed her.

"Tell me what?"

Ev beamed, 300 watts at least. "I talked to Mayrene McAllister Sunday morning. Yesterday morning."

"Hal's nemesis, who filed the grievance."

"An administrative grievance against the selecting official for failure to follow merit promotion procedures. And she had a solid case, Jack. He blatantly disregarded the regulations." Ev's head bobbed; her hair floated. "I got her address and stopped by when I figured she would be home. I told her I heard that Hal was trying to talk her out of asking for the position."

"Which is true."

Ev nodded again. "I never lied once the whole time, or even misled at all, really. I told her I was afraid she would back out, and I wanted to reassure her what a great job it is. Exciting and all that. Now here, I may have sort of . . . kind of . . . painted Hal as a . . . well . . . jerk."

Jack grimaced. "So far, still telling the truth."

"Then we happened to get talking about the cast on my foot, and I just casually mentioned, since she asked, about going over the cliff at Death Valley, and getting into the fights at Acadia, like when Marlette attacked me in the van . . ."

"A painful life you've been leading."

"Well, I didn't really emphasize it. If that's the conclusion she drew . . ."

"Tell him the good part!" Laurel goaded.

"I mentioned wrecking the rental at Mt. Rainier, and now my own car here. Then she asked me if I ever drew a gun —"

"This is the good part," Laurel crowed.

"And I went on and on about how I hate guns and having to be around them every day. You know, all these fire fights, like putting a hole in the ceiling of that tavern. You getting shot at, and they took your windshield out at Death Valley. You had to get your windshield replaced, but I didn't mention that was months ago. It happened, right?"

Ev looked positively peacock smug. "Then she asked about uniform allowance and stuff like that. I said — very truthfully, mind you — that Hal claims he's going to get right on that. She asked when did he say that, and I said, 'Last year, but I'm sure he will. And he's promised he'll get our per diem payments caught up real soon.'

"She said why didn't I file a grievance, and I said I was in budget, and I knew he didn't have any money. It wouldn't do any good, but that will change soon, I'm sure."

Jack wagged his head. "Ev. You might have messed Hal up royally by approaching her."

"And then we chatted for another hour or so, and I took her out to lunch. She's really not that bad a person. A bit more intense than I'm comfortable with, but we got along fine."

"The best part." Laurel jabbed her again. "We stopped for lunch today, and she called Hal's office asking if some faxes got there. Go on."

Ev picked it up. "And he said, 'Forget about being closed down. We're back in business. The McAllister broad withdrew her grievance this morning.' I think I was telling the truth about Hal being a jerk. She's certainly not a broad, Jack."

Jack just stood there gaping. Then he chuckled. Then he laughed.

A car with Virginia plates drew up behind. Jack stepped back, and Laurel drove off to park. The visitors pulled in beyond her.

Ev was back! He couldn't quit grinning. He had a job again. That was probably part of the elation, but right now it didn't seem to matter. Ev was back.

Suddenly Maxx broke into a frenzied spate of barking. He peeled off down the lot, yanking the leash out of Jack's hand. What . . .

The dog had recognized a motor sound, and now Jack did too — the big, bad twelve-cylinder Lincoln. Howling, it came speeding around the corner. And suddenly Jack knew who it was. Of course!

"Maxx! No! Come!" Jack broke into a run. "Maa-axx, come!"

The stupid, gallant mutt was going to tackle the Lincoln bare-handed! "Maxx, no!!"

Oblivious, Maxx lunged at the moving driver-side window. The Lincoln could have squashed him — should have squashed him — but it veered. It sent him flying anyway, a glancing blow.

Jack ducked behind a maroon Volvo. He barely made it beyond the front fender as the Lincoln struck it. The Volvo skidded sideways and slammed against the Ford minivan beside it. Jack continued right on around the Volvo and stretched himself across the flat trunk. The Lincoln would be back for another try. He knew it.

Two-handed, steadied prone across the Volvo trunk, Jack leveled his gun on the lane beyond the Ford. He heard the Lincoln's tires screech on the hot dry asphalt, listened to the motor rev. Somewhere on the periphery of his awareness, Ev was shouting.

Maxx . . .

Here it came, straight at him. He held off until the last moment. The driver must have seen the gun pointing at him. He hit the brakes. Jack let go at the windshield. The FBI standard is three feet, three shots, three seconds. Jack met it.

The Lincoln hit the Volvo again but not solidly. The Ford was in the way. Jack felt himself tumbling, found himself on asphalt, saw blue sky. It took him a few breaths to gather himself enough to move. He rolled to his knees, listening for the motor.

Right behind him! He flipped around to sitting and blasted at the tires. He watched the left front tire explode, literally, as the Lincoln whipped past. It swerved wildly. With a roar, the rubber ripped away, and the left rim gouged into the asphalt. Sparks flew like the Fourth of July.

Here came another rollover, and for once Jack wasn't in it. With thunder that rattled heaven, the Lincoln screed out across the asphalt on its driver side, hit the cement parking bumpers, and flipped onto its back. It slid wheels-up over the grassy berm into the brush beyond the pavement and slammed against a tree.

Jack struggled to his feet, giddy. His elbow wasn't functioning. He started forward toward the Lincoln not at a run but at a stagger.

Clump! Clump! Clump! Ev came galumphing up beside him, cast and all. Her face was hard, all business, and totally focused on the Lincoln. "Laurel's tending Maxx. She ignored the danger and ran right to him." She held her Sig two-handed, as clearly and completely a cop as any twenty-year veteran.

"I'll swing out around there." Jack didn't dare think about Maxx now. The Lincoln wobbled slightly. "Ev, down!" Jack dived to the side.

The driver fired. Ev returned fire. Jack's gun clicked, empty.

Still in his black ski mask and gloves, the driver loomed behind the Lincoln. He was on his feet. He must have crawled out a window. He took off through the trees toward the entrance to the Dome walk.

Ev braced herself and emptied her gun in his direction, but the distance was too great and the deflecting, interfering trees and shrubs too numerous. She took off running, sort of, popping the clip and jamming in her reload as she went.

Jack wanted to yell, "No, Ev!" but she was doing her job. He peeled out after her, he the guy who ran a couple times a week trying to catch up to a woman with her foot in a cast.

She paused to aim and suddenly swung her gun skyward. Just beyond the running perp, two tourists appeared on the Dome walk. They stood transfixed as the man in a ski mask ran past them.

Jack still couldn't get his breath. How could Ev run so fast with that foot? She blazed past the tourists, yelling, "Down!"

They bellied out and covered their heads as Jack thundered by.

Once the perp left the pavement and went over the side onto the hiking trail, they'd never catch him, especially if Maxx was out of commission. To Jack's amazement, the man continued on up past the rest rooms. He was obviously out of breath, and Ev was not. She saw a clear shot and paused to fire. He returned fire, but nothing came close. She emptied her clip. Jack could see cement chips fly near the target.

Ev was still ahead of Jack by a hundred feet. He wanted to say, "Stand aside! Let me take him!" but he couldn't. He was getting his breath back — he was almost up to full speed — but this was Ev's takedown as much as his.

The fellow slowed to a walk as the ramp curved up away from the ground. He hesitated, then took off again. Ev yelled at him, leveled her gun. He tossed a single shot her way. Did Jack hear the click of an empty chamber? The perp ran up around the bend, stopped and hunched over, apparently struggling with his own weapon. Something wasn't working right.

They were above treetop level now, nearly as high as they could go. He turned slowly around and raised his arms, his pistol still in his hand. Jack could hear his heavy breathing from away back here.

Ev moved in on him, ordered him to drop the gun. He did. Did he know hers was empty? It's not something you want to take a chance with unless you know.

His foot lashed out suddenly and kicked Ev's cast. It slid down the pavement, throwing her off balance. He darted forward, grabbed her, clamped her securely in a headlock. Ev struggled.

Jack closed the distance between them to fifteen feet. Ev's eyes bulged, and her face was turning blue. With a flick the perp snapped a switchblade open and pressed it to her throat.

Jack stopped cold, literally and figuratively. "You hurt her in the least little way, and you're dead meat."

"Back up. Back the way you came." Bugs Bunny's voice.

"No. Cut your losses now."

"It's her I'll cut. Back up."

"No." Jack kept his voice low, smooth, even, and — he hoped — menacing. He moved forward a few steps and stopped. "Why didn't you turn aside onto the trail back there? This is a dead end."

"I missed it. I didn't realize where it was."

So Bugs Bunny has never been up here before. Jack stepped forward, moving slowly and deliberately.

Bugs Bunny squeaks when he's excited. "Stay back!"

"You tried to kill my dog. For all I know, this time you succeeded. You tried more than once to kill me. Now you're threatening to kill Ev. Whatever makes you think I'm in a mood to back off?"

Ev suddenly exploded in a wild paroxysm, gripping his knife arm, jerking her head toward his. They tumbled together against the railing. He was losing it. He must realize he was losing it.

Jack rushed forward and grabbed him, trying to drag him off her.

With a howling, shrieking, insane roar, the perp flung Ev against the rail — onto it — tipped her over. With a choked scream she disappeared over the side.

Jack lunged for her, grabbed a piece of sweater — it slipped out of his hand. The perp took advantage of the distraction and butted him in the ribs. Jack lashed out blindly toward him. The fellow tried to run. Jack stopped him with a wild, uncoordinated swing. He recovered, stumbled, took off down the long ramp.

Where was the knife? Jack didn't notice, and he didn't care. His fury toward the electrocuter, his fury toward Abcoff, was nothing compared to what he felt now. He was hot with it, blind with it, charged with it.

306

Running downhill obviously suited the perp. But Jack was faster, Jack was heavier, Jack was by far the more desperate. He caught up to the man on the pavement below the spiral, a broad, open floor. He didn't try fancy police techniques. He plowed into the guy with a plain old high school football tackle, dragging him to the ground.

His weight knocked out any breath the perp may have had left. For good measure, though, Jack slammed the man's head into the paving stones. From his hip pocket, he pulled his portacuffs, the little plastic strip that looks like something a TV huckster would pitch — and that could hold an elephant in abeyance. He locked the guy down. A little puddle of blood formed by the ski-mask mouth, probably from the perp's nose.

Barely audible, the murderer, the caped crusader, no longer bothered with the Bugs Bunny voice. "In the parking lot. At the funeral." He had trouble talking, with no breath to talk with effectively. "That was the first . . . time a . . . a subject ever resisted . . . ever shot back . . . I can't tell you . . . the . . . the fantastic . . . thrill that was."

"Yeah, I bet."

The voice told him. Jack had guessed right.

"Jack . . ."

He wheeled.

Ev! She came stumbling out of the brush, slightly unsteady. Her face was scratched and bloody, her sweater torn, her cast cracked. And she was grinning. He should guard his perp. His fury dissolved as rapidly as it had flared, and he ran to her, wrapped arms around her, and clung desperately.

She sobbed and laughed and babbled. "What a ride! Bouncing branch to branch down through those trees. I'd have to pay fifty cents for a ride like that at Coney Island." She lifted her head away from his shoulder presently, and he was reluctant to let her do it. "We got him."

"We got him."

"Who is he? You didn't look to see who it is?"

Jack wrapped an arm around her waist and walked her slowly back to their perp. "Only one person knew where I was this afternoon. Weineke. But a second could have been listening. In fact, the second could have eavesdropped on any or all of my phone conversations, including the one with you yesterday afternoon. You know, where we decided we were going to get him. The beeper would have alerted him to tap in. Only that second person knew I saw the pattern of a masked avenger. Someone taking the law into his own hands. You and I became too dangerous to tolerate.

"Weineke would have known where the trail leaves the paved path there by the rest rooms. The other one never went out prowling here in the park. He might not know."

"But the hair samples. He didn't try to get you at Carl Sandburg?"

"Yes, he did. I don't recall in your report that you thought to get a sample from him."

Jack reached down and pulled the ski mask off Homer Clarence Symes.

29

The Great Problem
Is at Length Solved!

— Edgar Allen Poe, "The Balloon-hoax"

Jack loved it when a problem found solution. Here was a letter from Hal. Hal never bothered to write unless it was something official that needed hard copy. This had to be the cap on the Smokies case.

He pulled the rest of the wad out of his apartment mailbox and carried it inside. He stepped over Maxx — the mutt sprawled out asleep right in the way, of course — and took the mail out onto his little veranda in the waning sweetness of the summer day. He laid it on the patio table beside him, tossed the catalogue and junk mail on the floor under the chair, and opened the top envelope.

The phone rang. He walked back inside, stepped over Maxx, got the portable off its cradle, and helloed it on the way back out onto the terrace.

"Jack, guess where I am."

"The phone booth at Third and Main, trying to figure out how to get that bulky cast into that little cubicle with you."

"I got the cast off a month ago. My foot's doing fine. A little swelled, but the doctor says that's normal."

"Good! So where are you?"

"Yellowstone. Jack, I've been hearing about Yellowstone my whole life. And here I am!"

"That bear mauling?"

"They didn't tell the papers, but they suspect the bear had help. It's a great case."

"I'm very happy for you." *Sort of.*

"Jack, I realize it's been three months, and you've been very nice about not pushing me about the subject, but I owe you an answer."

"OK. What was the question?" He knew what question.

"You asked me to think about marriage."

"And . . ."

"This is my first solo, you might say. I want to see how I can fly on my own. Can we talk about it again, say, the first of the year?"

"Sure." He had known what her answer would be before she gave it. It disappointed him anyway. Immensely so.

She gave him her local number, they traded small talk a few minutes more, and she hung up.

Yawning, Maxx came out and flopped down on Jack's foot. He belched loudly and licked his toes, totally bored.

Back to the mail.

Here was Hal's stamp of approval on Jack's final report. Symes was apparently asking to waive a jury trial in return for certain concessions. If Hal acquiesced on that one, Jack would be mad enough to eat ant eggs.

They placed Symes at Sandburg with the hair and testimony from his wife's relatives. They placed him in the Lincoln and found forensic evidence of no other drivers. They got him boasting about the child molester's death, but they'd probably never pin that one on him. Uncorroborated confessions never do well in court.

He even boasted about how he managed to swipe his own wife's purse by slipping out the delivery door of the drugstore. Mr. Sneaky.

The caped-crusader analysis had been right on. Heady

with success after success, Symes had considered himself invincible. In fact, apparently he still did, viewing his arrest as a minor setback. Yeah, sure. Jack skimmed through the rest of Hal's letter. He'd read it in detail later.

Next on the pile was a letter from Lovey, thick enough to need two ounces worth of postage. He dumped the whole thing out into his lap and read the letter first.

August 12

Dear Jack,

    How are you? I'm fine.
    I don't write many letters but you said calling on the telephone is too easy, and you're right. I want to tell you the news.
    I got my GED, and it wasn't as hard as I thought it would be. Well, almost as hard. But I got it. I made a copy for you, enclosed. Don't need to return it. The copy, I mean.
    And guess what. I'm working at Uncle Gene's. Boy said I oughta. I was really scared but I made an appointment and went in one morning and told him I wanted to make him a real breakfast and see how he liked it. I made him a breakfast like that one I made for you. Boy was I nervous! Using a gas stove is hard. It doesn't turn out the same as a wood stove unless you turn the heat down real real low. Well, he didn't say a thing, he just ate it all, kind of thoughtful like. And then he said, "We'll start you out mornings. Come in at four." No "You're hired" or "Do you need a job Miss Hempett?" Just come in at four. So I did, and now I'm in charge of the kitchen five days a week until two every

day, and you wouldn't ever guess how much
he's paying me!

Bugle whelped another litter of puppies,
five of them this time. They're awful cute,
and really fat little things. I already got
four of them sold, and Hiram says he wants
the fifth. The money came in handy. I got
my school all paid off with it.

Hiram has those hunting magazines, and
he saw a picture that looks just like the
puppies, and he gave it to me. I tore out
the page with the picture. It's enclosed.
Don't need to return it.

I know you're busy, but write if you can.
God bless you.

                    Your sister in Jesus,
                    Lovey

Jack laid the letter aside and unfolded the Xerox. So that's
what a general equivalency diploma looks like. Beautiful. He
felt a flush of pride, as if Lovey were his kin. She was, in the
most important way — a sister in Christ. He never knew before that her Christian name was Lovetia.

He smoothed out the tear sheet. From a recent *Sports
Afield*, it was an ad for a series of ready-to-frame matted art
prints depicting puppies of various sporting breeds. She had
circled the black Lab.